Miss Davis and the Architect
Copyright © 2025 by Rogue Press. All rights reserved.
Published by Rogue Press

All rights reserved. No part of this book may be used or reproduced in any form by any means—except in the case of brief quotations embodied in critical articles or reviews—without written permission.

This is a work of fiction. Names, characters, places, and incidents are products of the author's imagination or are used fictitiously and are not to be construed as real. Any resemblance to actual events, locales, organizations, or persons, living or dead, is entirely coincidental.

This e-book is licensed for your personal enjoyment only. This e-book may not be re-sold or given away to other people. If you would like to share this book with another person, please purchase an additional copy for each reader. If you are reading this book and did not purchase it, or it was not purchased for your use only, please return to your favorite retailer and purchase your own copy. Thank you for respecting the hard work of the author.

Stay in touch through the C. N. Jarrett newsletter!

Miss Davis and the Architect

DAZZLING DEBUTANTES
BOOK FOUR

C. N. JARRETT

ROGUE

To my family.

For being able to count on you, no matter how dark or late the hour.

I love you all.

PROLOGUE

"I am not fond of the idea of my shrubberies being always approachable."

Jane Austen

LATE JULY 1820, LONDON

Barclay descended the stairs, sliding his hand over the banister, the muscles in his back protesting the movement. It had been a long journey from one of their minor Yorkshire building sites, and even a night stretched out in his own bed had not eased the stiffness brought on by too many hours in the carriage over the past days.

As his foot hit the bottom stair, he looked up to find an unknown gentleman staring at him from the doorway of his grandfather's study. His grandfather, Tsar, stood behind the man's shoulder.

Noticing his descent, Tsar called out, "Barclay, there you are! I just sent Robins to find you. Join us for coffee?"

Barclay frowned. Was the gentleman a prospective client? He certainly looked moneyed in his black Hessians, expensive buckskins, snowy cravat, and immaculate wool coat. His sable curls were artfully cut and his face clean-shaven.

But they rarely met clients in the family home. And something about how the visitor's emerald green eyes followed him was unnerving. Barclay sensed this was not a typical client meeting.

He entered the study in their wake and took a seat in a leather armchair beside the unknown guest, who fidgeted nervously with his cravat. Barclay's unease mounted.

"Allow me to make introductions. This is Lord Richard Balfour, the Earl of Saunton."

Barclay was startled. He made to rise to his feet to bow. "My lord—"

"Please, it is unnecessary, Mr. Thompson. I am quite embarrassed about this situation, so we shall not observe formalities."

Barclay raised a hand to run it through his hair, puzzled about what was happening. He shot a glance at his grandfather, who looked away. Barclay's own tension increased.

Thomas Thompson, better known as Tsar, was a renowned architect now in his mid-seventies. He had apprenticed and worked with Robert Adams himself in his youth, before being discharged along with three thousand other workers because of the failing Adelphi project in 1772. With a young Italian wife, whom he had met on his Grand Tour, and a two-year-old daughter to provide for, Tsar had risked everything to begin his own firm. He had quickly built his name and reputation with grand Palladian designs, crafting country homes for the wealthy over the subsequent decades.

Known as Tsar because of his commitment to purchasing quality timber and supplies from the Baltics and St. Petersburg, he was famous for his relationships with merchants from that region. Timber had become highly priced over the past decade or two because of heavy taxation during the troubles with France, but everyone knew that timber from Northern America was inferior due to the extended sea journey, often arriving with dry rot set in. Tsar was unwilling to compromise.

If one wished to conduct business in St. Petersburg, one called upon Tsar, well known to be a determined man of ideals and fierce loyalties. A man of integrity. He had taken part in thousands of negotiations with clients and suppliers over the decades, and he never looked nervous.

Of course, today proved that the observation was inaccurate. Tsar was distinctly nervous as he fiddled with papers on his desk. Eventually, the gentleman to Barclay's left broke the awkward silence by clearing his throat.

"If I may explain?"

His grandfather grunted a bashful consent, his cheeks growing suspiciously red.

What on earth is going on?

"This is a rather indelicate subject to discuss, so I shall be blunt." Despite the announcement, Lord Saunton hesitated. He stared down at his hands folded on his lap.

Barclay did not like to express emotion in public. He was a man of restraint, except with his close family, whom he adored, but even he could not maintain his patience any longer. He frowned, then demanded, "What is this?"

His lordship took a deep breath. "I have recently discovered through extensive investigation that you and I are brothers ... well ... half-brothers. A fact that your grandfather has just confirmed this morning."

Barclay's jaw dropped. After several heart-pounding moments, he turned to Tsar. "The late Earl of Saunton was my father?"

Tsar kept his eyes lowered, dropping his head in a curt nod.

"You and Mother informed me my father was an officer in the Royal Navy, lost at sea before they wed!"

"It was ... easier. It was what your mother desired," he mumbled.

Aurora Thompson! He was going to have words with his mother when he saw her next. She and Tsar had lied to him. He was a man in his early thirties, discovering his parentage for the first time. He felt like a callow youth discussing this subject in front of a stranger, with his shock and outrage on display.

Nay, not a stranger, but a brother!

He attempted to gather his wits, but could not make sense of what was unfolding. "Grandfather, I have always appreciated that you did the right thing by my mother and me—standing by her when she ... but this is ... Why did you lie about who my father was?"

Lord Saunton coughed quietly into his fist. "I believe, if you think on it, that the idea of an officer lost at sea with a wedding planned was a more romantic notion for a young lad than ..." The earl pulled at the knot of his cravat in agitation before finishing, "Than ... the Earl of Satan seduced the young daughter of his architect and abandoned her to her fate."

"Satan?"

Wincing, Lord Saunton's face gradually turned red while he struggled to respond. "Rest assured, your ignorance of my—our—disgraceful father is a blessing. Now that I am the head of the Balfour family, it is my responsibility to acknowledge our connection and ensure you receive the benefits of our relationship ... brother."

Barclay's thoughts were swimming, and his customary composure was nowhere to be found. He straightened, ready to spring to his feet. "I do not want it!"

"Barclay." His grandfather spoke quietly, but firmly. Barclay had always trusted and respected Tsar, so, despite his struggle, he could not rise and stride away.

Reluctantly, Barclay paused before settling back into his chair, his hands resting on his knees while he drew a calming breath. "Yes, Grandfather?"

"Barclay, these many years your mother has struggled with the burden of being unwed. My reputation has assisted her to maintain some relationships, but she is not accepted in general society. One day, my great-granddaughter ... Tatiana will struggle with the burden that her father is a illegitimate. When I am gone in the not-too-distant future, none of you will enjoy the benefit of my protection any longer. Lord Saunton's offer to acknowledge the connection will elevate you from a by-blow to the brother of an earl. It will open doors for you, as well as for your daughter and mother ... All this will provide me with the solace I sorely need."

Tsar ran his fingers through his short, curling gray hair in a gesture reminiscent of Barclay's own a few moments earlier. His rounded face was creased in concern when he continued. "I ... often worry about what will happen to my family when my reputation and relationships from fifty years of professional excellence are no longer available to all of you to facilitate your social and professional interactions."

Barclay hung his head, closing his eyes while he thought. "I am an excellent architect in my own right. My awards attest to that."

"I will not deny that, but you have yet a decade of work, which simply does not compare to my five decades. You must acknowledge that, as a by-blow of an unknown officer, you will encounter difficulty when I am no longer here to lend you my support. Lord Saunton can make that difficulty disappear, which will benefit our womenfolk. Society is much harder on them than it is on men."

Barclay leaned his head back in the chair to stare at the ceiling, swallowing hard while his thoughts raced.

The earl leaned forward to speak in earnest. "Mr. Thompson, it would be my great pleasure to acknowledge you publicly and unite our families. You will gain two brothers, along with extended family, for your mother and daughter. My—our—cousin is the Duke of Halmesbury. He and his duchess are certain to sponsor Tatiana in society when that time comes. Even now, we can open doors for your mother."

Barclay wanted to walk out of the room, but reflecting on the advantages to both his mother and Tatiana, he realized that would be the immature act of an excessively proud man. A duke? And not just any duke, but the much-lauded Duke of Halmesbury? Only a fool would reject such a prestigious connection.

He might tolerate the challenges he faced as a natural-born son, but if that burden could be lifted for Tatiana ... if his late wife were still with them, she would place her much smaller hand gently over his and counsel him to accept the offer. His heart squeezed at the thought of Natalya and the words she would have said if she had been here to say them, but it had been two lonely years since she had died. Tatiana no longer had a mother, and he no longer had a wife, yet now his young daughter would gain uncles, aunts, and cousins in the peerage.

He swept a trembling hand through his hair, leaning forward to place his elbows on his knees before mumbling to his boots, "What does this entail, Lord Saunton?"

"Please ... Barclay ... we are brothers—blood. If our father had done right by your mother, even now you would be the earl, instead of myself. My family address me as Richard."

Barclay sighed. "What does this entail ... Richard?"

CHAPTER ONE

"A large income is the best recipe for happiness I ever heard of."

Jane Austen

Jane Davis stood at the window, watching the guests arriving. The Earl of Saunton was hosting a grand house party at his Somerset country seat, and many of the guests were young gentlemen earmarked to meet Jane. Despite the impending festivities, she was feeling rather melancholy as she observed the hive of servants, guests, carriages, and trunks, all bathed in the sunshine that filtered through a bank of distant clouds.

"I cannot believe you are married and leaving us."

Her older sister, Emma, came to stand next to her by the window. "You encouraged me to accept him."

Jane sniffed. "I merely informed you that Peregrine Balfour was your Darcy."

"How strange that I am now married to the brother of

the earl. You should have been there when Perry and his friends serenaded me. I shall never forget his proposal as long as I live."

"Perry truly sings that poorly?"

Emma smiled lovingly, looking down on her groom who was assisting the earl to greet his guests. Perry and Emma had been married a few days earlier and were eager to leave for their new home. Shepton Abbey was a fine country estate, and her sister was elated to assist with managing it. "He promised to never sing again."

Jane huffed a quick laugh. "To think our entire family was there to witness it except for me."

"And Ethan."

Jane nodded. "And Ethan."

The Davis family was connected to the earl in an unusual manner. A few years earlier, during the time the earl had been a notorious rake, he had dallied with their cousin, Kitty, who had been in service.

Kitty, being with child as a consequence, had retreated to the Davises' tenant farm where she had died in childbirth and left Ethan in their care. No one had known who his father was until the earl had begun a crusade to make amends for his past earlier this year and unexpectedly learned about Ethan. Lord Richard Balfour had claimed his four-year-old son, gifting their father with a small country estate in gratitude for taking care of his first child.

A few weeks earlier, wanting Emma's assistance with settling Ethan into his new household, the earl had invited Emma and Jane for a Season in London. Perry had acted as their tutor to prepare them for entry into high society, but Emma and he had quickly fallen in love.

Both of their families had just gathered at Saunton Park for the wedding in the chapel a few days earlier, before bidding the Davis family farewell when they had returned to nearby Rose Ash to make room for arriving guests.

Perry and Emma had delayed their own departure for Shepton Abbey because Perry was to meet a very important guest who was arriving today—a brother who had just been discovered by the earl.

Jane was grateful for the additional time with Emma. Her sister was a year older than her own eighteen years, but infinitely wiser. A bluestocking who had raised Ethan. And now she was leaving. Embarking on a new adventure while Jane tried to sort through her thoughts of what she wanted from her own life.

"Have you thought about what we talked about?" It was as if Emma were reading her thoughts aloud.

Jane drew a deep breath. "I do not know what I want my future to hold. If you were anyone else, you would accept my first answer. That a young landowner would likely suffice."

"The husband you choose will greatly influence your future. Please assure me you will not follow society's dictates on what a successful match consists of and that you will think on what your own desires are."

"How will I know when I meet the right man?"

Emma sighed. "You must know your own heart, your own dreams. Then you will know if the gentleman will make the appropriate partner."

"I have no dreams beyond a happy family with lots of children."

Emma snorted. "One moment I am impressed with your maturity and the next you sound like a silly child once more."

"Why?"

"You answer my question as if you have no thoughts of

your own. You like to write. Your prospective husband should support that. Not so many years ago you spoke of traveling, of seeing the length and breadth of our fine kingdom, and perhaps voyaging to parts of the Continent. You appreciate fashion plates, and family, and you wish to have children. And you plan to spend time with your children and not relegate them to a nursery as some of those fops plan to do." Emma waved her hand at the arriving guests below.

"Hmm ... you make it sound as if I have a mind of my own."

Emma tilted her head back to look up at her with thoughtful coal-black eyes. Jane's sister might be older than her, but she was diminutive in stature. "You do! I have seen many gentlemen gravitate towards you, but you have not yet shown interest in any of them."

"They seem so dull. I am looking for a gent who engages my mind, as you have with your Perry."

Her sister beamed. "Excellent. Keep that in mind and you should be fine."

Jane yawned, shaking her head to invigorate her thoughts.

"You still do not sleep?"

"I am just too excited. Just think, the next time we meet, it could be for my own wedding. How can one sleep with so much to consider?"

Emma frowned. "I wish you would see the earl's physician to discuss what might be causing you to stay awake all night."

Jane shrugged. "I am young and in good health. It is the excitement of this unexpected Season."

"If it persists, will you at least consult a herbalist? There should be one nearby."

Jane bent forward to embrace her sister. "I shall be lost without you. You are my dearest friend."

"I shall miss you so much, Jane!"

"Nonsense! You have a handsome husband and a new estate to manage. You will barely think of me while I am left bereft to meet all these strangers."

They both turned to the window once more. Another carriage had arrived, and Jane watched as an intriguing man descended from its depths.

He was tall, the same height as the earl, who hurried over to greet him, but he appeared taller because he was so slim. There was not an ounce of extra flesh anywhere on his form. A very fine form at that, with shining black Hessians covering his lower legs, buckskins stretched over long, muscular thighs, and a black coat draped over wide shoulders and a lean torso. The coat was in an unusual choice of color but suited his black waves of hair, which he wore a little too long. He had a close-cropped beard and a strong, narrow face.

Jane found her attention riveted by the sense of energy and purpose he exuded, wondering who he was as he thrust out a large hand to greet the earl. Was this one of the gents whom Richard intended for her to meet?

Beyond them, the clipped yews and broad lawn glistened in the soft morning light, a curving gravel lane sweeping away toward a hedge-framed garden path. The house party was truly underway.

A pang of disappointment followed when the man turned to assist an elegant woman from the carriage. Her jet-black hair and olive skin suggested an Italian or Spanish heritage. This must be his wife. As if to confirm her assumption, he reached into the carriage and turned back with a little girl in his arms. The only oddity was that the child had thick, silver-blonde hair. Perhaps this was a child from an earlier marriage?

Jane yawned again and turned away from the window. Walking across the room, she leaned over and breathed deeply of the coffee aroma wafting from the tray. Taking a seat, she poured a cup, adding cream and sugar before settling back to drink, her fingers brushing the worn brocade arm of the chair where she had curled many a night with a book.

Emma came over and joined her, pouring a cup of tea. "I cannot believe that you have taken up drinking that foul beverage, Jane. I do not know why Perry agreed to let you try it."

"It awakens me, especially when I have not slept until the early hours."

Emma rolled her eyes. "I still think it is a mistake. Not least because it is noxious."

Jane did not comment. Draining her cup, she put it down and crossed the room to pick up the gift she had made for her sister. "I wanted to give you this ... for your new life at Shepton Abbey."

"What is it?"

"Some needlework to celebrate your nuptials."

Emma came over, and Jane handed her the embroidered cloth. Her sister stretched it out, gasping in surprise. "Jane! It is beautiful. I swear you are a veritable artiste with the floss! When did you find time to do it?"

Jane smiled. "I am not sleeping, Emma. I have plenty of time on my hands."

They both gazed at the embroidered scene. It depicted a towering oak tree surrounded by a field of colorful wildflowers—*wildflower* was a private sobriquet she had overheard Perry calling her sister since their wedding ceremony.

"May your marriage grow strong while allowing you the freedom to follow your own way, sister."

Emma reached over to embrace her sister once more. "Thank you."

BARCLAY TILTED his head back to view the grand Palladian manor that Tsar had completed building in early 1787, glimpsing two women standing at a window in what would be the family block to the left of the main house.

The house had been completed the year Barclay was conceived, when a seventeen-year-old Aurora Thompson had been seduced by the then-owner, the late Earl of Saunton.

Or *Satan*, as the current earl had referred to our sire.

A rusticated lower level was crowned by a towering upper level, perfectly cut, symmetrical planes soaring into the deep blue vaults of the Somerset sky. The many windowpanes shimmered in the light, reflecting the bucolic lawns and the great oaks that rolled outward across the parkland to where the earth and firmament met—a marriage of the solid and the ethereal.

High above them, classically inspired statues stood as silent sentinels, while twin majestic staircases converged on a landing in front of the Corinthian columns beneath their feet. Sunlight played across the pale stone, casting sharp shadows that emphasized the grandeur of the facade. It was one of Tsar's finest works, a testament to his talent, but until this day Barclay had only seen it in his grandfather's architectural plans.

His newly discovered brother, Richard, had walked away to fetch someone for Barclay to meet, while he gazed up with fascination at the monumental house. This building was the legacy Tsar would leave behind, and his grandfather's creation impressed Barclay.

Tatiana gazed up with him. "Grandpapa built this?"

"He did. Or rather he designed it, and then supervised the master builder who built it over the next fifteen years."

"It is beautiful," she said reverently.

Barclay smiled down at his daughter, her small hand clasped in his. "As are you."

At that moment, a servant approached them. Barclay assumed it was the butler, based on his rigid decorum and immaculate attire.

"Mr. Thompson, one of the maids will escort your daughter to the nursery."

Barclay narrowed his eyes. "Nursery?"

The ginger-haired servant straightened up, looking down his hawkish nose with the utmost dignity. "Indeed, sir. The nursery."

Barclay's lips thinned as he thought. The Thompson family was inseparable, and Tatiana had never been sequestered on a different floor, with only servants to interact with. Not only that, but his child had struggled with night terrors since her mother died, and he frequently attended her at night. When he was traveling, his mother took his place in comforting her.

Barclay shot a perturbed look at Aurora, who held up her hands in question. They had failed to think about what the arrangements for his young daughter would be at such a country house, but Barclay should have predicted these circumstances as a man who drew plans of these homes for the wealthy. However, he personally had never subscribed to the notion that children should be kept separate from the family.

He frowned. Agreeing to attend the house party was a mistake. He should have insisted they remain in London. Now Tsar was handling his work for him, which was more than the old man should deal with, and his daughter was peering up in fright at the servant.

"Papa?" Her voice quavered.

"It will not do."

The butler tensed, clearly uncertain how to respond. "Sir, I assure you that the nursery is well-attended and there are several children already arrived. We set aside a place of honor for your daughter—"

"It will not do." Barclay ensured his voice was firm but low. He did not want to alarm Tatiana any more than she already was. "Do not worry, Tatiana. We will return home if we must."

From the corner of his eye, he saw the earl rushing over. His new brother must have noticed the stiffness of the interaction, as he appeared mildly alarmed.

"Is there an issue?"

"Your butler wishes to remove my daughter to the attics, like some sort of prisoner. I know how the peerage treat their children, and it will not be tolerated in the Thompson family."

Richard bit his lip. "Barclay, I assure you we are not a traditional family of the nobility. My son, Ethan, joins me for breakfast each morning before we ride together. Then he goes to the lovely and well-equipped nursery for lessons and whatnot before coming back downstairs for family time."

Barclay straightened to his full height, satisfied to discover he was a good inch taller than his younger brother. "I thought you married earlier this year?"

"Yes, that is correct."

"You are a young man. The countess must be your first wife?"

Richard's expression reflected strain. "Yes."

His new brother was turning out to be no better than his debauched sire, who had ruined his mother. Barclay struck without sympathy. "How do you have a son old enough to breakfast with you?"

"An astute question," a velvet voice drawled from behind his shoulder, but Barclay did not react. He merely listened while firming his jaw to glare at the earl. "I thought the entire kingdom knew my brother had sired a son on the wrong side of the blanket."

Barclay narrowed his eyes into an accusing stare. The earl fidgeted uncomfortably with his cravat, a telling gesture. "It is not what you think. I did not know about Ethan ... I mean ..."

"Calm yourself, brother." The voice moved as a man stepped around into Barclay's view to reveal the earl's apparent twin, who bowed. "Good afternoon, Barclay. I am Peregrine Balfour. Your younger brother." The gentleman's sable locks, square jaw, and emerald eyes were a mirror of his older brother's. "I assure you that my brother claimed Ethan as his own the moment he learned of him. Subsequently, he posed that perhaps our father had sired children we did not know of and set his men to finding you. There is little resemblance between him and the late Earl of Satan."

Barclay sized up the newcomer carefully. "You just married?"

Peregrine inclined his head in acknowledgment. "I did. I married Ethan's cousin, Emma Davis. The entire Davis family has just departed for their estate, which my brother gifted them. As I said—no resemblance. My brother is a good man with a notorious past, which he has taken pains to set right."

Richard closed his eyes. When he reopened them, he appeared more composed, his cravat only slightly crumpled. "I apologize for not explaining the circumstances before your visit. It was difficult to inform you, considering your circumstances. I had hoped to discuss it in my study before Ethan came down to play chess with the family this afternoon."

Barclay sighed in capitulation, relaxing his stance. "I appreciate that this is an awkward situation we find ourselves in. However, my daughter is accustomed to being close to her family."

The men turned to acknowledge Aurora, who had joined them and appeared disconcerted by the two brothers, her eyes darting from one to the other. Barclay wondered if they resembled the late Earl of Satan in their coloring, their features and height being similar to his own. Was it a strain for her to return to the site of her social ruin after these many years?

Stepping forward, the earl took up her hand, bowing solemnly. "Miss Thompson, it is our great pleasure to host you. Please allow me to introduce my brother, Peregrine Balfour." Perry stepped forward, bowing deeply.

Barclay's mother responded with a dignified curtsy. "My lord. The pleasure is mine, I assure you." Then she moved her head to the side to pout at Tatiana, who giggled in response, hiding behind Barclay.

"I am afraid both the family wing and the guest wing are fully occupied. There are no rooms left for Tatiana."

She smiled graciously. "Then Tatiana will sleep in my room. In the guest wing."

Richard's tension visibly eased. "If that is acceptable …"

He glanced at Barclay for confirmation, who inclined his head. "... then we shall have a cot brought to your room. But, Miss Thompson, we have situated you and Barclay in the family wing."

Barclay's mother was a woman well accustomed to keeping her composure under trying circumstances. She had been forced to acquire the skill when she had kept her natural-born son despite society's censure of her as an unwed mother. At the news she was to stay in the family wing of Saunton Park as an honored relation of the earl, Aurora threw a hand over her mouth in consternation. "My lord ... that is not necessary."

To Barclay's ear, it sounded like his mother might be overcome with emotion, her words quavering and tight. Was she fighting back tears?

The earl bowed deeply. "I assure you ... it is long overdue." Then he turned to drop a bow to Tatiana, who was peeking around Barclay's elbow at the scene. "Welcome, Miss Tatiana. It will be the great honor of the Balfour family to host you in our family rooms."

Tatiana blinked her big blue eyes, then stepped forward to curtsy, craning her neck up to address the tall nobleman. "Thank you, milord."

Richard delivered an exaggerated wink. "I am your Uncle Richard." The earl glanced over to Barclay, as if seeking permission to continue. Barclay gave a brief nod, and Richard turned back to Tatiana. "Here, come meet your Uncle Perry."

As Barclay observed the introductions, he wondered what more surprises lay in store for him on this unanticipated jaunt to the country.

CHAPTER
TWO

"I declare after all there is no enjoyment like reading! How much sooner one tires of anything than of a book!"

Jane Austen

Emma and Jane spent their final hours together while Perry and Richard were somewhere in the manor acquainting themselves with their new brother. Finally, Jane bid her sister and Perry a tearful farewell before watching their carriages depart for Shepton Abbey. It was late afternoon, and the manor cast long shadows across the drive as the carriages disappeared around a corner.

Turning back to the house, Jane addressed the earl's wife. "Sophia, I think I shall retire to my room to eat dinner. I did not sleep, and I rose early to spend these last hours with Emma."

The countess walked over to clasp her hands with

concern. "Of course, Jane. There is no pressing need to attend dinner this evening. Our guests are still arriving, so I believe it will be an informal gathering, and you can meet Mr. Thompson and his family in the morning. Should we send for the physician?"

Jane shook her head. "It is nothing that a nap will not set right."

Sophia's stormy blue eyes displayed her worry. "Please do not hesitate to have us summon him."

Jane smiled in acknowledgment before departing for the family wing. Soon she was undressed and attired in her nightclothes, settling her weary head to the pillow.

Some hours later, she awoke. Night had fallen, and the room was dark, the familiar silhouettes of the furniture softened in shadow. Rising from the bed, she lit a beeswax candle and watched as the flame flickered to life, casting a pool of golden light against the dimness.

Crossing to the dressing table, she uncapped her dental elixir and poured a portion into a glass before adding water from the pitcher. Then she raised it to her lips to take a mouthful, swishing it gently before leaning over to spit into the empty pitcher beside it.

"What are you doing?"

Jane jumped in fright, spilling several drops of the watered-down elixir over the table, but managing to hold on to the remainder of the contents. Her hand came up to clutch her chest, where her heart beat like that of a panicked rabbit while she gasped for breath.

Turning around, she saw a tiny form in the corner of her room.

The figure stood up and stepped into the light, and Jane realized it was the little girl from earlier, her silver-blonde hair shining like rays of moonlight in the dimly lit room.

"Hallo?"

The girl's cherubic face broke into a smile. "Hallo."

"Are you lost?"

Her little face grew thoughtful. "No, but I am a little bored. I am not accustomed to traveling anymore, and I believe I should have brought more books with me."

Jane fumbled mentally. She was familiar with dealing with children, and this girl appeared to be about the same age as her youngest sister, little Maddie, but she was groggy from her nap and not sure how the child had come to be in her room.

"What were you doing?" The girl pointed a slender finger at the bottle of elixir and the water glass standing on the table. "Why did you spit that out? Did it not taste good?"

Jane gathered her wits about her. "It is a dental elixir that the countess's French maid prepared for me. It is not intended for drinking."

"What is it for?"

"It cleans the mouth. I had sensitive gums recently, so Miss Toussaint made the elixir for me. You swirl it around in your mouth, then spit it out."

"Curious." The waif wandered closer to inspect the glass, diminutive compared to the height of the dressing table. "What is in it?"

"Pyrethrum, some rosemary essence, nutmeg, a little bergamot, and some very strong brandy. Which is why I water it down before I use it."

"What is pyrethrum?"

"It is a daisy."

The girl reached out and took up the glass, raising it to her nose to sniff it. "It smells good and foul at the same time."

Jane grinned. "Indeed."

The girl tilted her head back, her deep blue gaze so intense that Jane unintentionally stepped back.

"May I try it? My gums have been bothering me." She stretched her mouth open to reveal pearly white teeth. The front two were missing to give her a gap-toothed smile.

Jane found herself rather charmed by the child. She gave a nod. "If you promise not to swallow any?"

Raising the glass, the girl took a mouthful to swirl it around for several seconds exactly as Jane had done, then turned to spit it into the empty pitcher. She straightened back up, smacking her lips. "It does taste foul!"

Laughing, Jane took the glass from her. "How are your gums?"

"They feel clean."

"Excellent." Putting the glass down, Jane dropped a little curtsy. "I am Miss Jane Davis. Who might you be?"

"Tatiana Thompson. The earl is my uncle." The last was said with reverent pride.

Jane realized that the gentleman she had seen disembark from the carriage earlier that day must be the new brother of the earl.

Well, not new, per se. Just newly discovered.

"Then we are related ... distantly. The earl's son is my cousin."

"Ethan?"

"That is correct."

"My papa grew quite stern when he heard about Ethan."

"Did he?"

"He did. I think he had an issue with how long the earl had been married."

Jane rubbed her face, not sure how to respond. "Um ..."

"Is it because Ethan is a bastard? Like my papa?"

Jane could not prevent a grimace from flickering across her face. How did she wind up being the unfortunate party to address this question?

"I think it best you ask your papa about that."

"Is Ethan a bastard?"

Jane shook her head. "Ethan is a very nice boy. A true gentleman. It is true his mother and the earl were not wed, so he is natural born. But it is not polite to call someone … that."

"Why?"

Tucking a curl behind her ear, Jane dropped into the chair so she might be more of a height with the little girl. "It is an impolite word. Ethan cannot help the circumstances of his birth. It is more polite to say natural born."

Tatiana contemplated her for several seconds. "Then the person who called Papa that was being rude?"

"Yes, it was an insult."

"I did not like the man. He was complaining to his companion the entire time he waited in the drawing room, and I thought he was not very nice. Or correct about his complaints."

"How did you know what a bastard is?"

"The man sort of explained it during his complaining. He did not know I was hiding behind the sofa. It was enlightening."

Jane chuckled. "It is not polite to eavesdrop."

"What is that?"

"It means to listen to another's conversation."

Tatiana shrugged. "What they do not know cannot offend them."

At this, Jane could not hold back a laugh. *From the mouth of babes.*

Tatiana stepped forward, placing a hand on Jane's cheek as she stared deep into her eyes. "I like you."

She smiled in response. "Thank you. I like you, too."

"You treat me like a person."

"Thank you. I have several younger brothers and a sister who just went home, so it is pleasant to talk with you in their stead."

"Will you marry my papa?"

Jane sputtered, turning her head to cough into her hand in her surprise. After several moments, she responded in a dry, hoarse voice, "Does your papa not have a wife?"

"No." Tatiana leaned closer so her face was just inches away from Jane's. "Mama died. I am sad, but I think it is worse for him. Papa is very lonely, and he does not smile like he did before. I think he needs a new wife."

"Well ... that is a choice your father must make."

Tatiana's cherubic face fell in disappointment, her little lip quivering as she bit it. "You will not marry him?"

"Your father must decide when he is ready. And he must choose his own wife."

The little girl walked away, standing in the shadows with her back turned. "I am worried about him."

Jane felt her eyes prickle with threatening tears. The child was so sweet, and her heart went out to the little one who had lost her mother so young. "How long has it been?"

The blonde hair bobbed as she inclined her head. Jane thought she might be counting on her fingers. "It is two years."

"That is a long time to be without a mama."

"I miss her."

Jane could not help it. A tear of sympathy escaped the corner of her eye at the little girl's plight. Reaching up, she brushed it away, and when she was ready, she spoke in a steady voice. "I am sorry, Tatiana. I cannot imagine how that must be."

"I miss Papa, too. We used to go with him to see his buildings, but since Mama died, he leaves me at home with Grandmama. I want to go with him, and have a mother to read me stories at night ... and I want ... I want to see him smile." The little girl's voice was thick as she stated the last.

Jane hurried across the room. Dropping to her haunches, she embraced the little girl, burying her face in her sweet-smelling silver hair.

"I am sure when he is ready, your papa will find a wife."

Tatiana hugged her back. "I hope so."

They spoke for several more minutes before Jane escorted the girl back to her room down the hall. Knocking quietly, she waited hand in hand with Tatiana until the door opened to reveal the black-haired beauty she had observed earlier that day.

"Miss Thompson? I believe I have something of yours."

The woman was lively, and although she must have been close to fifty to have a Tatiana as a granddaughter, her olive face was barely lined. Her high cheekbones and flawless skin spoke to a Mediterranean heritage, while her thick black hair fell to her waist in a gleaming plait. She had risen from bed, her brown eyes bleary and unfocused—until she caught sight of her granddaughter peeking from behind the skirts of Jane's wrap. She looked back into the room to the cot near the bed, as if expecting to see a replica of the girl lying there.

Turning back, she wailed, "Tatiana! What are you doing out of bed?"

Jane noted a slight Mediterranean lilt to the older woman's voice. "She came to find me in my room."

Over the next few moments, they made their introductions. Jane led the child into the room, and then, with a nod of her head, gestured that she needed to speak in the hall with the grandmother.

Miss Thompson understood her. After tucking Tatiana back into the cot, she followed Jane from the room and closed the door behind her.

Jane told her of the conversation that they had had. When they parted ways, the grandmother had a look of worry on her face, but Jane felt better for meeting the woman, who appeared genuinely concerned about Tatiana's request. She was certain that the woman would address the matter.

Walking away as the door clicked shut behind her, Jane visited the library in search of a new book. She was wide awake in the middle of the night, and recent evenings had taught her it would be some hours before she fell asleep once more. With no sister left in residence, a good novel was needed to keep her company.

BARCLAY LEANED on the ledge of his bedroom window, staring up at the moon which cast a silver light across the landscape. The chamber behind him was quiet, the hearth embers long gone to ash, and the only sound was the soft stir of the drapes as the breeze moved through the crack in the casement. Pale ribbons of moonlight spilled across the polished floorboards, and from somewhere in the distance came the solitary hoot of an owl.

He pondered what Natalya would say about this recent turn of events.

They had acquired a whole new family. An important earl, his various relations, and tonight, at dinner, he had met the Duke of Halmesbury and his duchess. The man had been imposing in stature, several inches taller than Barclay, who was himself six feet. But the big, blond Viking had a steady manner and calm gray eyes, and appeared genuinely honored to meet him.

After dinner, the earl and the duke had met with him in the study to converse—the younger brother with the smooth manners and even smoother tongue had departed earlier in the day with his new bride.

Once in the study, the duke had taken the time to explain their connection. The late earl, whom no one seemed to remember with any relish, was the younger brother of the duke's late mother. As Richard had stated, Barclay was indeed a first cousin to the duke, which was still a fact he was having difficulty assimilating.

If Natalya had been by his side tonight, she would have been so pleased on his behalf. His late wife had never been tolerant of anyone who socially snubbed the Thompsons because of Barclay's parentage, and she would have heartily approved of the earl's decision to find him and acknowledge him as kin.

With that thought, his memories turned to his young wife.

When Barclay had been a much younger man, Tsar had sent him to negotiate new contracts with suppliers in St. Petersburg. He had arrived in late spring, when the Neva River shimmered beneath nearly endless skies and lilacs bloomed along the embankments. The light never seemed to fade, and the scent of warmed stone and birchwood drifted through the city streets, where merchant families in fine carriages passed beneath rows of wrought iron balconies and bell towers.

He had stayed in the home of a respected merchant—an

old friend of his grandfather—where he met the merchant's youngest daughter, recently returned from finishing school.

Natalya had caught his attention at once, acting as his interpreter at social events. He still recalled what she had worn that first night—a gown of soft lilac silk, the hem embroidered with tiny white wildflowers, and a sheer shawl fastened with a silver filigree brooch. Her hair, the color of moonlight, was plaited into elegant coils and adorned with a carved ivory comb. Her manner was warm and graceful, her voice low and precise as she translated jokes and proposals with equal poise. She smelled faintly of rose attar and orange blossom water.

To her, his parentage had meant nothing. She had not blinked at the mention of his unmarried mother. She only cared for him.

Her father had considered the match an honor—uniting with the family of Tsar was no small matter, even if Barclay bore the stain of illegitimacy. The man had looked beyond society's snubs and seen a future son-in-law worthy of his daughter.

Barclay had intended to stay a month. He had remained for three.

And when the ship set sail for home, his Russian bride had stood beside him—his Natalya, silver-haired and smiling, her hand wrapped tightly in his.

When Natalya had accepted his proposal and embarked on a new life in England, they had both known their days together were numbered. She suffered from a weak heart, but she had refused to allow her condition to hold her back. She had been determined to live life to its fullest, and Barclay was grateful for every moment he had shared with her on this earth.

When she had decided to have a child—something the doctors had cautioned her against—his wife could not be dissuaded. She had wanted to leave a piece of herself behind.

"You must allow this, Barclay. One day I will no longer be here, and then you will be grateful to have our child to remember me by."

He had reluctantly agreed, and Natalya had bravely taken the journey of motherhood, taking every precaution to protect herself during that time. And she had been proved right in her quest. She had survived the ordeal to bring Tatiana into the world and lived another six years as her mother. Long enough to see their daughter walk for the first time, to hear her laugh, and to watch her grow from a tiny babe into a spirited young girl.

Barclay could regret none of their time together—made all the more sweet because his beloved had fulfilled her dream of motherhood, and had been there to witness their daughter bloom into a small, radiant version of herself. Then Natalya's heart had taken its last beat, and she had slipped away from them for the final time.

Even as her health declined, she had continued to dress with quiet elegance—her beloved shawl always around her shoulders, her silver hair still pinned with the comb he had given her on their wedding night.

Tatiana tilted her head just like her mother once had, her laughter on certain days so like Natalya's that it startled him.

His wife would have been so pleased for him this evening. So happy that Aurora and Tatiana would gain a new level of social status with this recent development. She had believed in family, in honor, and would have admired the earl for searching him out and elevating their name.

He wished she were here to view this beautiful moonlit night with him. To discuss the events of the day and their arrival at this magnificent country home. "Barclay, you did well, bringing our family here."

As he had so often done since her death, Barclay had summoned Natalya from his memories to stand at his side. She appeared just as she had in life—wrapped in her amethyst shawl, the ivory comb catching the moonlight in her pale hair, her expression serene and steady.

"I knew it was what you would want."

She smiled, resting her delicate head against his shoulder. "You were right."

Barclay's heart squeezed tight. He knew this phantasy could only survive so much—he could not attempt to touch her, or his imagination would fail and his grief would return. He missed his wife so much, it was a physical pain.

"Anything for you."

"But, my love, you promised me you would find a new wife. A new mother for Tatiana."

Barclay grimaced. Recently, every time he called Natalya from the recesses of his mind, she admonished him for not fulfilling his last promise to her.

"I am not ready, Talie."

"It is ... *vremya* ..." She searched for the English word, as she often had in the past. "Time. It is time, Barclay. I have been gone two years now, and Tatiana needs a mother."

"I cannot, my love. I still hear your voice. I still turn to find you when I wake. I cannot ... replace you."

She smiled, tears dampening her silver lashes. "Not replace. Someone new. Someone different to provide you comfort. An English girl, perhaps, who does not care about your lack of a father. Who cares for you."

Her voice was a balm and a blade—soft as silk, but it cut him all the same.

"Please, Natalya. I cannot."

Natalya frowned lightly, turning to place a hand on his chest as she always had when imparting advice. He could almost feel the remembered warmth of her palm, though he dared not look directly at her hand.

"You must let me go, Barclay. My child needs a mother. And you need a new partner."

"Talie—"

A knock at the door interrupted his thoughts. He blinked. The moon slipped behind a cloud as she faded, the silver light dimming, as if taking her with it. Shaking his head, he returned to the moment, crossing the room as the memory of Natalya departed as quietly as it had arrived.

Jane sat in a wingback chair in the far corner of the library, reading the book of poetry she had found on the shelves. Since arriving in the Balfour household, she had been struggling with insomnia, but had grown to enjoy the late hours when the household had retired to bed. It allowed her to read in peace.

A single candelabrum flickered on the table beside her, casting long, wavering shadows across the book-lined walls. She turned the page to her favorite sonnet, tracing a finger over the familiar lines from the Bard as she mouthed the words to herself.

In the distance, she heard footsteps approaching.

Not sure who might be entering the library so late at night, she drew her long legs up onto the seat, adjusting her wrap to conceal herself until she knew who had interrupted her solitude.

"Why is it we need to converse in the library at this hour, Mother?"

Jane shivered at the husky quality of the man's voice, her skin tingling in response to the warm, textured sound. It wrapped around her like the velvet lining of a winter cloak.

Leaning around the wing of her chair, she stole a peek.

It was him. Tatiana's father.

Jane realized she should announce her presence, but she found herself reluctant to do so. She wanted to enjoy listening to him for a few minutes more. If she made herself known, there would be polite introductions, awkward greetings—and all of it while they were in their nightclothes, which did not seem an auspicious beginning.

"Barclay, it is important that Tatiana not overhear us. You know how she is. I thought if we talk here in the library, we will leave her undisturbed. The poor mite only just fell asleep."

The accented voice confirmed that his mother was the companion who had followed him into the room.

He gave a dry laugh, which skidded over Jane's scalp like warm honey. His tone had such a dark and unique timbre, thrilling to listen to, and unlike any she had heard before.

"Are you certain she was not feigning?"

Miss Thompson responded pertly, "Quite certain. She already snuck out for the evening while I was asleep, but a charming young woman returned her to me."

It sounded like the pair had taken the seats near the entrance of the library. Jane considered rising to inform them of her presence, but she held back. Once again, she found her romantic nature stirred by the presence of the gentleman, and this was her chance to gain insight into him.

"What was so urgent we needed to meet at this late hour?"

"We need to discuss your future, Barclay. This house party represents an opportunity for you to move forward. Natalya has been gone for two years now, and you need to think about the future."

Barclay was quiet for several seconds before making a low sound of dissension.

"I do not wish to talk about Natalya. Or the future, for that matter."

"Barclay, I just want to help. You are not aware that Tatiana approached a stranger this evening and asked the young lady to be her new mother?"

"What?"

"You heard me correctly. She found a young woman in the family wing. Miss Davis is a distant relation to the earl, and Tatiana was quite taken with her—so much so that she proposed that Miss Davis marry you."

The gentleman paused before replying.

"Why would she do that?"

"Tatiana is worried about you. Which is why I insist we need to discuss this situation … for Tatiana's sake. It has been a long time since Natalya left us. It is time for you to pursue a new relationship. To start again."

The gentleman sighed, while Jane held her breath, awaiting his response. The precocious daughter and the melancholy father captivated her attention. If only she knew how to help them.

"We will be fine."

Miss Thompson snorted delicately.

"Barclay, something must be missing from your lives if your daughter is proposing on your behalf to strangers. We must deal with this, son. Are you sleeping?"

"No, but who can sleep when the most beautiful woman in the world was stolen to the heavens by greedy angels, leaving us mere mortals behind to grieve?"

Jane felt a pang shoot through her chest. The raw honesty of the man's grief was almost too much to hear. There was poetry in his pain, in the way he spoke of his wife—so vivid, so undiminished. She lowered her eyes to the book in her lap, though the words had long since blurred. A single line from the sonnet lingered in her thoughts.

"I all alone beweep my outcast state..."

She should not be here, eavesdropping like some schoolgirl. And yet she could not bring herself to rise.

It was poignant, his love for his lost wife. Jane wished to comfort him in his sadness—and wished, with a sudden sharpness, that a man might one day love her in that way.

"Son, your child needs a mother. And you need a wife. It is time to consider the future."

"How can I consider the future?"

There was silence. Then came the question, soft and deliberate:

"Do you think you could love again?"

Jane rested her chin on her knees, scarcely breathing in her anticipation of what he might say.

"That seems an impossibility."

"Then what will you do?"

"I will ... continue. I will rise in the morning and go about my day. I will spend time with Tatiana and then return to bed in the evening and remember my dear wife until …"

"Until?"

"Until one day I wake up and this terrible sense of loss has faded, and I can forget how wonderful it was when we were a family. When my silver faerie was at my side … and my child had a mother."

In the silence that followed, Jane could swear she could hear the gentleman's heart cracking in two. The discussion had become so intimate, so raw, that there was no possibility of announcing her presence now. Her body was tense with the need to vanish. She barely dared to breathe, terrified they might hear the faint intake of her breath in the deep stillness.

And yet, she could not pull herself away. She wanted to offer comfort, to soothe his grief—do something. *Anything.*

If she were older, more worldly, had something to offer him … she might find the courage to act. Offer him solace?

But what could a young girl such as she, with no life experience, offer a single father in his thirties, haunted by the ghost of a beloved wife? Jane had never felt so helpless. She would seem an immature flibbertigibbet beside this weary, grieving gentleman.

His mother interrupted the gloom that had descended on the conversation.

"I appreciate you loved Natalya with all your heart, but you understand this cannot continue?"

There was a long pause.

"I … know."

"So you will make an effort to meet some women at this house party? Ask the earl and his countess to make introductions to eligible women?"

Another pause, deeper and heavier.

"I ... suppose ... I must ... for Tatiana's sake."

CHAPTER
THREE

"We are all fools in love."

Jane Austen

Barclay had grown weary of the house party, and it was only the second day. Tatiana and Aurora were having tea with the countess in the family drawing room, but he was unaccustomed to idle days. Idle houseguests made it even worse, drawing him into annoying discussions.

After escaping an inane conversation with a spoilt young beau who had introduced himself as Lord Julius Trafford, Barclay sought the library. Surely anyone he encountered in that venerated room would be inclined to be more intelligent than the pontificating fool—with his insipid poetry—whom he had just left behind in the billiard room?

Barclay relaxed as he entered the room of shelves and books, even considering shutting the door behind him when ... when he saw her.

The earl's son, Ethan, was playing chess. Barclay had met the lad the afternoon before when he had been bullied into his own match with the boy, whose current companion distracted Barclay beyond reason.

She was utterly glorious. A mane of ebony curls poised on her elegant head, smooth, creamy skin to draw the eye, and long limbs.

The young woman finished her move and then sat back in her chair, her ice-blue eyes flickering toward the doorway. She blinked in surprise, gazing at Barclay intently as she nervously tucked a lock of silky hair behind her ear. It was a magical moment, intensity sparking between them in visceral awareness. Something he had not experienced since the first time he had laid eyes on Natalya upon his arrival in St. Petersburg.

The profound connection was abruptly severed when Ethan spoke to her from across the table. Barclay resumed his breathing, blinking several times as the room came back into focus.

"Uncle *Bar-clee!*"

The little boy had just noticed his presence, hopping off his chair, careful not to disturb the board, before racing over. He lifted his arms, and Barclay realized the boy wanted him to lift him.

He bent over to scoop the lad up, who embraced him in a hug.

"Are you here to play chess with me? I am in the middle of a game at the moment, so you will have to wait a bit."

Barclay chuckled. Ethan was unbearably sweet, only

four or five years old, but Richard had informed him that the lad had grown up with a large, exuberant family, so he was in his element to have new relations in residence.

"I suppose I might wait my turn. Who is your lovely opponent?"

Ethan wriggled out of his arms as Barclay gently lowered him, racing back across the room.

"Miss Jane Davis, may I present my Uncle *Bar-clee Tom ... Tom's son ...*"

The boy's face fell at his failed attempt to formally introduce him.

"Thompson."

Ethan tried again, determined.

"May I present my Uncle *Bar-clee Tom-son?*"

The lovely creature he addressed stood up and politely curtsied. "Good afternoon, Mr. Thompson. I am glad we finally meet."

This was who his daughter had proposed to? She was heavenly. Barclay bowed deeply, deeper than he intended. *Blazes,* was he nervous about meeting the young woman?

"The pleasure is mine, Miss Davis."

She laughed, the sound harmonious, like the ringing of one of the perfectly pitched bells his firm had recently arranged to be hung in the spire of St. Michael's Church in Yorkshire. He remembered the gleaming bronze shimmering in the morning sun as the workmen hoisted it into place. The parishioners had gathered in the square to listen as its first clear peal swept across the dales. That was how her laughter sounded—pure and bright, like a stroke of joy carried on the wind.

"Please, we are all extended family of a sort, so there is no need for formalities." She frowned slightly, as if that statement made her uncomfortable, before elucidating. "That is, you are Ethan's uncle on his father's side of the family, and I am his cousin on his mother's side."

Barclay quirked an eyebrow. Was Miss Davis subtly elaborating that they were *not* blood relations?

"Of course, we are more directly related because my sister married your half-brother, Perry."

Her face fell at this announcement before she finished her thoughts in defeat.

"You may call me Jane."

Barclay was having trouble focusing on her words, fascinated by her glowing countenance. There was a vibrancy to her—a spark, like sunlight glancing off glass. He managed to bob his head in a brief bow.

"Please call me Barclay ... Jane."

They stared at each other, wordless, until Ethan broke the crackling tension.

"Will you wait for me to finish my game, Uncle *Bar-clee?*"

He nodded, following them back to the game they had set up. He took a seat to observe them play, using the opportunity to run his eyes over the fascinating woman. She was beautiful. Her eyes were framed by sooty black lashes, and she was taller than most women, a mere hand shorter than him. Willowy and graceful, she fueled his overpowering desire to sweep her into his arms in a waltz.

His eyes fell to her bow-shaped mouth, soft and unpainted, which was when he realized he was in trouble. He might not have noticed a single woman other than his own wife in ten years, but now he found himself entranced by a young girl who could be no more than eighteen, considering she had not the faintest line on her flawless skin.

She is too young, Barclay. You cannot possibly be thinking there is a possibility of courtship!

He closed his eyes as Jane moved a piece across the board, collecting his wits. When he opened them once more, he focused on the board and the strategy his young nephew was employing. He looked up to find Jane watching him, but her eyes quickly skittered away. It would appear she was just as aware of him—of the frisson of excitement that her presence evoked.

This is horribly inappropriate, Barclay. You need a mature woman who can be a mother for your daughter. Are you your father's son, to have your head turned by a woman who has not yet reached her majority?

He shivered in repulsion. Jane could not be more than a year or two older than his own mother had been when she had been seduced by his lecherous sire. He needed to seek an appropriate woman of ... appropriate years, not have his head turned by a young girl.

And yet ... there was something about her. A hint of magic.

It is not magic. It is lust! Latent hereditary impulses.

On the other hand, she seemed just as enamored as he was.

Faith! It is certain that is precisely what the Earl of Satan said to himself just before he seduced Aurora in this very house more than three decades ago.

His chest tightened, and Barclay wished he were back in London to discuss the events of the past day with his grandfather. Tsar was a pragmatic man who could assist Barclay to make sense of all this confusion with Tatiana and now ... this ... surprising fascination for this radiant new relation who had just made a point of their lack of shared blood.

A few minutes later, Ethan announced his triumph.

"Checkmate!"

"You won," she replied in her tinkling voice.

Then the boy frowned.

"That was too easy. Did you allow me to win?"

Barclay watched as a delicate blush rose over her neck to color her creamy cheeks, while her lashes fluttered down in her embarrassment, accentuating the high cheekbones.

"Nay, little cousin. I am distracted. We shall play again tomorrow when I shall challenge you more fiercely than today."

Ethan dropped onto his feet and walked over to peer up at her face. His small hands rested on his hips, his stance as authoritative as a young squire addressing his lady.

"Did you not sleep, Jane?"

Jane flicked a glance at Barclay, looking decidedly uncomfortable at the personal question.

"I slept fine."

"At what time?"

"I fell asleep at dawn."

Barclay noted the dark smudges under her eyes, visible evidence of the nocturnal habits his nephew was questioning her about, which did nothing to mar her graceful splendor. Quite the contrary, they lent her an air of mystery —as though she wandered moonlit halls when the rest of the world slumbered.

The boy shook his head in admonishment, his arms akimbo on his chubby waist.

"You are no country lass anymore, Jane!"

Jane lifted her hand to cover a smile. Barclay himself pressed his lips together to restrain a chuckle at the boy's antics.

"I shall attempt to do better."

Ethan gave a quick nod of approval, setting his sable locks bouncing about his little head.

"You will stay and drink your *cough-ee* while I play Uncle *Bar-clee*?"

She dropped her hand, inclining her head graciously.

"Of course."

Rising, Jane took the seat near to Barclay, who now noticed the tray laid out on the table between them as he rose to his feet. She poured out a cup of coffee, just as the boy had suggested. As Barclay took his seat to play with his nephew, he noted her pour cream and stir sugar into the cup with a practiced hand.

The steam curled above the porcelain rim, and Barclay found himself strangely fascinated by the sight. He had never seen a woman drink the beverage before—especially not a refined young woman. Coffee was typically the domain of gentlemen in their clubs or after dinner in their studies. For a young woman of gentle birth to partake so openly spoke of a quiet boldness, a subtle rebellion against expectations.

Did she know of the potential troubles related to drinking coffee? Restlessness, nerves, even melancholia—it was whispered about by some of the more strait-laced matrons in London. Yet there she was, taking a sip with the serene grace of a duchess.

He was just about to ask her about it when Ethan broke his reverie with a tug on his sleeve, instructing him to prepare the chessboard for their game.

JANE WAS FINISHING her last sip of coffee, for all appearances watching the chess match between Ethan and his uncle.

Surreptitiously, she was using it as an opportunity to observe the gentleman up close.

He was a splendid specimen of manhood. Slim, long-limbed, with olive skin inherited from his mother. His hair was a mane of black waves that brushed his broad shoulders. A close-cropped beard suited his strong but narrow face. Once again, he wore a black coat, which Jane had come to realize was probably a sign of his extended mourning and the deep regard he held for his departed love.

The man needed a wife, which was clear from both the conversation of the night before and his hair, just a little too long. She yearned to brush it back from his cheek.

And he did everything with sincere attention. Even now, matched against the four-year-old Ethan, he paid every attention to the game, deliberating his moves while his nephew squirmed in his chair, his little legs swinging beneath him.

"There you are, Ethan!" The earl walked in and made his way to the board, his stride confident and brisk. "I see you started chess early today?"

The boy tilted his head back quite far to look up at his father.

"I found Jane, and she wanted to play."

Richard chuckled.

"She wanted to play, or you made her?"

The lad's face broke into a huge grin.

"I made her."

"Well, all I can say is it is a pity you are busy, because I was going to teach you to play cricket this afternoon."

Ethan stood up in riveted surprise.

"Cricket?"

"Have you played?"

"No! Oliver and Max play with the local boys, and Jane and Emma have played with them."

Jane smiled at Ethan's mention of her younger brothers, who would wheedle her into playing when they were short of boys for their teams. In a dejected voice, he lamented, "But I was too small to hold a bat."

Richard raised his brows in theatrical contemplation.

"Hmm ... if only there was a bat small enough for a little boy to learn cricket at Saunton Park?"

The earl lifted his arm to reveal what he had carried behind his back. It was a miniature bat—a shortened blade of polished ashwood, with a cloth-wrapped cylindrical handle and a thick edge. The craftsmanship was exquisite, the varnish catching the light from the window as he held it aloft. With his other hand, the earl produced a leather-seamed ball, the stitching pristine against the deep red polished to a gleaming shine.

Her cousin almost launched into the air with his excitement.

"Where did you get that? I have never seen one so small before!"

"I had it made for you in London."

Ethan had reddened in his excitement, scrambling to join his father and take it reverently in his hands. His little fingers traced the seam of the ball, as if he could scarcely believe it was real.

"We are to play cricket? Together?"

"I will have to help you when it is your turn at the wicket."

"Do you mind, Uncle *Bar-clee*? Can we play chess later?"

Barclay inclined his head, a rare smile touching his features.

"Of course, we shall leave the board set up for when we return."

Jane stood up and walked over, gathering the pieces with gentle care.

"Shall I place the board on that table? The servants know to leave it alone if it is resting there."

Ethan nodded vigorously, not able to take his eyes from the specially commissioned club.

"Are you playing with us, Uncle *Bar-clee*?"

"Say yes, Barclay, and I promise a full-length bat for you," Richard joked, his emerald eyes as bright with enthusiasm as his son's. Jane had never seen the sophisticated earl so eager and boyish. His laughter rang through the room, unrestrained and free.

The gentleman chuckled, running a hand through his slightly unruly hair.

"It has been some time since I played, but I suppose I might rack my memory to recall the rules. Will you play with us, Jane?"

Her breath caught in delight at the invitation. His brown eyes were studying her as he waited for her reply, and Jane had difficulty finding her voice as she became lost in his warm gaze. For all the reasons that made no sense for a match between them, something inexplicably drew her to the man.

"Yes! Do join us, Jane?" Richard spoke from behind Barclay's shoulder, oblivious to the heat between his half brother and his houseguest. Jane reluctantly turned her gaze to him as he continued. "Sophia is coming to watch, and a few ladies have expressed an interest in joining in. One of them attended that women's match at Ball's Pond nearly ten years ago. She claims she is one of the spectators depicted in the drawing by Thomas

Rowlandson. We are short players to make a proper match of it."

Jane blinked in surprise. She knew the Rowlandson drawing—it had been quite a spectacle, widely talked about for its depiction of women engaging in cricket with unapologetic vigor. The earl's zeal for the sport was unexpected, and she suddenly wondered if her family, who had just departed after Emma's wedding, might have relished a match of their own had they known of his fondness for it.

Realizing that Barclay would be there, she inclined her head in assent.

"Of course, it has been a year or two, but I am sure I can manage. I shall go change into my boots. Where are we playing?"

"We have created a playing field on the west lawn to take full advantage of the afternoon sun."

Ethan grasped his bat, tugging on his father's sleeve.

"How long will we play? For three days? Must I tell Miss Lovell we will not be doing lessons in the morning?"

Richard and Barclay both burst out laughing. Jane herself pressed her palm against her mouth to keep a giggle back at Ethan's transparent attempt to evade his governess.

"We are all amateurs," his father replied. "We shall see if we can even make it last the afternoon."

Ethan's face fell.

"Oh. We were going to practice Latin tomorrow morning. I was hoping to tell her I was busy."

The earl pursed his lips as if giving the matter serious consideration.

"If you learn Latin, we can practice talking to each other. Latin is important, is it not, Barclay?"

Barclay nodded solemnly, his expression the perfect imitation of a master tutor.

"Without my Latin lessons, I would not have been able to visit Florence and Rome and learn to draw plans for important buildings."

Ethan grumbled but appeared mollified as they departed the library. Jane was too distracted to pay him any mind. She headed to her room to change her shoes, the fabric of her skirts swishing against her legs with each hurried step. Nervous excitement bubbled up within her, quickening her pace as if a gust of wind pushed her down the hall.

It means nothing, you silly chit! He was just being polite.

Yet she could not shake the flutter of anticipation that accompanied the thought of seeing him again so soon.

WHEN JANE REACHED the western lawns, she found that most of the houseguests had gathered. The field had been marked off with lines scored into the turf and dusted with lime, and wicker chairs were set up beneath the shade of sprawling oak trees. The smell of freshly cut grass mingled with the scent of flowers from the gardens, lending a sense of idyllic calm to the cheerful chaos of assembling teams.

Because the countess was increasing, she sat on a bench in the shade to watch, lamenting that she also wanted to play. She looked lovely in her blue day gown with her red-blonde hair in a simple chignon, having removed her bonnet to take advantage of a breeze that rustled the verdant leaves above her.

The Duchess of Halmesbury elected to sit with her, though there was envy in her brandy eyes as the teams assembled. Jane thought she might have wanted to play but felt obligated to keep the countess company.

"I suppose it is only fair I sit out if my husband is one of the umpires," she remarked to Jane before making her way to join Sophia.

Tatiana was standing by to join a team, looking exuberant. Her eyes shone with excitement, and she waved enthusiastically when she spotted Jane. The little girl raced over, grabbing her hand.

"Are you playing, Jane?"

Jane agreed she was, and Tatiana immediately begged to be on her team.

"Please, may we? Then you can show me how it is done!"

The girl's enthusiasm was infectious, and Jane found herself smiling. *How could I refuse her?*

When Jane reached the crowd of gathered players, her smile dimmed as she discovered that Barclay had already been assigned to a team that was now full. The organizers had clearly been mindful to balance men, women, and children on each team, and Barclay, Richard, and Ethan were paired together.

She was to play against him.

Jane could not deny the drop in her spirits at this news. It would have been much easier to spend time in his company if they were on the same team, but she could hardly make a fuss without rousing suspicions. No, she would have to endure watching him from a distance—and worse yet, competing against him.

Instead, she found herself grouped with Peregrine Balfour's friend, Lord Julius Trafford. The foppish heir to the Earl of Stirling had a bizarre thatch of wheat-colored hair at the crown of his head, while the rest of his hair was a deep chocolate color. Jane could not help but suspect the gentleman's valet was using lemon juice or vinegar to lighten the nobleman's hair in some sort of fashionable folly, but she considered it to be a silly affectation.

Lord Trafford and the duchess's brother, Mr. Brendan Ridley, were both friends of Perry's who had remained for the house party after attending his wedding a few days earlier. Jane preferred Mr. Ridley over the spoilt young lord. Despite his reputation for cavorting with widows, Mr. Ridley was an affable young man who had spent a great deal of time doting on his infant nephew, Jasper—the duke's heir—who shared the same rich chestnut locks as his uncle and mother.

Additional members of her team included a Mr. Adam Dunsford, Mr. Ridley, Tatiana, another child, and several men and women she had not yet become acquainted with.

Mr. Ridley was elected team captain. The duke himself oversaw the coin toss, and Jane's team won. Two batters strode to the pitch, brandishing their bats with a confident air, while Tatiana and Jane hurried off the field along with the other batters to await their turn.

Barclay, Richard, and Ethan spread across the grassy field while Jane watched Barclay's long strides intently as he took his place, his dark hair catching the sunlight, his coat flaring slightly as he moved. *He looks at home out here,* she thought, then scolded herself for noticing.

Determined not to let her thoughts wander too much, Jane found a bat suitable for Tatiana's height from the collection that had been laid out. She showed her how to grasp and swing it, being mindful of their skirts. Then she explained how to score a run, including how to scarper to the other wicket without tripping over petticoats.

The little girl was brimming with excitement, chattering questions at Jane as they went through the rules. It gladdened her to see the child so animated after their first encounter, when Tatiana had been so sad about her mother. Unable to resist, Jane reached out a hand to smooth the girl's hair affectionately.

"You are going to be splendid," she whispered.

Tatiana beamed up at her, cheeks flushed with happiness.

"I am glad you are on my team."

BARCLAY TOOK his place on the field, bemused as he observed Tatiana interacting with Jane across the way. When he had agreed to play, he had not realized Tatiana was participating, or he would have made sure they were on the same team in order to help her learn the game.

By the time he had realized she was there, she had already latched onto the intriguing young woman from the library, and he had been loath to interrupt the *bonhomie* he saw forming between the two. It had been some time since Tatiana had laughed or chattered as much as she was now, her face lit up as Jane demonstrated how to swing the bat and run while wearing skirts, then smoothed his daughter's silver-blonde hair with affection.

Jane truly was a unique young woman in how she took such an interest in children, playing with Ethan in the library and now with his daughter. Natalya would have approved of such engagement. His eyes ran over her willowy form with appreciation as his thoughts returned to the notion of courting her.

She is still a child herself! There are no more than ten years between her and your daughter, you degenerate lech!

Barclay grimaced. His thoughts were only on courtship because of his conversation with his mother the night before. He needed to find a woman more suitable and forget about the vivacious girl who was far too young for a man at his stage of life.

Looking about the field, he noticed a blonde glancing his way in admiration.

Mrs. Agnes Gordon.

He searched the archives of his mind and remembered she was the widow of the vicar from the local village. The earl had provided her with a cottage at Saunton Park when her husband had unexpectedly died three years earlier.

Mrs. Gordon flickered a flirtatious smile from under the brim of her bonnet before approaching him while Barclay contemplated her. *A woman closer to my own age. A more mature woman who would be of Natalya's age, if she had still been here with us.*

Mrs. Gordon had experience running a household and assisting a vicar—certainly she would make a good wife to a professional man like him.

"Mr. Thompson, I hope I might impose on you to explain the rules of the game?"

Barclay smiled, bowing in acknowledgment. With an appreciative eye, he noted she had a lively manner and was quite comely in her striped muslin dress. Her blonde curls were neatly arranged beneath a wide-brimmed bonnet adorned with pale yellow ribbon, lending her a touch of gracefulness that he had not noticed before.

"Of course, Mrs. Gordon. I would be most happy to oblige."

She stepped a bit closer, the soft scent of lavender drifting from her as she lifted her eyes to his.

"I must confess, I have watched the matches from a distance, but I have never quite understood how it is played."

Barclay felt a stirring of satisfaction at her gentle manner.

This is the kind of woman I should pursue.

Someone practical, with experience in managing a household, and with the poise of a widow who understood both loss and survival.

"It is quite simple," he began, gesturing toward the field. "The bowler attempts to hit the wicket with the ball, while the batter attempts to send the ball across the field. Scoring is achieved by running between the two wickets while the fielders attempt to return the ball to the bowler."

Mrs. Gordon nodded, her attention fixed on him as he spoke.

"Would you like me to show you?" he offered.

Her smile brightened, and she inclined her head. "I would be delighted."

Mr. Adam Dunsford, the sole heir to a local Somerset landowner, had just been bowled out. Rambling over, he sank down beside Jane beneath the shade of the great oak, its branches swaying gently above them. The whisper of leaves provided a soothing backdrop to the lively shouts from the cricket field. After a nod of greeting, they both turned their gazes back to the field where Tatiana held her bat aloft proudly as she walked away to take his place at the crease.

Mr Dunsford was a handsome young man, with a mop of curling brown waves that must have taken his valet endless time each morning to perfect into looking effortlessly unaffected. It was flattering that he picked the seat next to her, an obvious compliment considering the other alternatives to watching the match.

"You played rather well for a woman, Miss Davis. Twenty runs, was it?"

Jane smiled in return, while wishing she had had more sleep the night before because all the sunshine and activity were making her drowsy. It was not the most effusive compliment—*for a woman?*—but it was well intended, and the gentleman had such a warm manner, it was difficult to take offense.

"Yes. Thank you, Mr. Dunsford."

"I am afraid I batted rather poorly. Barely made twelve runs before a child bowled me out. They are getting more and more talented each year. It has nothing to do with my deplorable talents, I assure you."

She chuckled in response. His self-deprecation was endearing as he threaded his fingers together and pulled a slight face, leaning forward on his elbows to observe the game. Jane had been watching Barclay with Mrs. Gordon across the field, but now she averted her eyes to watch the bowling.

"Have you known the earl for long, Mr. Dunsford?"

"Yes, but I must admit, not very well. It is his brother, Peregrine Balfour, with whom I attended Oxford."

"Oh? Perry just wed my sister a few days ago!"

"I heard he had just wed. Your sister must be a lovely woman if she is related to you."

Jane warmed at the compliment. The admiration of a charming young man was almost enough to take her attention off the intriguing architect across the field who was currently demonstrating how to bowl to the lovely Mrs. Gordon before she took her turn at the pitch.

Almost.

Jane had the sinking feeling that she had lost an opportunity when she left his side to find her boots. Now he and Mrs. Gordon were making a connection. All the times she had encountered Barclay, he had been so serious. Now he was laughing while Mrs. Gordon attempted to mimic his bowling demonstration, and the widow was laughing with him.

You are too young for him. He could never take you seriously when he has achieved so much and you have done so little.

It was disappointing. It was the first time she felt a genuine attraction for a man, and he would have to be someone unattainable. If only she had anything to offer a man who had been through so much, but she was merely a country lass who was away from her immediate family for the first time in her brief life.

What could she possibly offer such a gentleman? She could play the pianoforte. She was excellent with a needle and thread. But, despite her fascination for the handsome widower, she had no experience with the kind of loss the Thompsons were recovering from.

Are you going to embroider his heart back together?

Jane sighed and turned her attentions to Mr. Dunsford, sitting up straight to force some energy into her tired limbs. She wished ... she could sleep a full night and consider her future with a fresh mind.

Failing that, the architect was beyond her reach and she needed to set her sights on a gentleman interested in pursuing her. What had she said to Emma last week? A landowner who was young and fun? Mr. Dunsford fit the bill rather well.

Emma's advice to pursue a gentleman with whom she shared a connection of the minds seemed a poor option in the bright sunlight when a young man was at her side to exhibit his regard, and the object of her desire flirted with an eminently suitable widow who had all the right qualifications to be a wife and mother to his daughter.

Jane was well disposed to be the spouse of a young gentleman of the gentry, such as Mr. Dunsford, and she need never feel gauche or awkward with such a safe choice.

Perhaps she should discover how deep the young man's interest ran?

CHAPTER
FOUR

"Seven years would be insufficient to make some people acquainted with each other, and seven days are more than enough for others."

Jane Austen

It was late morning when Jane woke up. She had not fallen asleep until dawn yet again. Perhaps she should visit a herbalist in Saunton to discuss the matter as Emma had suggested because she was wearing down from so little sleep.

The evening before had been wonderful. She had been seated with Adam Dunsford for dinner. The gentleman had a quirky sense of humor and had kept her laughing the entire evening. After dinner, they had paired up for parlor games, which Jane had enjoyed all the more for his charming company.

Then she had retired to bed, where she had been unable

to fall asleep. Eventually, she had found a captivating book from the library and stayed up reading until the first threads of dawn had stolen into her room.

Stretching her limbs out, Jane yawned widely before sitting up. Then she remembered her plans for this morning, and with a burst of vigor, she scampered from her bed to pull on a wrap before loping over to her door. Opening it wide, she found the tray she had requested.

Her breakfast tray was still warm, and a fat, silver pot of tea was speckled with drops of condensation which promised a piping hot drink to pour.

In addition, the extra supplies she had requested were heaped on a tray of their own. Jane clapped her hands in excitement. She had been looking forward to trying this ever since she had read about it in a women's periodical.

"What are you doing?"

Jane shrieked and jumped in surprise. Clutching a hand to her pounding heart, she found Tatiana staring at her from the door of her and her grandmother's bedroom.

"My goodness, you startled the wits from me, Tatiana!"

"You are very twitchy. I noticed it the other night."

"I ... have had trouble sleeping. It has me on edge."

"Why all the strawberries? And what are those nuts for?"

Jane beamed in delight as she recalled this morning's task. "Do you wish to join me? I can show you what I am about?"

The girl nodded her head enthusiastically, skipping over to follow Jane into her room with a broad smile on her little face. "Shall I close the door?"

"No, leave it ajar in case your family wishes to find you."

Jane carried the tray over to the table and chairs at the end of the room. Sitting down, she poured out a cup of tea.

Adding cream and sugar, she sat back and breathed in the floral flavor with a radiant smile. "You may eat one of the strawberries, if you like. Just not too many because we will need them."

Tatiana's face lit up. She inspected the bowl and then delicately took hold of the largest strawberry she could find, pulling it up by its cap and holding it in front of her face to sniff it. With a deep breath, she took a bite, smiling in pleasure while she chewed.

"Have you thought more about courting my father?"

Jane choked, quickly putting the cup down while she coughed into her hand. "I thought we agreed your papa needed to find his own wife?"

"I went around meeting all the women since then. You are the only one who is right for Papa."

"Perhaps this house party is not the right place to find his wife? If you did not like any of the women here, there will be more women in London for him to meet."

"No, I did not mean you are the best woman at the house party." Tatiana shook her head, clearly exasperated with Jane's simpleness. "You *are* the right woman for him. I know it! Did you meet him yet?"

"I did, and your papa is a gracious gentleman. But I must confess there is a difference in our ages, and he might prefer someone with more maturity than me. He seemed quite taken with Mrs. Gordon."

Blue eyes narrowed at this suggestion. "The blonde woman? She is awful!"

"Your papa seemed to like her. He played cricket with her and sat with her at dinner."

Tatiana stood up, outrage quivering in every line of her body. "Not Mrs. Gordon. She does not like children!"

Jane frowned. "What do you mean?"

"I could tell when I met her. She smiled, but it did not reach her eyes, and she asked me if I had a doll to go play with like I was a simpleton."

Jane bit her lip, uncertain how to respond. "I am sure if you give her time, she will grow accustomed to you."

Tatiana clenched her jaw. "Promise me you will think about it. I know you are perfect for Papa. You must spend more time with him, and then you will see what I mean."

Jane hesitated. She did not want to encourage the girl's hope of a match, but she would distract her and then search out the grandmother to discuss the matter. The older woman seemed sensible, and she had a warm manner. Perhaps they could meet for tea to work out how to address Tatiana's surprising desires.

"Do you want to see what the strawberries are for?"

The child's face lit up, her appreciation of the aromatic fruit obvious as her eyes darted back to the bowl.

"I recently read directions for preparing strawberry water. It softens and lightens the skin."

Tatiana grinned. "We are going to smell like strawberries?"

"That is the plan."

Reaching out her hand, Jane took hold of one of the plumpest fruits and brought it to her lips. Breathing in deeply, she took a bite, tasting the sweetness of its flesh, and finished it quickly. "Pass me that empty bowl."

Tatiana solemnly handed over the extra bowl, along with the pestle resting in it. Jane selected several well-ripened strawberries, dropping them into the empty bowl and offering the girl one of the remaining fruits to eat.

Then she crushed the strawberries, pulling the caps out to discard them. The vibrant red juice pooled at the bottom of the bowl, staining the muslin cloth she placed over the second vessel. Jane poured the pulp onto the muslin, pressing it through diligently until the bright juice flowed into the waiting dish. A sweet, heady aroma filled the room, and Tatiana leaned over to breathe it in with an appreciative sigh.

Jane discarded the muslin and its pulpy mess onto the tray before popping one of the remaining strawberries into her mouth, biting it off at the cap before setting it aside.

Walking over to the washstand, she used the pitcher of water to rinse her hands, the cool water splashing over her fingers and carrying away the sticky residue. When she returned, Tatiana was still hovering over the bowl, breathing in the scent as if it were a bouquet of flowers.

"Now what happens?"

"Now I mix it with milk and a little water, and then we can dab it on our faces. After our long afternoon in the sun yesterday, it should be quite soothing."

"And what about the almonds?"

"That is for afterward."

"I want to do things like this with you every day."

Jane smiled. The girl was sweet, and she enjoyed her company. Tatiana had a calm presence unless she was excited, as she had been to play cricket the day before. "I enjoy spending time with you, too."

Tatiana hesitated, her small hands resting on the edge of the table. Then she spoke, her voice soft and wistful. "If you were my mama ..."

BARCLAY HAD SEARCHED for Tatiana throughout the splendid home of Saunton Park. When he had drawn his first plans for a similar large and extravagant building, it had been the greatest of honors, but now that he searched for one small girl who liked to hide, he could curse the wasteful spending that created such long halls with so many ridiculous rooms sprawling in every direction.

How the peerage lived in such vast spaces was something he could not comprehend. If he, Tsar, Aurora, and Tatiana lived in such a home, they would not see each other for days on end. Their London townhouse was quite sufficient for a family of means.

Stopping in the great hall, he glanced up at the richly colored, oversized oil paintings of Balfour ancestors in ornate gilded frames and tried to think where else he might look for his child. He had been certain she was with her grandmother, but when he had found Aurora sitting with the ladies for tea in a large drawing room of blue and gold, she had not seen Tatiana since breakfast when she thought the child had left with him.

Barclay encouraged her to continue her tea, mindful that his mother was making important connections with well-placed women of high society, which would elevate her status when they returned to London.

Aurora had mentioned Jane in parting, but Barclay had not found her in his search for Tatiana. Was it possible they were together somewhere? Tatiana seemed quite taken with the young woman, so she might have sought her out.

Ethan had mentioned during the chess match the day before that Jane had trouble sleeping.

Could she be in the family wing still?

He turned and began the long walk to the family wing, where he heard his daughter's voice echoing down the hall. Following the sound, he reached a door that stood ajar.

This had to be the young lady's room. He noted it was right next to his mother's as he raised his hand to knock and then lowered it to listen to the conversation floating out into the corridor.

"Mama used to read to me every night."

"Every night!" exclaimed Jane. "That is an admirable mother. What did she read to you?"

"My favorite were the ones she read from *Abian Nights*."

"Do you mean *Arabian Nights' Entertainments*?"

"Yes! That is it!"

"I was just reading *Aladdin* last evening. See, it is there next to my bed."

"Oooh! It has been so long since I heard that one."

Tatiana sounded both excited and disappointed at the same time, leaving Barclay feeling guilty. Had he not paid sufficient attention to his child since Natalya had left them? He ensured he spent time with her and took her to the park regularly, but somehow he had not realized that she might miss the simple joy of a story at bedtime. Perhaps he had been too consumed by his own grief and failed to notice how his daughter was suffering.

"I can read it to you, if you wish?"

Jane's offer surprised him. She had no obligation to his daughter, but she freely offered her time. It was a generous gesture. Surely a young woman like her had more absorbing ways to pass her time than in the company of a child. What of the fidgety young gentleman she had been spending time with since the cricket match the day before?

Realizing he was shamelessly eavesdropping, Barclay raised his hand to knock. He heard a chair shifting and then Tatiana's light footsteps as she raced across the room to peer around the corner of the door, which was only open by a few inches.

"Papa!"

"There you are, young lady. I have been searching

everywhere for you." He noticed the fragrance of strawberries and almonds wafting in the air. It was a pleasant scent, sweet and fresh, mingling with the sunlight streaming in from the window.

"Jane and I were using strawberry water and almond oil for our faces."

Barclay tilted his head in confusion. *What on earth does that entail?*

At that moment, Jane swung the door open to appear in her night rail and wrap, looking a little embarrassed by her attire as she crossed her arms. The gesture pulled the soft fabric snug, highlighting the gentle curves of her form. Barclay did his best to keep his eyes on her face—which only drew his attention to the glorious ebony hair plaited to drape over her shoulder, a few tendrils curling loose to frame her cheeks.

Her cheeks were flushed, likely from the warmth of the room and whatever ritual she had been engaged in with his daughter. The delicate scent of strawberries and almonds wafted from the room, mingling with the sunlight streaming in from the window.

She is too young for you, Barclay. What are you doing, noticing her like this?

"I apologize if I interrupted," he managed, his voice hoarse.

Every rational instinct Barclay possessed screamed at him to maintain his composure, and he firmed his jaw to prevent himself from acting on any foolish impulses.

"I hope you do not mind? Tatiana joined me when I awoke, but I left my door open in the event you came looking for her."

The young lady was decidedly nervous, lowering a hand to fidget with the edge of the wrap. The motion drew his gaze to the soft fabric where her fingers toyed with it. Barclay found himself ill-equipped for the situation, taking several moments to respond because of his scrambled wits. He would not usually be speaking with a young woman in her nightclothes, but as they were both considered family of the earl, staying in the same wing, there was nothing particularly improper about it with Tatiana acting as a chaperon of sorts.

He found his tongue. "Not at all. I hope she is not bothering you?"

Jane smiled, the curving of her pink bow lips lighting her face with unexpected charm. Good heavens, she was lovely.

"Tatiana is good company. She could never bother me."

"Papa, Jane said she would read me *Ladin, and the Lamp*. Can she put me to bed tonight?"

"Tatiana, I would not want to impose on the young lady. During your bedtime, she should attend the games in the parlor."

"I can come up and read to her. No one will miss me if I leave for a short time after dinner."

"I would not wish to interrupt your entertainment."

Jane shook her head. "It is no bother. I miss my younger brothers and sister, so this will be fun for me ... unless I am imposing?" Her face fell, and she appeared genuinely disappointed. "Would you prefer to do it? I can lend you my book."

Barclay was grateful for the reminder of their age disparity. He had just caught a whiff of the strawberries, cream, and almonds clinging to her skin, and the scent was unexpectedly soothing.

Clearing his throat, he struggled to recall her question as his breathing evened out. Tearing his gaze away from those fascinating ice-blue eyes that reminded him of a frozen lake in winter, he composed himself before replying, "Tatiana does not like my reading. She says I do the voices wrong. If you are sure it is not an imposition ..." He looked back at her, and she shook her head once more. "... then we would be honored if you would join her at bedtime ... for a short time, mind you. I do not wish to take you away from your leisure."

Both girls clapped their hands at the news. Jane's smile widened, her eyes brightening with happiness. She is so lovely, he thought, and it struck him that the word sweet suited her. Not just in her appearance but in her nature.

And far too young, you fool.

Had visiting his father's home somehow triggered his own roguish impulses? He must set aside these musings before they grew any stronger. Steeling his nerve in the manner he would when entering a tough negotiation, Barclay took Tatiana's little hand in his.

"Come, little one. I wish to play some chess with you in the library."

Tatiana beamed. "Good. Ethan made me play after cricket yesterday, and he beat me. It was most embarrassing. I should have paid more attention when you were teaching me to play."

"We will improve your skills." He gave a brief bow. "We shall see you later, Jane?"

Jane inclined her head in agreement, then gently closed the door as they walked away.

While Tatiana chattered about the beauty treatment that she and Jane had partaken in, Barclay scolded himself mentally. No matter how charming or kind the young woman was, it bore remembering that she was not for him. She could make a much better match than a man born on the wrong side of the blanket who also happened to be at least fourteen years her senior.

This attraction was … so inconvenient.

He really needed to find someone more suitable if he was to hunt for a new wife. When he was finished with his chess game, he would seek out Mrs. Gordon. She was good company and pleasing to the eye, not to mention mature enough to mother a nine-year-old girl.

CHAPTER FIVE

"Birth and good manners are essential."

Jane Austen

J ane was a keen observer of people, thus she wondered what she had done to anger the widower. One moment, he had been gazing at her with admiration, so that she had swayed toward him. The next, he had been staring at the ceiling, his jaw tight and his husky voice tighter when he next spoke.

Closing the door on the retreating pair, she turned and leaned against it. The cool wood pressed against her back, grounding her in the moment. Brushing her fingertips over her lips, she wondered what it might be like to kiss such a man. He smelled of leather, ink, and some sort of spice she could not quite place, a fragrance that lingered in the air long after he had departed. Her fingers drifted to her cheeks, which still felt warm from his presence, and she wanted—with every ounce of her being—to reach out a hand and feel the shape of his broad chest. To lean in and feel the roughness of his beard against her skin as their lips met in a moment of intense affinity.

She had been kissed a couple of times, as a girl back in Derby, when she had been the daughter of a tenant farmer. It had been pleasant, but nothing momentous.

When her sister and Perry had met, Jane had seen the sparks flying. Their passion for each other, despite their constant confrontations, had been unmistakable, and Jane had lamented in the recesses of her mind that she had never felt such intensity for a man before.

Gentlemen had pursued her, especially now that she was a member of the gentry. Jane knew well that she was a woman of fine looks. Her ink-black curls were often admired, and her eyes, a piercing blue, had been compared to sapphire glass. Today, she wore a day dress of soft muslin in pale lavender, the kind of elegant simplicity she had become accustomed to since living at Saunton Park. She had excellent prospects. Yet she wanted to find what Emma had—a deep understanding with a gentleman that transcended society's expectations. She wanted to find her Darcy, no matter how much Emma teased her for her whimsy.

Jane perceived that Barclay Thompson was aware of them bonding but, inexplicably, it angered him. She supposed that, like her family was inclined to do, he saw her as an immature girl who could not offer a worldly man much in the way of useful skills. Or perhaps his parentage posed some sort of problem? She was well aware of the challenges he must have faced, what cousin Ethan would face in his future as the son of an unwed mother.

It was a pity because Jane had never felt such a connection to any gentleman before him. She hoped Barclay did not think she minded such trivial matters. A man's worth was displayed by his actions, not those of his father. Neither she nor her family would snub a person for something they had no control over.

Whatever the problem was, whatever was causing Barclay to grow stiff in her presence despite their mutual attraction, she knew when a gentleman was interested in her, and it was clear he was not. It caused such a sense of disappointment to see him harden himself against her. If only Emma was still in residence, so she could discuss this puzzling development, but Jane was alone at Saunton Park and dealing with a decidedly adult situation for the first time.

Regardless of his reasoning, he and his daughter were recovering from a great loss, and it was not Jane's place to assert herself into their lives. Only Barclay could know what was best for his little family in the wake of his wife's death.

Jane turned to wash up and get dressed. She had assured the countess that she could manage without a lady's maid until they hired a new one. Their last one had left with Emma, but Jane was accustomed to preparing herself, despite enjoying the luxury of assistance, and Sophia's abigail was occupied with other tasks with so many guests in residence. She walked to the washstand, poured fresh water from the porcelain pitcher into the basin, and dipped her hands in. The coolness of it was refreshing as she splashed her face, banishing any lingering sleepiness.

Later that afternoon, Jane arrived for her match with Ethan in the library. Richard was there, showing his son a strategy with a reference book at hand. The scent of leather bindings and ink hung in the air, mingling with the faint crackle of the fire that had been stoked against the chill. Ethan's face lit up when Jane arrived.

"Jane! I just finished playing with Papa. Are you here to play?"

"Of course. You asked me to come at this time."

The earl rose. "I am happy you are here. I am to meet the duke and Barclay in my study, but I thought I would have to find Daisy to take care of Ethan."

"That is unnecessary. I can return him to the nursery when we are done playing."

Richard smiled in gratitude, heading for the door. "You are an excellent houseguest, Jane."

A maid arrived with her tray of coffee, leaving it on the side table as Jane took a seat across from Ethan. The silver pot gleamed in the firelight, the scent of roasted beans filling the room as she poured herself a cup. Soon they were absorbed by their game, so that Jane barely noticed when Mr. Dunsford entered the room.

"Miss Davis! I am so glad to find you. I was hoping we could take a walk on the front lawn? Lady Saunton and Her Grace are seated on the terrace, so several couples are taking a turn around the garden under their watchful eyes."

Jane smiled politely. "Certainly, Mr. Dunsford. I will join you once I finish this match with Ethan."

The young man glanced at her cousin as if noticing him for the first time. Ethan shot him a glance, dissatisfied at the interruption to their game, before turning back to contemplate the pieces on the board.

"I shall wait for you." With that, the lanky gentleman sat on a chair. "Oh my! The servants here are so attentive. They must have placed this coffeepot here for the guests. I wonder how frequently they replace it?"

He picked up the tall, tapered coffeepot and poured it into the single cup provided. Ethan swung his head to scowl at the man in outrage. "Hey! That *cough-ee* is for J—"

Jane shot out a hand to caution Ethan. Her little cousin stopped, shooting her a look of inquiry. She shook her head, which he understood. He closed his mouth abruptly, but his expression remained irritated as he resumed play. It was fortunate Emma had taught the boy how to hold his tongue in public, but Jane would be required to explain it to him once they were alone again. To her relief, Mr. Dunsford barely noticed the boy had exclaimed at him, too engaged in drinking the coffee he had poured.

WHEN BARCLAY ENTERED the earl's study at the designated time, he was surprised to find both the duke and the earl with cups of tea in their hands. A dainty china cup looked especially fragile in the duke's large, bronzed hand.

The room was a bastion of aristocratic luxury, with dark mahogany paneling polished to a deep gleam and floor-to-ceiling bookshelves crowded with leather-bound volumes. Afternoon sunlight spilled through the windows, casting golden slants of light across the thick Turkish carpet beneath their feet, its intricate patterns of crimson and gold adding warmth to the solemn decor.

Barclay rubbed his cheek in perplexment. "When you said I should join you for a drink in the study, I did not understand that to mean tea?" His gaze flickered to the crystal decanters that stood on a silver tray upon the sideboard, their contents glimmering amber and russet in the sunlight.

"Barclay, there you are. Please help yourself." The earl

gestured to the sideboard, the silver stoppers of the decanters catching the light as he spoke. "Halmesbury does not like spirits, and I suppose I might reveal to my own brother that Sophia's father drank himself into an early grave. She asked me to not partake in liquor, and I find my mind is much clearer since I switched to tea."

Barclay lifted a hand to stroke his beard while he thought, his fingers brushing over the coarse texture of his neatly trimmed whiskers. He looked between the sideboard with its rich offerings of brandy and whiskey and the teapot set upon a porcelain tray, painted with delicate blue forget-me-nots. "I suppose a cup of tea would be a pleasure. I have always had a preference for it."

He took his seat, the leather of the high-backed chair creaking slightly under his weight, and leaned forward to pour a cup before settling back. The aroma of Earl Grey—fragrant with bergamot and faintly floral—curled up from his cup in delicate ribbons of steam. He took a sip, letting the warmth spread through his chest, while the sunlight glimmered off the gold rim of the cup, casting a faint sparkle onto the surface of the dark liquid.

"Thank you for joining us, Barclay. Halmesbury and I were..." His brother stopped, fidgeting with his cravat, his fingers worrying the neatly folded linen as if it were suddenly too tight. Barclay frowned with suspicion. He had noted that his brother would toy with his neck linen when he was anxious.

The duke set down his cup with a faint clink against the saucer and leaned forward. His movements were deliberate, and his broad shoulders filled the space with an air of command. "My cousin and I are thinking about the future. Ethan's future. I know it is impudent to ask, but ... how has it been for you?"

Barclay exhaled, the tension in his shoulders ebbing away. His brother merely sought insight on a delicate matter. "To be illegitimate, you mean?" he asked, his voice level and unflinching. The word hung in the room, heavy and stark.

The duke blinked, his gray eyes clouding like storm-tossed skies. "Please be assured I have never used that word ... not in that context." His Grace's tone was low and measured, the kind of voice that commanded attention without raising itself. There was a flicker of discomfort in the man's gaze, as if the very syllables of the word held a charge of impropriety too strong for the confines of polite society.

Contemplating His Grace, Barclay toyed with the cuff of his sleeve, his fingertips brushing the fine linen with an absent rhythm. The duke was widely regarded for his philanthropic works, and his reputation for decency preceded him wherever he went. Barclay reflected on this, noting the stark difference from the many lords he had encountered—men of power who wielded it carelessly, indifferent to those whose stations lay beneath their own. Even his own brother continued to surprise him, taking pains to include the Thompsons as valued family members, contrite for his—their—sire's actions. The study, with its heavy oak paneling and towering shelves of leather-bound tomes, seemed to cocoon them from the judgment of the outside world, granting the conversation a solemn intimacy.

This conversation was decidedly uncomfortable, yet there was no hint of malice. Only genuine concern. "I understand," Barclay said, his tone softening. "You wish to anticipate the troubles that the child might endure in the future. To predict and take measures to prepare the boy for the challenges he will face." He ran his thumb along the edge of his teacup, the motion steady and sure.

The duke's face relaxed, a touch of relief smoothing out the lines of tension across his brow. He set his teacup down with deliberate grace, the porcelain clinking softly against the saucer. "I understand it is an imposition, but you are uniquely experienced to deliver insight. You are a lauded professional in your field despite your mother's unwed status, so we felt that your situation would have some parity to Ethan's as the acknowledged son of a peer, yet with similar parental circumstances."

Barclay leaned back in his chair, the leather creaking as he shifted. "It will not be easy for him," he said, his voice tempered with certainty. "Some will accept him for his connections and his own merit. Others will mock him or turn from him without explanation. Unwarranted antagonism is assured."

He paused, gathering his thoughts. "I would prepare him for school. Take measures to teach him how to defend himself in the event of a physical scuffle, but instruct him on how to ignore taunting and follow his own path when he can. Some battles are unavoidable, but diplomacy is always best to pursue."

Richard shook his head in disgust, his hand coming up to fidget with his cravat once more, the linen twisting under his fingers. "I cannot believe I have created this situation for my son." His voice cracked slightly, the edge of remorse unmistakable.

Barclay tilted his head back to study the intricate patterns of the painted ceiling. His own grandfather had overseen the artistry there—the sweeping arcs of vines intertwined with heraldic symbols and bursts of floral detail that whispered of grandeur and tradition. When he was prepared to speak, he leaned forward to peer directly into his brother's eyes.

"Richard, you are here for him now, and that is worth something. Tsar could have had me raised by strangers, but he did not. I owe everything to the old man for standing by me. Ethan is fortunate to have a father who feels responsible for the situation and who takes care to pave the way for his future."

Richard's hand came up to fidget with his cravat once more, his expression tight with concern. "How did you handle it? All those issues you referred to?"

"Tsar is a man skilled in negotiation. From a young age, he taught me how to handle men. How to make self-important lords pay their bills in a timely manner, how to manipulate suppliers when they attempt to raise prices or delay deliveries, how to contend with competitors and maintain good relationships with all of these men while refusing to be taken advantage of. You will do the same for Ethan. The boy is intelligent, and he will turn this situation to his advantage."

The duke cleared his throat, setting his teacup down with careful precision. "The question that really lingers is ... are you accepted socially?"

"No. I am tolerated for my professional prowess, but I am not invited into their homes." He allowed his gaze to drift to the window, where sunlight spilled in patterns across the parquet floor. "Tsar assures me that will change now that Richard has acknowledged me as his brother, but I have to say I am not excited by such a prospect. If I was not acceptable in my own right, I cannot respect these people for changing their minds because of my new connection to the wealthy Earl of Saunton." His voice grew firm. "However, if it will ease the path for Tatiana, or allow my mother entry to places she wishes to access, then I will ignore the slights of the past. I will grin and bear it, so to speak."

Richard's face displayed his alarm, his hand stilling from its fidgeting. "You are not accepted socially? Not anywhere?"

"I have good relationships with tradesmen and suppliers. Some clients. They are more accepting of my situation, especially given my talents, but my mother has struggled." His voice softened, and he stared into his teacup as if the swirling liquid held answers. "She has been attempting to join a lady's society for some time, but she has been rejected on several occasions. Now she has reapplied on the strength of our change in circumstances. I prefer to not pursue unworthy connections, but it is important to her because my grandmother was a member, and she wishes to follow in her footsteps."

A thoughtful silence stretched between the three men, the ticking of the longcase clock in the corner marking the seconds. Finally, Barclay looked back up. "I have yet to discover how my own situation will be altered once word of this new ... kinship ... gets around."

"What of your wife? Was she affected by the situation?"

"Natalya was a private woman who valued her time on this earth. Her days were numbered, and she had no patience to pursue relationships with English families that were hostile." Barclay's gaze grew distant, his hands curling around his teacup as if it might anchor him. "She made friends where she could easily do so, despite being wed to a by-blow, and ignored the rest to spend her time with Tatiana and myself."

Richard slumped back in his chair, his cravat now askew from his compulsive fidgeting. The tall windows behind him cast long ribbons of light across the polished surface of the desk, flickering like sunlight on water. "I am sorry I did not learn of you sooner."

Barclay smiled, the expression gentle but firm. "It is not your cross to bear, brother. The blame is squarely at the feet of the man who is not here to answer for his actions." He leaned forward, his gaze steady. "I respect what you have done for Ethan, and I hope his path will be easier than mine. After all, he has the advantage of your support."

The three men sipped on their tea, the silence settling comfortably between them as the clock on the mantel ticked away the passing moments. Eventually, Richard broke the silence, setting his cup down with a soft clink.

"On another matter, I could do with some advice."

The duke chuckled, the sound low and smooth. "Is that not what we have been doing here? Advising you?" He raised his brow with mild amusement, his gaze flickering between the two brothers.

"I meant on a less strenuous subject." Richard rubbed the back of his neck, his eyes brightening with sudden purpose. "This matter involves Jane Davis."

Barclay nearly choked on his tea. He carefully placed his cup and saucer back on the tray, drawing a fortifying breath as he willed his composure to return. "Should I leave you to it?"

Richard frowned, shaking his head. "No, you are family now. I would appreciate your thoughts."

Halmesbury finished his tea, setting his cup down with deliberate grace. "What of the young lady?"

Barclay leaned back in his chair, the soft leather creaking beneath his weight. He found his head tilting back so he might study the painted ceiling once more—the familiar swirls of delicate flora and scrollwork that had once been merely lines on Tsar's drafting table. The discussion about his own situation had been uncomfortable enough, but the notion of sitting through Richard's musings on the young woman he admired felt distinctly more troubling. His hand tightened imperceptibly on the armrest.

This is deuced awkward.

"I received a letter from London. Lord Lawson has written to me to pose the possibility of his courting her. He states he was quite taken with her at the ball we held for Emma and Jane earlier this month." Richard's green eyes clouded with discomfort.

Halmesbury frowned, setting his teacup down with a decisive click against the saucer. "The man is forty years of age! He has daughters of an age as Jane." His brow furrowed as if the very notion caused him physical discomfort.

Richard rose to his feet, his long strides carrying him back and forth before the window. "Precisely. I know that the man is yet to have an heir, but his wife has been gone only two years and now he wishes to pursue a young woman under my protection." He halted to stare out over the grounds, fingers clasped tightly behind his back. "I cannot quite bring myself to consider it."

The duke sighed, his hands folded loosely over his knees. "Unfortunately, it is common amongst the peerage for such disparate ages to exist between a husband and wife."

Richard's mouth flattened into a grim line. "Not in our particular set. The man is a good friend, but I find myself quite repelled by the notion, and I do not know how to reply to his letter." He turned back to face the room, eyes shadowed with indecision. "Jane is lovely and young. She could marry a gentleman with far more in common with her. There is no hurry to marry her off, and I know from Sophia that she is a romantic who wishes to marry for love."

Guilt twisted and churned in Barclay's gut, sharp and unrelenting. He was in his thirties. He had a daughter only nine or ten years younger than Jane, and yet he was coveting the young lady like a degenerate old man. Not dissimilar to the late Earl of Satan, in fact. His hands curled into fists in his lap, the knuckles whitening. How had he arrived in this situation, where he sat beside the earl repressing his shameful secret?

He clenched his jaw and forced his gaze to the ceiling, tracing the familiar patterns that his grandfather had designed decades ago. Ornate flourishes and golden-leafed vines wove across the surface, beautiful and endless. The ceiling was safe, distant—far easier to look upon than the reality of his own failings. He reminded himself that a young Aurora had been robbed of her virtue in this very building, her life irrevocably altered. It was why he needed to stay away from Jane Davis, despite his daughter's encouragement to pursue her. His hands relaxed slightly, his fingers uncurling as he exhaled.

"Perhaps Jane will find a gentleman at this house party, and it will not be necessary to dissuade Lord Lawson's inquiry?" Halmesbury mused, his voice thoughtful. He picked up his cup again, cradling it between his large hands.

"Blazes, I hope so. This is deuced awkward!" Richard raked a hand through his hair, his composure faltering.

Barclay nearly flinched as his own thoughts from moments ago were echoed out loud. The air in the room felt heavier, thicker somehow. There were so many issues, he did not know which to focus on—setting a young woman up to be rejected by society because she was married to a man born on the wrong side of the sheets, or that she was far too young to foist a nine-year-old child onto. The warmth of the tea he had swallowed earlier now sat uneasily in his stomach, curdling with his thoughts.

And if he had had any thoughts of approaching his brother about the possibility of courting Jane, they had been soundly put to rest. All he knew was that he needed to stay away from her before he gave in to temptation. Her smile, her laughter, the way she lit up a room with her mere presence—it was not for him. It could not be.

If Tatiana needed a new mother, he would need to look elsewhere than the lovely Jane Davis.

CHAPTER SIX

"To begin imperfectly is better than to postpone indefinitely."

Jane Austen

After dinner, Barclay discreetly signaled to Jane from across the parlor where the guests had gathered for games. Making her excuses, she rose gracefully and followed him out of the room, finding him waiting for her in the hallway. He extended his arm, and she accepted, slipping her hand over his forearm. A warm, roiling sensation of awareness unfurled from her fingertips, winding its way up her arm to ignite a slow-burning flame of yearning in her heart. His powerful forearm was solid beneath her touch, a tangible reminder of his strength and the quiet confidence that marked his every step. She could not deny her fascination with the gentleman, no matter how unattainable he might seem.

He walked beside her in silence, his expression solemn

as they made their way down the connecting corridor to the family wing. Jane soaked up every moment of their silent journey, wishing it could last longer. But, alas, all too soon, they reached the door of his mother's room.

Barclay raised his hand to knock, while Jane, lost in thought, wistfully imagined what it might be like to be his wife. To tuck Tatiana into bed each night. To travel to towns across the realm, just as Tatiana had described with such enthusiasm.

It was disheartening to envy a dead woman, but Jane could not deny that the late Mrs. Thompson had lived the life she herself had always dreamed of—a loving husband, a beautiful child, and the freedom to travel and explore.

The door opened, revealing Tatiana's grandmother, who smiled warmly. "Miss Davis, this is so generous of you. Tatiana is beside herself with excitement!"

"Please, Miss Thompson, you must call me Jane," she replied, her smile softening.

The older woman's eyes brightened with delight. "I would love to! You must do me the honor of calling me by my given name. Aurora."

"Aurora? That is a beautiful name."

Aurora inclined her head gracefully. "Thank you, my dear. My mother was Italian," she explained, a touch of nostalgia coloring her voice.

Barclay, Aurora, and Jane quickly conferred, and it was decided that Aurora would return to the guests in the main house, leaving Barclay to accompany Jane to the little girl's room. When they entered, Tatiana sat upright in her cot, her silver-blonde curls tumbling over her shoulders. She clapped her hands with delight, her eyes shining with excitement. Jane could not help but smile at the child's enthusiasm as she crossed the room to sit beside her. The book had been delivered earlier that evening, so she picked it up and settled comfortably before beginning to read aloud.

With four younger brothers and sisters at home, Jane was confident in her storytelling abilities. Oliver and Max, the rambunctious twins, were never shy to criticize her reading, which meant she had long since learned how children preferred their stories told—plenty of expression, with dramatic pauses and just the right inflection to keep them enraptured.

Tatiana was entirely absorbed, her delicate face reflecting every twist and turn of the tale as Jane spoke of the treasure-laden cave and the glittering jewels hidden within. Barclay had taken a seat in an armchair across the room, his presence a steady, watchful silhouette in the dim light. He did not interrupt or draw attention to himself, yet Jane could feel his gaze on her as she read.

As she described Aladdin's discovery of the magic lamp, Tatiana's eyes began to flutter closed, her little body curling into the cot as she fought to stay awake. Jane softened her voice, letting it lull the girl toward sleep, and soon enough, a gentle snore escaped Tatiana's lips—a sound so sweet and innocent that Jane found herself pausing to simply gaze at the child's peaceful face.

Carefully, she closed the book, her movements light and practiced. With a tender hand, she smoothed the blankets around Tatiana's shoulders, her heart aching with a longing she had not known she possessed. To have such moments every night, to bring peace and comfort to a child ... it stirred something deep within her.

She straightened and turned to Barclay, who rose as well, his expression inscrutable. Together, they moved to the door, Barclay closing it with a soft click. In the quiet hush of the corridor, he turned to her, his eyes searching hers. "Thank you ... Jane. It has been a long time since I have seen Tatiana so content. What you did tonight was exceedingly kind."

Jane looked up at his solemn face, taking in the faint lines at the corners of his eyes and the close-cropped beard that lent him an air of guardedness. Her lips curved into a smile. "It was my great honor, Barclay."

For a heartbeat, neither spoke. Then he inclined his head and offered his arm once more. She accepted, and he escorted her back to the main house, his stride slow and measured, as if unwilling to rush the moment.

When they reached the parlor, Jane rejoined the countess on a satin-upholstered sofa, her mind still lingering on the tender moment she had shared with Tatiana. It had been a curious experience—one she suspected she would always cherish. Bringing comfort to both the child and, she hoped, her father, had filled her with an unexpected sense of fulfillment.

As the countess resumed her conversation with a cluster of ladies, Jane's mind wandered back to Tatiana's sleepy smile, to Barclay's soft-spoken gratitude. The evening had brought clarity to her own desires—she yearned for such moments with her own family. To be needed. To offer warmth and affection to those she loved.

Since Emma had left to embark on her new life as a married woman, Jane had felt the pangs of loneliness keenly. She had no wish to return to Rose Ash Manor, only to wait for the next event or visitor to punctuate the quiet of her days. She longed for a husband and children of her own. To tuck them in with bedtime stories. To watch them grow, to share in their triumphs and soothe their hurts.

It was time she began the next chapter of her life. Emma had done it. So could she.

You are grown now, Jane Davis. You must find your own happiness.

BARCLAY SAT on the wide stone ledge of his window, watching the fog roll in over the sprawling parkland. The mist crept along the earth, shrouding the moon and stars, leaving him staring into the abyss of midnight. It was ... unsettling.

He could no longer summon Natalya to his side as he had done that first night at Saunton Park. He supposed that some unspoken decision must have been made—some quiet acceptance that he would move forward after learning that Tatiana wished for a new mother. It was what Natalya had wanted, and her continued absence from his midnight reveries suggested it was too late to turn back.

He considered the widow, Mrs. Gordon, whose pleasant company and kind manner made her a reasonable choice. She did not mind his situation. She had laughed at his jokes and spoken warmly of Tatiana. There was an ease to her presence that Barclay could appreciate. He shifted his back against the chilly pane, inspecting the ceiling with an expert eye out of habit. How was he to sleep? And what was he to do if, now that he had released Natalya from the binds of memory, she refused to return and soothe his sleepless hours as she had always done before?

Eventually, the restlessness became too much, and he rose from the window ledge to roam the silent halls. The manor was draped in stillness, its grand corridors bereft of guests and family, all retired for the evening. His footsteps were muffled by thick Persian runners that stretched the length of the hall, and the sconces cast soft amber light, just enough to avoid stumbling in the dark.

It felt strange to wander the corridors of this grand home his grandfather had designed. So much history lingered in the walls. Tsar had made his reputation with this very estate. Aurora had been seduced under its soaring ceilings. Barclay himself had been conceived here. And now, whimsically, it was the place where memories of Natalya had finally been released from the living, as if she might now pursue her own journey while he struggled onward in this mortal coil.

Contemplating these heavy matters in the middle of the night did nothing to settle his mind. He needed distraction —something to occupy his thoughts, or he would find himself pacing the halls until dawn.

Approaching the main block of the manor, he stilled as he noticed the library was still lit. Who would make use of the room at such an hour? Curiosity stirred him, and he headed in that direction, craving company—any company —to dispel the lingering shadows of grief and relentless solitude.

When he entered the room, he came to a sharp halt. Jane was bent over a library table, her brow furrowed in concentration as she scratched over a page with a quill. He should leave. He should turn around and return to his chambers. It was entirely inappropriate for him to be alone with her in the dead of night.

But the hour was late, and his soul was weary. He could not command his feet to walk away. The room was warm and inviting, and she … she was a vision of serenity, her dark hair tumbling over her shoulder, her lashes low as she concentrated. She looked like something out of a dream, bent over her writing with such absorption that he almost hated to disturb her.

But he could not resist. He wanted to enjoy this quiet hour alone with her. In the morning, he would do the right thing. He would be honorable. He would keep his distance as he had promised himself. But tonight ... tonight, he was so profoundly lonely, and this captivating creature was the only solace he had found in two long years.

"What are you writing?" He moved to take a seat by the fireplace, his gaze steady and curious.

Jane flinched, startled by his presence. Her hand moved reflexively to cover the page, as if shielding the words from him. His curiosity only deepened.

"It is nothing."

Barclay raised a brow. "Jane ... it is midnight, and evidently neither of us can sleep. Share your thoughts with me."

Her face contorted with hesitation, twin spots of color appearing high on her cheeks. "It is poetry," she mumbled, barely above a whisper.

His brows rose. "You write verse?"

She nodded, seemingly unable to meet his eyes. Her fingers trembled slightly as they smoothed over the page.

"Tell me about it."

She chewed her lip before replying, the words tumbling out in a rush, as if speaking too slowly would break her courage. "I wrote it in the style of Shakespeare—each line is five feet of two syllables to create the ten syllables of iambic pentameter. But I used variations of the iambs, so not all my lines are the traditional *duh-DUH* rhythm. Some of the stresses are reversed—*DUH-duh*—while others are not stressed—*duh-duh*—to draw attention to certain phrases and to add emphasis ... I am a bumbling amateur at best."

MISS DAVIS AND THE ARCHITECT

Barclay hid a smile. The endearing young woman was babbling, clearly flustered to be caught with her poetry. The flush of her cheeks, the nervous way she spoke—he found it all unexpectedly charming. "Read one to me."

Jane straightened in her seat, her eyes wide with alarm. "Oh, no! I never share my work. Even Emma has never heard my lines."

"Poetry is food for the soul. It is meant to be shared, and I wish to hear what you have written."

"No. I cannot—"

"I will not judge." His tone was gentle but firm. "I know the challenge of creating something and showing it to another for the first time. My first design, I was certain Tsar would hate it. I had to find the courage to display it. Now I have won awards and am paid to design monumental buildings."

His gaze wandered to her mouth, where she nibbled on her soft pink lip, clearly caught in the throes of indecision. Barclay quickly averted his eyes, repressing an urge to steal a kiss.

"What if it is terrible?" she whispered.

"Then I shall be the only one who knows it. Just look down at that page of yours, and wherever your gaze happens to fall, read me that verse."

She gazed at him, searching his eyes as if testing his sincerity. At last, she nodded, closing her eyes to gather her breath. When she opened them, she glanced down, found a place on the page, and read it aloud, her voice soft but steady.

"Old eyes, cold eyes, eyes that have seen too much.
Aware of what it is to love and lose.
How my heart cries out to ease his burden.

To banish the dark shadows from those depths,
And bring back a sure smile to his firmed lips."

Barclay went still. Were the lines about him? Was that how she perceived him? Was his grief so evident?

Staring at the flames in the hearth, he found himself spellbound by their flicker, their hypnotic dance mirroring the tumult of his thoughts. The silence in the room grew thick and heavy with indolent meaning, settling around them like a shroud. Finally, he turned his head to look at her, searching her face for confirmation.

Jane was blushing so fiercely, staring down at the page before her, that he feared she might singe her glorious mane of ebony locks with the heat emanating from her cheeks. He could not help but marvel at her—the way her fingers trembled slightly as they clutched the paper, the gentle rise and fall of her breath, the vulnerability she displayed in that fragile moment.

"That was ..." Barclay hesitated, seeking the right word, one that would do justice to the delicate beauty of her verse. "Evocative."

"Uh ... thank you?" Jane mumbled, her voice barely above a whisper. She did not look up, her lashes fluttering as if the mere act of meeting his gaze would undo her.

"Truly, Miss Davis. You should share your verses more often. I think you could write a volume and seek a publisher."

Her eyes shot up, wide with disbelief. "What? Why would the musings of a country lass be worth publishing? You are funning me!"

Barclay's expression grew earnest, his gaze steady and unwavering. "Women are the jewels of our civilization. They are grace and kindness incarnate. They are the beauty of our world. Without them, men would be mere barbarians in the mud." He leaned forward, his voice dropping. "We would all do well to hear more from the feminine perspective."

Jane blinked, her lips parting slightly in surprise. "My sister is the one with something to declare. I am not."

"I beg to differ. Your words contain profound insight. It is not simply the words—it is your perspective ... the way you capture what is unspoken and yet deeply felt."

Her gaze softened as she glanced back at the page, fingertips tracing the inked lines. "I observe people. Most of my poems are about what I think I see."

Barclay swallowed, the room seeming to grow warmer. "You see much, if that verse is any indication."

A small smile touched her lips. "You are most encouraging."

He shrugged nonchalantly, though inwardly he was still reeling from the observation she had read aloud. "There are plenty of people who could criticize you for your effort," he said gently. "I prefer to be the sort of man who encourages worthy individuals to pursue their dreams. I owe my grandfather for taking a chance on me, so I feel obligated to create opportunities for others. In that vein, I have publisher acquaintances if you ever wish to submit your work for consideration."

Jane sat back in her chair, her hands resting lightly in her lap as she studied him with a curious intensity. "You are an unusual man, Barclay Thompson."

Barclay found himself held captive by the blue depths of her gaze. Her eyes shone with earnestness and sincerity, like pools of clear water untouched by shadow. He imagined—not for the first time—what it would be like to have this bright, gentle soul by his side. To walk with her in the garden, sharing quiet moments beneath the spreading branches of ancient oaks. To sit beside her by a crackling fire, her laughter filling the room as Tatiana played at their feet. To wake each morning to her smile, sunlight filtering through the curtains to warm their faces.

For the first time in years, he allowed himself to think of the future—not one laced with grief and longing, but one filled with light and possibility. Jane's presence, her softness, her unguarded joy, had reminded him of what it meant to hope.

He blinked, and the idyllic fantasy vanished, the firelight flickering back into focus. *She is not for you, Barclay.*

But he wished she were. His entire being longed to spend more time with this graceful young woman who treated his daughter with such kindness and, somehow, had begun to soothe the ache of loss he had carried for so long.

They spoke for a while longer, discovering a mutual love of Shakespeare and Wordsworth. Barclay found himself charmed by the quickness of her mind and the way her eyes sparkled with understanding as they discussed their favorite passages. It was the most pleasant conversation he had experienced in years, and when he finally returned to the family wing, he could not help but feel lighter.

The corridor was dark, the fog pressing against the windows and blocking all moonlight from weaving its way in. Barclay could barely see his way because the sconces cast little light. He supposed that on most nights, the large sash windows allowed plenty of moonlight in and that the sconces were sufficient. But tonight, the fog hung heavy and thick, so the servants had not taken pains to increase the light for the gloomy conditions.

Just then, a flash of lightning lit the hall. A clap of thunder masked Barclay's yelp of surprise when a small, ghostly figure was revealed several feet in front of him.

"Papa?"

Barclay caught his breath, realizing that it was Tatiana who had startled him out of his wits. "What are you doing out of bed, little one?"

"I miss Mama." She broke into tears when she responded, causing Barclay to hurry over to her side.

Dropping to his haunches, he folded her into his arms. "Oh, Tatiana. I promise wherever your mama is right now, she misses you dreadfully, too."

Tatiana's little shoulders shook as she cried into his shoulder, breaking Barclay's heart as he swept her up against him and carried her to his room. Walking over to a sofa by the fireplace, he settled her down next to him. "What is it?"

"I woke from a dream. Mama was there, but I couldn't see her face. When I awoke, I realized I have forgotten what she looked like." Barclay's heart fractured as he stared down at the tear-streaked face of his little girl and thought about what he should say.

He reached out a finger to wipe away her tears. "That is ridiculous, little one. Of course you remember how she looks. Why, you look just like her!"

Tatiana's tears stopped. "I do?"

"All you need to do is look in the mirror. Come, see here."

Barclay ushered his daughter over to a mirror on the wall. Holding her up with one arm, he raised his hand to finger her hair. "She had silken hair woven from moonbeams . . ."

"Like mine?"

"That is correct. And, see, she had eyes as blue as the Baltic Sea."

Tatiana gazed at her reflection. "Like mine?"

Barclay bobbed his head. "And her skin was as smooth as fresh cream."

Tatiana stared intently into the mirror, raising a hand to touch her cheek. "Like mine?"

"Just like you, little one. Just like you."

"She will always be here with us?"

"Always." Barclay's voice was hoarse when he responded, and he accepted the truth. Their mutual grieving must come to an end. He could not live in the past any longer, and he must help his child to find joy once more, as she had during the reading of *Aladdin* earlier that evening.

Somehow, this visit to Saunton Park had unlocked a door, and Barclay could see clearly that he had been keeping them trapped in the past with his lingering state of mourning. Natalya had instructed him to find a new wife once she was gone. Barclay had failed to pay her heed, and it would disappoint his late wife that her child suffered for his neglect in fulfilling his promise to her.

He must accept that Natalya was gone. Come morning, he needed to make a serious attempt to find a new mother for Tatiana. No more mourning. No more woolgathering over the beautiful young woman he had met a couple of days ago, but a genuine effort to find a suitable mother.

CHAPTER
SEVEN

"It is not what we think or feel that makes us who we are. It is what we do. Or fail to do ..."

Jane Austen

Jane woke late the following morning, having stayed awake until dawn before finally drifting off as the first light crept over the horizon. This inability to slumber was becoming maddening. She had never struggled with sleep before, but ever since she had joined the Balfour household in London—and now Saunton Park—her nights had grown longer and more restless.

Before her visit, she could sleep anywhere and at any time, but that was now a distant memory. Insomnia had become a persistent companion for many weeks.

She prepared for the day, eating breakfast from a tray brought in by a maid. Fortunately, her strange hours were not widely known outside her family. What kind of denizen of the country kept such late hours? Her twin brothers, Oliver and Max, had teased her mercilessly during the few days they had been in residence for Emma's wedding the week before.

Eager to read, yet nervous to encounter Barclay after the intimate words they had shared the night before, Jane left the family wing and headed for the library. Upon entering, she was greeted by the familiar scent of roasted beans and found a tray of coffee waiting for her—the servants had grown accustomed to her unusual habits.

"Miss Davis, there you are. Did you hear me coming?" he asked, his voice smooth and easy. The young gentleman wore a finely tailored burgundy coat that fit him like a second skin. His waves of curls were both wild and perfectly arranged, a testament to a valet's deft touch.

Jane blinked in confusion.

"You were pouring me a cup?"

Her smile was pasted on out of sheer habit. Her head pounded from lack of sleep, and she had been yearning for that first sip of coffee to fully rouse her before encountering company. But now that Mr. Dunsford had seen her reaching for the gentlemen's beverage, she had little choice but to forfeit her cup. "Of course," she replied with forced cheer.

She poured, breathing in the rich aroma with unspoken longing before setting the pot down. Reluctantly, she picked up the cup and handed it to him, feeling the pang of sacrifice as the warmth left her fingertips.

"One wonders why the servants are providing cream and sugar?" he mused, gesturing toward the tray.

Because that is how I prefer to drink it!

Jane shrugged. "Perhaps some guests prefer to add it."

"Fie! That is something a lady might do. What type of man would drink it in such a feminine manner?"

Her fingers tightened around the edge of the tray. It was time to change the subject, lest she reach over and snatch the cup back from his hands. She had noticed a certain propensity for grumpiness before her first coffee of the day, and she was liable to say something unladylike if she lingered too long on the injustice. Mr. Dunsford was blissfully unaware of the havoc he was wreaking on her patience. It would hardly be fair to take it out on him.

"Were you looking for me, Mr. Dunsford?"

"I was. I was hoping you might be available to play lawn bowls? Several guests have gathered on the east lawn. Do you play? I can teach you!"

Jane suppressed a smile. She had grown up in the country as one of six children. They played bowls every Sunday, and Jane was the best player among them. Again, it was not Mr. Dunsford's fault that his comments grated on her nerves. Her mood had everything to do with the absence of that dark, glorious brew she so craved. Perhaps she should call for tea instead?

"I have played it before." The temptation to refuse and hunt down another cup of coffee flared in her mind, but she recalled her resolution after reading to Tatiana. It was time to consider her future—time to seek a husband and turn the page to her life's next chapter. "I would love to play."

Mr. Dunsford's boyish face brightened. "Excellent!" He stood, placing the cup down with careless abandon.

Jane's gaze flickered to the untouched coffee, her mouth practically watering at the sight. How she longed to take it up, savor its warmth, and let it work its magic. She forced a smile at the young gentleman, but her eyes drifted back to the cup. "I shall need to collect my bonnet, Mr. Dunsford. How about I meet you on the lawn?"

"Of course! A lady as fair as yourself must take care of

her complexion. I shall wait for you by the terrace." He bowed, his expression brimming with hope. Jane realized that with a bit of encouragement, she might easily secure a proposal from him. He was clearly keen. All she had to do was spend time with him and decide if he was the sort of man she could tolerate for the rest of her days.

The moment he left the room, Jane sprang into action. She prepared her coffee with swift, efficient hands, her heart lifting as the rich aroma filled the air. Lifting the cup to her lips, she breathed deeply before downing it in one long, indulgent sip. The tension in her shoulders melted, and the pounding in her head dissipated, leaving only the hum of satisfaction in its wake. She dabbed her lips with a handkerchief to remove any evidence. It was not the leisurely ritual she craved, but at least she was fortified for whatever lay ahead.

Feeling invigorated once more, Jane collected her bonnet from her room and washed her mouth with the dental elixir before making her way through the manor. The sun streamed through tall, mullioned windows, casting long beams of light across the polished floors. She exited onto the terrace, where several guests had already gathered, their laughter drifting through the manicured gardens. Tables were laid out with neatly arranged lawn bowls, the polished wood gleaming in the late morning sun.

Mr. Dunsford spotted her arrival and hastened over, his long legs carrying him swiftly across the lawn. He took her hand and bowed deeply. "Miss Davis, I am very much looking forward to demonstrating the nuances of play to you."

"That would be delightful." She returned his smile, her eyes bright with amusement.

"We are playing in teams of two. Mr. Ridley and his sister will play against us."

Jane glanced over the bowling green, its smooth surface bordered by trimmed hedges and shaded by towering oaks. The duchess approached, her jaunty bonnet bedecked with elegant feathers that bobbed lightly with each step. Sunlight caught the rich color of her brandy eyes, making them gleam with anticipation.

"Jane, we finally play a game together. I grow weary of sitting as a spectator."

"Which rink is ours, Your Grace?"

"We are playing on the first one."

They strolled over to where Mr. Dunsford and Mr. Ridley stood waiting, the men deep in conversation. Upon their arrival, Mr. Dunsford tipped his beaver hat with a modest bow. "Your Grace, I am honored to play against you."

The duchess beamed in response. "And I, you, Mr. Dunsford. I must warn you that my brother and I have played together many times."

"If you win, I shall be able to say the Duchess of Halmesbury bested me," he replied with a polite grin.

"Excellent. Let the best team win."

Mr. Dunsford and Mr. Ridley performed the coin toss, the bright glint of silver catching the sunlight as it spun through the air. The duchess won the right to toss the jack, her smile triumphant. Her brother dashed forward to collect it, running out to center it on the pitch after it came to rest.

Jane walked over to the table where the bowls were laid out, their polished surfaces smooth beneath her fingertips. Mr. Dunsford joined her, his hands clasped behind his back in an imitation of gentlemanly leisure. "I shall bowl last because it will be more difficult. You should do your best to place your bowl near the jack."

She smiled amiably, masking her amusement. They had not discussed who would bowl first, but she saw no need to quibble. Her focus turned back to the pitch as the duchess approached the mat, skirts sweeping elegantly around her legs. With a practiced drop, she rolled her bowl, the polished wood curving outward before arcing back and coming to rest just four inches from the jack.

Jane's eyes widened. The duchess must possess considerable experience to send her bowl so far up the pitch with such precision. Clearly, she had played as often as she claimed.

"Well done, Annabel." Mr. Ridley leaned down to peck his sister on the cheek, holding the brim of his hat to prevent it from toppling off.

Mr. Dunsford rubbed a hand over his jaw, his gaze fixed on the placement of the duchess's bowl. "Her Grace has done very well. Please do not be alarmed if you cannot place yours closer than hers, Miss Davis. Just do the best you can."

Jane nodded without comment. Taking her place at the mat, she surveyed the arrangement of the bowls and the jack with practiced precision. The lawn stretched before her, the sunlight casting long shadows over the pitch, the whisper of a breeze rustling through the nearby hedges. Kneeling gracefully, she bowed and sent her bowl gliding forward. It rolled in a smooth, deliberate arc, coming to rest a mere two inches from the target.

Mr. Dunsford walked forward, his jaw slack with disbelief.

Mr. Ridley, too, approached, squinting down at the placement before turning to call out instructions to his sister. The duchess, unruffled, picked up another bowl. With a look of determination, she returned to the mat and rolled her shot with steady elegance. The bowl curved, slowed, and settled just a hair closer to the jack than Jane's, claiming the winning position.

As the game continued, the duchess formed a strategic head with her remaining bowls, expertly blocking any clear path to the jack. Jane studied the layout, her eyes narrowed with concentration. Then, with measured steps, she approached the mat. A hush fell as she knelt and bowled a fast run shot. The bowl sped down the pitch, striking two of the duchess's well-placed bowls. They skidded apart, one tumbling into the ditch and out of play, while Jane's own bowl collided with the jack. Both quivered, then rolled gently apart.

Jane quelled the grin that threatened to spread across her face. Her run shot had been quick and precise, a testament to her years of practice.

Mr. Dunsford shook his head, his beaver hat teetering dangerously before settling back into place. "Miss Davis, I believe you should have been the last to play! I hope Mr. Ridley is a poor player, for I cannot do better than you."

"Not at all, Mr. Dunsford. I am certain you could have thrown a run shot more impressive than mine. You are stronger, after all." Her tone was gracious, but Jane was undeniably pleased. Let Mr. Dunsford see she was a sensible young woman—one who would not dim her light to stroke a gentleman's pride. She might forgo drinking coffee before him, but she would not restrain her talents.

The game progressed slowly, with tension building as each end was played. Eventually, the duchess and Mr. Ridley triumphed by a single shot. It had been exhilarating, neither team certain of victory until the very last play. Mr.

Dunsford had performed adequately but lacked the accuracy to break apart the head Mr. Ridley had so expertly formed. That decisive move won the final point for the opposing team.

They congratulated each other with genuine smiles, complimenting notable shots before making their way back to the terrace. The sun had dipped behind the manor, casting the terrace in cool shade, and the heat of the afternoon had eased. Jane's spirits lifted further when she saw that tea and biscuits had been laid out on a linen-draped table.

She joined the duchess, taking a seat beside her. Together, they watched the ongoing game on the third pitch, the only match still in play. The soft clack of bowls and the murmur of conversation drifted around them, lending the afternoon a pleasant, genteel atmosphere.

"I must say, Jane, I was pleased to observe that you did not restrain your skill to pander to the gentleman." The duchess spoke quietly so as not to be overheard, nodding her head subtly in Mr. Dunsford's direction. "Many young ladies would have done so."

Jane sipped her tea, the delicate porcelain warming her hands. "I think there should be some honesty during courtship. I would not want the gentleman to get the wrong idea of who I am."

"You seem quite a competitive young woman," the duchess remarked, her eyes sparkling with mirth.

"Not really. I love feminine pursuits. I embroider well. I am adequate at the pianoforte. But I do not wish to be controlled when I marry. I would like a partnership such as the one my sister and Perry share."

The duchess chuckled, the sound light and unrestrained. "I see. It was a demonstration for the young buck —that you have a mind of your own."

"Precisely."

"I appreciate that. When my husband and I met, there could be no doubt that I was an independent hoyden. I am still uncertain if the duke was impressed with my audacious behavior, or if he married me to protect me from my wild spirit."

Jane tilted her head, her interest piqued. "You were audacious?"

The duchess shook her head in mock remonstration. "My goodness, I hope I am still. Perhaps more refined, but under this regal exterior beats the heart of a rebel."

Jane giggled, the sound as light as a bell. "I would not say that I am a rebel. However, I would like a husband who respects my needs as I respect his. I wanted to ensure the gentleman noted me as an individual and not just a pretty face."

"That is well advised. He will have to acknowledge that you are a person in your own right after the way you played today."

"Then I have succeeded in making my point. All that remains is to discover if his pursuit continues now that he has been informed of my skills."

As if on cue, Mr. Ridley and Mr. Dunsford joined them, teacups balanced in their hands.

"My word, Miss Davis. You play exceptionally well!" Mr. Dunsford's youthful face shone with admiration, and Jane found his praise to be quite validating.

"I come from a large family who loves to play. We have competed on many a Sunday afternoon."

"I am most impressed with your run shot. You must

have quite a bit of steel running through you to bowl so fast and hard."

Jane smiled, satisfaction blooming in her chest. Mr. Dunsford had seen her as capable and strong—and still wanted her company. Woolgathering over Barclay Thompson be dashed. This budding connection showed promise. Perhaps she might be betrothed to a suitable young man who genuinely admired her before summer's end.

Behind them, the terrace door swung open with a soft creak. "Jane!"

Mr. Dunsford flinched, nearly spilling his tea. Jane turned just in time to see Tatiana's bright face, brimming with joy, before the little girl flew across the stone floor and threw her arms about Jane's neck. Jane laughed warmly, raising her hands to embrace the child, though she noted with some amusement how Mr. Dunsford leapt aside as if she had unleashed a wild hare. His expression was one of pure consternation.

"Jane, have you been playing bowls with Papa? I cannot find him anywhere."

"I am afraid not. I have not seen your papa today, Tatiana."

"Oh." Tatiana's little face fell, her silver-blonde curls bobbing as she dropped her gaze. A pang of sympathy tugged at Jane's heart. Gently, she reached up and tucked a stray curl behind the girl's ear.

Mr. Ridley cleared his throat politely. "Some guests are playing ninepins beyond the rose garden. Perhaps Mr. Thompson is there?"

Tatiana's eyes brightened with hope. "Where is that?"

"I can take you, if you wish. I was going to join a friend."

His expression was kind, and Jane noted the ease with which he offered assistance.

"Yes, do that," Mr. Dunsford interjected quickly, his relief poorly disguised.

Tatiana clapped her hands, turning to Mr. Ridley. "Yes, please, Mr. *Riddee*."

The gentleman chuckled at the mispronunciation of his name, his brandy eyes twinkling with good humor. He extended his bronzed hand, and Tatiana slipped her tiny one into it trustingly. Together, they walked off, as she peppered him with questions about ninepins.

Jane watched them go, a strange wistfulness stirring in her chest. Despite her newfound appreciation for Mr. Dunsford's attentions, there was an undeniable ache in watching the little girl wander off in search of her father.

Barclay had been sorely disappointed when Mrs. Gordon elected to play ninepins. He had hoped they might engage in a game of bowls—a sport of precision and skill—but she had declared that the game made her head hurt to think so hard.

Given that he was making a sincere effort to determine whether the woman would be a suitable wife and mother, not to mention that the only gentlemanly response was to agree, he had found himself rolling heavy balls at wooden pins instead.

The gathering was composed predominantly of ladies in lavish bonnets, their pastel skirts flaring as they chattered and laughed over the so-called sport. Barclay noted with no small amount of irony that there were precious few gentlemen present. His mother stood among the group, her hands clasped before her as she observed the scene with amusement. When she caught sight of him, she pressed her lips together in a poor attempt to stifle her laughter at his evident discomfort.

Bowls might make Mrs. Gordon's head hurt from the excess of challenge, but *ninepins* made *his* head ache from the sheer lack of it. As a man accustomed to mathematical formulas, angles, and precise measurements, bowls was a game he could appreciate. A gentleman's game—one that required strategy and finesse.

I would wager coin that the brilliant Miss Davis is partaking in bowls right at this very moment, he mused, but he swiftly banished the thought. That way lay distraction, and he had resolved to give Mrs. Gordon his full attention, no matter how tedious he found the exercise.

When the widow eventually lamented the strength of the sun, fanning herself with a gloved hand and complaining of the heat, Barclay seized the opportunity. He suggested that they retire to the shade of a nearby oak tree, assuring her with barely disguised relief that he would not mind in the least. She accepted gratefully, and they made their way to a curved bench nestled around the base of the majestic tree, its thick canopy casting cool shadows over the lawn.

Barclay smoothed his hands over his buckskins as he sat, acutely aware of the monochromatic nature of his attire. With his recent decision to come out of mourning, he had realized only that very morning that he could not continue to wear the black coats that had become something of a uniform. How had he not noticed before?

Change is coming, he thought with a twinge of melancholy. If he were at a work site, he might have loosened his cravat to breathe easier, but here among the houseguests, such an action would be considered a breach of etiquette. And so, he suffered through the rigid dress standards—stiff collars and tightly knotted cravats—throughout the long hours of tedious games and trivial pleasantries.

Nevertheless, he reminded himself, *I must try to find a new mother for Tatiana.* Inhaling deeply, he resolved to persist.

For the next half hour, Barclay made small talk with Mrs. Gordon, his tone polite and his attention fixed, if not entirely sincere. He fetched lemonade and biscuits from a refreshment table the earl's staff had set up under the canopy of another oak. The beverages were chilled, the biscuits crisp, and the company tolerable. Mrs. Gordon prattled on about London's latest fashions, her bonnet bobbing as she spoke, while Barclay nodded in the appropriate places, his thoughts occasionally drifting despite his best intentions.

Eventually, Mrs. Gordon sighed, her gloved hands smoothing the skirts of her lavender muslin gown. "Would you mind terribly if we no longer partook in small talk? Perhaps we could share more entertaining tales if we relax the proprieties a little?"

Barclay straightened, his interest piqued. He needed to learn more about the attractive woman at his side, and polite chitchat revealed precious little of a person's true character. "Indeed. It can become dreadfully dull. Did you have a subject in mind?"

Mrs. Gordon tilted her head, her eyes sparkling with mischief. "Tell me, Mr. Thompson, do you ever have difficulty with a client? Does anyone refuse their plans or whatnot?"

Barclay chuckled, the sound low and rich. "It is the constant dread of an architect when an important client changes their mind midway through a project. Just recently, I planned a Neo-classical folly for a client up north. I traveled to visit the building site, where he met with me. The foundations were already dug and construction had begun, which we inspected together."

Mrs. Gordon leaned forward, the feathers of her bonnet trembling with her eagerness. "What did he do?"

"The client mentioned he had recently visited Stourhead near Wiltshire and inquired if we might adjust the foundations to make the building round—like the Temple of Apollo at that grand estate designed by Colen Campbell."

Her gloved hand flew to her mouth as she giggled. "My word! How far along were the foundations?"

"We had already constructed them and had begun on the first level."

"That is a ridiculous request to have made! What did the gentleman think you were to do?"

Barclay's eyes twinkled with amusement. "He asked me if we could simply leave what we had constructed but knock out the corners of the square to form a circle."

The widow burst out laughing, the sound bright and genuine, her hands coming up to cover her mouth as she shook with mirth. Her bonnet bobbed precariously, the ribbon under her chin fluttering as she tried to compose herself. Barclay could not deny that her absorption in his tale—and her unrestrained laughter—was flattering. It had been some time since he had enjoyed the company of a woman in so leisurely a manner, and Mrs. Gordon evidently found him amusing.

Gasping for breath, she wiped at her eyes with her gloved fingertips. "How did you address his request?"

"I told him, of course, we could do precisely as he requested. I would simply prepare an estimate for the change in specifications and bring it to him that evening."

"And did you do so?" she asked, her eyes shining with anticipation.

"I did." Barclay leaned back against the bench, crossing his arms comfortably. "When he saw the cost, he looked as if he might suffer an apoplexy right there on the spot. I asked him if I might commence work on the changes, and he sputtered that he would sleep on it and inform me in the morning."

Mrs. Gordon's shoulders shook with glee as she laughed even harder. Her bonnet wobbled precariously with each mirthful shake, and she brought a gloved hand to her lips in a vain attempt to stifle her giggles. "And then?"

Barclay leaned back, crossing his arms comfortably. "Come morning, the gentleman had left me a note stating that he was urgently required elsewhere. He also declared that the Hoares of Stourhead were pretentious tradesmen who knew not their place and that Colen Campbell was naught but an upstart from *louse land*."

Mrs. Gordon's eyes widened. "Louse land?"

Barclay chuckled. "My master builder—a proud Scotsman from Edinburgh—informed me that the contemptible phrase referred to Scotland. The note concluded by directing that I should proceed with the original design of 'taste and distinguishment' that he had, in his words, 'so masterfully conceived.'"

Mrs. Gordon clutched her stomach, practically doubling over with mirth. "What a rude man!" She gasped for breath between peals of laughter. "Well played, Mr. Thompson."

Barclay grinned back at her, the lines around his eyes softening. "One does not get far as an architect if one does not learn how to manage one's clients."

Mrs. Gordon leaned forward conspiratorially, her eyes

gleaming with curiosity. "Who was the gentleman in question? Was it someone I would have heard of?"

Barclay shook his head with a chuckle. "I am afraid I cannot speak out of turn. Suffice it to say that he was not quite as distinguished as he claimed."

Her eyes danced with amusement, and for the first time that afternoon, Barclay found himself fully at ease. The widow had proven to be far more engaging company than he had initially presumed. Perhaps they might form a comfortable companionship? She was attractive, pleasant, and had a sparkling sense of humor.

Not to mention that she is of an appropriate age.

He exhaled in contentment, feeling the tension in his shoulders ease. This might actually lead to something. It occurred to him that he was enjoying himself for the first time since Natalya had died. It was as if he had been locked in stasis these past two years, and this visit to Saunton Park had gently shaken him awake. He still did not sleep through the night, but mayhap once he had a wife in his bed once more, he would recover his ability to rest peacefully.

Certainly, he felt relaxed at this moment.

He had not realized how much tension had coiled through his body until this week—tension that was now unwinding in small, subtle increments. Perhaps by the time he returned to London, he might be engaged in a proper courtship with the handsome widow.

At that moment, movement beyond the shade of the oak caught his eye. A gentleman approached, his gait steady and purposeful, with a small child in tow. Mr. Ridley, upon spotting him beneath the sprawling branches, headed over. Barclay straightened, unexpectedly ashamed as he watched Tatiana skip up alongside him.

"Here is your papa."

Tatiana pulled her hand away from Mr. Ridley's grasp, crossing her small arms over her chest. Belligerence was etched in every stubborn line of her posture as she took in Barclay's proximity to Mrs. Gordon. Her curls shimmered in the sunlight, but her expression was thunderous. "What are you doing?"

Barclay arched a brow at her tone. "I am enjoying a conversation with Mrs. Gordon. What are you doing?"

Tatiana's frown deepened. "I was playing with the children in the nursery when I came to find you. I thought you would be with Jane, but—" Her sharp gaze swung to Mrs. Gordon, who blinked in surprise before giggling nervously, her gloved hand fluttering to her lips.

Mr. Ridley, observing the tension crackling in the air, raised his brows in mild amusement. He shot a sympathetic glance at Barclay before bowing, tipping his hat politely to Mrs. Gordon. "Mrs. Gordon, Miss Tatiana," he said with a flourish, and then strode away to join Lord Trafford—the only other gentleman participating in the languid game of ninepins.

Barclay firmed his jaw, leveling his daughter with a steady look. "Mind your manners, little one." His voice was low but authoritative, a hint of warning threaded through the words. Turning to his companion, he gestured politely. "Mrs. Gordon, may I present my daughter, Tatiana Thompson?"

Tatiana remained rigid, her eyes flashing defiantly.

"Please curtsy, Tatiana." His tone was measured but left no room for argument.

With great reluctance, Tatiana dropped into a slight curtsy, as her grandmother had painstakingly taught her.

The movement was executed perfectly but lacked any warmth or grace. "Can we go play chess now?"

Barclay drew himself up, straightening his shoulders. "I am not yet finished playing ninepins with Mrs. Gordon." His voice was firm, brooking no opposition. It would not do to allow his daughter to control him, particularly in front of an audience. Her behavior was nothing short of shocking, and he felt heat rise to his cheeks at her lack of decorum.

Bother! Had he just defended ninepins? He repressed a groan. There was no help for it now. He had committed to the game, and his word would stand. Rising to his feet, he held out his arm. Mrs. Gordon accepted it with a gracious smile, and together they fell into step, making their way back to where the players were assembled. *Ninepins, it is.*

From the corner of his eye, he caught sight of Tatiana bolting back toward the manor, her skirts flying behind her. Her face was scrunched, her little fists clenched at her sides, and he thought—though he could not be certain—that there might have been tears in her eyes.

A pang of guilt speared through him, sharp and unyielding. She had spoken often of wanting a new mother, and he was taking steps to fulfill that wish. So why did he feel like a scoundrel now?

Mrs. Gordon chattered pleasantly at his side, but her words barely registered. Barclay moved through the motions, setting up the pins, aligning them with care. He wondered grimly how long an appropriate length of time would be to make his point that he was the adult in their family.

Fortunately, the game passed swiftly. Less than an hour later, he accompanied Mrs. Gordon back to the manor, her arm nestled comfortably in his as they strolled along the gravel path.

Upon reaching the terrace, Mrs. Gordon joined the other guests who had gathered for refreshments and conversation. Barclay's gaze swept the scene, catching sight of Jane speaking animatedly with the countess. A surge of interest flared within him, surprising in its intensity, and he forced himself to look away. He was here to court Mrs. Gordon, not indulge in fancies.

He turned and strode into the house to search for Tatiana, his boots echoing softly against the polished floors. He checked the nursery, the library, even the morning room, but she was nowhere to be found. Her absence pulled a sigh from his lips—she was hiding. Hopefully, she would reappear in time for dinner.

Resigned to the wait, he returned to his chambers with a well-worn volume of *The Iliad* and took up residence in his armchair, its leather cushions creaking beneath him. He left the door ajar, a silent invitation for his daughter to come find him when she was ready.

When he awoke, the sun was setting. Barclay stretched his arms above his head, blinking against the warm glow of twilight. He marveled at the fact that he had dozed off—something he rarely did, especially in the middle of the day. His usual restlessness had given way to a sense of calm since his arrival at Saunton Park. It was unsettling, almost unfamiliar, to find himself relaxing when there was always an endless list of things to do.

He turned his gaze to the window, where the Somerset sunset stretched out over the manicured lawns and distant tree line, a sight both serene and majestic. The colors deepened as the sun dipped lower, staining the sky with hues of rose and amber. He watched in silence until the creak of the door behind him pulled him from his reverie.

It opened slowly, the hinges groaning in protest, and

then closed just as softly. He did not need to turn to know who had entered. The light, measured footsteps padded across the thick carpet.

"Papa?"

Barclay turned his head, his gaze softening as he met her eyes. "Tatiana."

Her hands twisted in front of her, her eyes downcast. "I am sorry I was rude."

Barclay set his book aside, his expression gentle. "I thank you for your apology. Will you come sit with me?" He gestured to the spot beside him, the cushions plush and inviting.

She approached, the patter of her feet as light as the treading of angels upon clouds. When she reached his side, Barclay leaned forward and lifted her up, settling her onto his knee with practiced ease. She was getting heavier—growing right before his eyes—but somehow, in his grief, he had failed to truly notice the subtle changes in his young daughter. The lengthening of her limbs, the slight curve of her cheeks losing their baby roundness—it struck him all at once.

Tatiana leaned back, resting her head against his chest as they both gazed out at the dramatic colors painted across the evening sky. Splashes of crimson, violet, and amber streaked the horizon, their brilliance reflected in her wide eyes. For a moment, they sat in companionable silence, watching the firmament slowly deepen as twilight crept in.

"Why were you so upset, little one?" he asked gently, his hand smoothing over her curls.

Tatiana sighed, her tiny shoulders rising and falling. "I want Jane to be my new mother. I do not understand why she was with that Mr. Dunsford fellow, and you were with that Mrs. Gordon."

Barclay blinked, momentarily taken aback. "Jane is too young to be your mother. I have to find a suitable woman to marry, and I am spending time with Mrs. Gordon so I can get to know her."

Tatiana twisted slightly to look up at him, her expression fierce with determination. "Mrs. Gordon is the wrong woman. You must court Jane."

Barclay raised his brows, suppressing a chuckle at her resolute tone. "You understand that I am the parent? I am the one who must decide what is best for us. For you."

Her lips pressed together stubbornly. "But if Mama were here, she would tell you that Jane is the one who is to be my mother."

Barclay froze, his heart clenching painfully in his chest. The room seemed to grow still, the air heavy with memories. "If your mother were here, we would not be discussing who should be your new mother."

Tatiana fell silent, her little hands clasped tightly in her lap. After a moment, she pushed away from him, slipping off his knee and landing lightly on her feet. She walked to the window, her small hands reaching up to toy with the heavy drapes, her back turned to him. Her voice, when she finally spoke, was barely above a whisper. "I do not wish to have Mrs. Gordon as my mother."

Barclay ran a hand over his face, steeling himself. "If matters progress with Mrs. Gordon, you will grow to like her."

Tatiana turned back to him, her delicate face set with surprising resolve, her eyes sparking with indignation. "If Mama were here, she would say to look into my heart. I looked into my heart, and Mrs. Gordon is nowhere to be found!"

Barclay stared at her, astonished by the conviction in her words. "What are you saying? That Jane is?"

Tatiana stepped forward, her little fingers clutching his hand tightly, her eyes pleading with his. "Yes. Jane likes to spend time with me. She reads me *Ladin!* That is what Mama used to do. It is a sign, Papa!"

Barclay shook his head slowly, regarding his daughter with a mixture of exasperation and affection. "How old are you, Tatiana?"

"Nine."

"And how old is Jane?"

Tatiana's brow furrowed. "I do not know."

"I believe she is eighteen or nineteen."

"Why does that matter?"

Barclay suppressed a sigh. "How many years older is she than you?"

Tatiana began counting on her fingers, her tiny brows drawn in concentration. "Nine?"

"And how much older am I than Jane?"

Her little face screwed up even tighter as she began counting again, her lips moving silently with each number.

"Aaah! One, two, three, four ..." He took her hand and smacked it rhythmically against his palm in time with the counting before throwing his hands up in mock frustration. "There is something like thirteen or fourteen years between us! She is closer in age to you than she is to me!"

Tatiana blinked up at him, her expression uncomprehending. Barclay exhaled sharply, running a hand through his hair before standing up and taking her hand. He led her out of the room, his stride brisk and determined as they crossed the carpeted hallway. The faint light of dusk spilled through the tall windows, casting elongated shadows on the walls as they made their way back to her chamber.

Inside, he settled her into a chair beside the supper tray that had been brought up for her. The soft glow of candlelight flickered over the silverware, illuminating the steam rising from the covered dishes. He placed his hands on his hips, his expression firm. "So there you are. It is a sign! I must pursue Mrs. Gordon. She is the same age as your mother was."

Tatiana scowled up at him, her arms crossing over her chest in clear defiance, but for once, she seemed to be at a loss for words.

Barclay's gaze softened. He leaned down, pressing a gentle kiss to her mulish little face before brushing a stray curl back from her forehead. She glared up at him, her eyes bright with rebellion, but she did not flinch away. He could not remain in her company just now. Not with all the memories of Natalya storming his thoughts and this tangled mess with Jane complicating everything further. His mind was a whirl of conflicting emotions, and he needed air. Space.

"I love you, little one," he said quietly, his voice rough with emotion. "Your grandmama will be here shortly."

With that, he straightened and strode across the room. He grasped the door handle firmly and yanked it open—only to find Aurora on the other side, her hand still extended as if to knock. Her eyes widened slightly, and she swiftly withdrew her hand, recovering her composure in a heartbeat.

"Mother," Barclay acknowledged politely, nodding his head. His tone was clipped, his need for escape evident.

Without waiting for a reply, he swept past her, his boots striking the floorboards with purpose as he strode down the hall, his thoughts already half a world away.

CHAPTER
EIGHT

"There could have been no two hearts so open, no tastes so similar, no feelings so in unison, no countenances so beloved."

Jane Austen

The clock announced the last few minutes of the midnight hour, its rhythmic ticking echoing through the stillness of the library. Jane's quill hovered over the page of her journal, the nib poised above the parchment, but no words came. All she could think was that the midnight hour was ending. *Their time.*

Would he make an appearance?

She had barely caught a glimpse of him all day, a mere shadow passing in the hall or a flicker of movement in the distance. But now, the manor was sleeping, its grand corridors silent and shrouded in darkness. Last night, he had startled her when he appeared. Then, he had encouraged her to speak her thoughts freely, to share her ideas in a way no man had ever done before.

Barclay appreciated her mind, and it was invigorating. No one had ever heard her verses before—those secret lines of poetry she scribbled in her quiet moments. But she knew, instinctively, that he had been the right person to share them with. He did not laugh or dismiss her efforts; he listened. He saw her.

And he had been right. She needed to take bigger risks. Even if Barclay was not interested in her, and even if she had to pursue a courtship elsewhere, she would steal this interlude for herself. She would use it to build her confidence, to embrace the idea that she was a woman with a mind of her own—one who had something to contribute to the world beyond needlework and polite conversation.

It was such a pity their courtship was not meant to be, for she was very much afraid she had found the man Emma had spoken of—the one with whom she shared a true meeting of minds. If only he could look at her as a woman. As a potential wife.

Her mind had connected with the wrong gentleman, and she feared she would never meet another like Barclay Thompson.

The hands of the clock crept forward, marking the passing of time with merciless precision. Midnight slipped away, and still, he did not come. Her heart sank with each tick of the longcase clock, disappointment settling like a stone in her stomach. She set her quill down with a soft clatter, staring at the empty page in front of her. Tonight, she had no muse. No lines to write.

Pushing back her chair, she gathered her things, smoothing her skirts and closing her journal. A book waited for her in her room—a poor substitute for conversation, but it would have to do. She would let its pages keep her company through her sleepless hours.

Turning toward the library door, she nearly jumped out of her skin.

"Barclay!" she gasped, her hand flying to her chest. He stood there, leaning against the doorframe, his gaze fixed upon her with the strangest expression. Candlelight flickered in the hallway behind him, casting long shadows over his white linen shirt, which hung loosely at the neck, revealing the strong column of his sun-bronzed throat. His hair was slightly tousled, as though he had run his hands through it in frustration.

"I knew you would be here," he murmured, his voice low and rough-edged.

Jane's heart thudded in her chest. "I hoped you might join me."

Silence stretched between them, heavy and charged.

"I tried to stay away," he admitted at last, his voice gruffer than she remembered. His hand flexed against the doorframe as if to steady himself.

"Why?"

"Because this does not make sense." Barclay waved a hand between them.

Jane blinked, her brow furrowing. "What does not make sense?"

His gaze locked with hers, his eyes darkening with something she could not quite name. "This attraction."

Jane's breath caught. He was admitting he felt it, too? Her pulse quickened, and a delightful shiver raced across her skin, as if she had caught a sudden chill. She turned back to the desk, placing her things down while she tried to gather her thoughts. She must have taken too long, for the next thing she knew, Barclay had come up behind her. The warmth of his presence radiated against her back, a solid reassurance that he was indeed real.

"Since I met you, it is as if I awoke from a deep slumber. The slumber of mourning. And you were the first face I saw when I finally opened my eyes."

Her breath came quicker, her heart thudding in her chest, barely daring to move in case she shattered the fragile magic of the moment—or woke to find herself in her own bed, with only the memory of yearning to keep her company.

Barclay waited in silence, as if studying her reaction. Jane did not move, frozen with wonder, while her heart fluttered with anticipation. He stepped closer, and she felt the warmth of his breath brush against her nape, teasing the delicate tendrils of her hair. His nearness sent a thrill down her spine, and she closed her eyes as he inhaled deeply near her ear. "You smell of strawberries and almonds again."

Her eyes drifted shut, and she held her breath. Gently, he leaned down and pressed his lips softly where her neck met her shoulder. A wave of warmth flooded through her, melting any lingering reservations. She tilted her head back, offering him silent permission, and his lips brushed against hers, feather-light and unhurried.

For the first time in her life, she felt the stirring of passion—tender, slow, and all-consuming. His long, muscular arms came up to encircle her waist, turning her to face him with gentle insistence.

Jane looked up at him, her eyes wide with wonder. He gazed back, the emotion in his brown eyes unguarded and genuine. Tentatively, she raised her hand and smoothed back the long strands of hair from his face, her fingertips grazing his cheek with delicate tenderness.

"Jane—" His voice was rough, threaded with longing. He dipped his head, capturing her mouth with his once more. His lips moved gently against hers, exploring, savoring. The rasp of his beard brushed her delicate skin, but she only pressed closer, her heart fluttering wildly in her chest.

The kiss was slow and reverent, a gentle exploration rather than a devouring. There was no rush—only the sweetness of discovery, the warmth of connection. When her lips parted slightly, he deepened the kiss just a fraction, his breath mingling with hers. She clung to him, her hands coming to rest on his shoulders, feeling the strength of him beneath her fingertips. He held her with care, his hands lightly resting on her back as if she were something precious.

After a long, lingering moment, he pulled back, resting his forehead against hers. His hands remained on her shoulders, but he took a steadying breath, his eyes closing briefly.

"You are temptation itself," he murmured, his voice laced with regret. He straightened, his hands dropping to his sides as he took a step back. "I must step away before I forget myself."

Their eyes met, a mixture of longing and restraint shimmering between them. "Jane, it is not my place to pursue this ... us. You are young, with a promising future. And I ... I am illegitimate. Too old for you."

Jane's brow furrowed as she processed his words, confusion evident in her eyes. "Are you saying you cannot pursue this because you are illegitimate? Or because of the age difference?"

Barclay released a half-chuckle, shaking his head. "Both, I suppose. But mostly the first. You do not know the repercussions, Jane. You are too young to understand."

Jane lifted her chin, her gaze steady. "I am willing to find out."

His expression softened with disbelief and something else—hope, perhaps. "What if I am not willing to put you through that?"

"It is your decision," she replied quietly, "but know that I am ... that is ... I would ... like to try."

Barclay lifted one of his large hands, the hands she had imagined countless times in her dreams, and ran his calloused fingertips gently down her cheek, as if she were made of the finest porcelain. "I must leave you now before I do something I will regret."

Barclay stepped back, his expression taut with restraint, and then turned to leave the room. Jane stood still, the warmth of his touch still lingering on her skin, her heart pounding in her chest as she tried to catch her breath. She stared after him long after he disappeared, her fingers touching her lips as if to hold the memory in place, wondering what would happen next.

BARCLAY WOKE, surprised at how well he had slept after the interlude in the library. He blinked up at the ceiling, its ornate moldings softened by the pale light of dawn filtering through the heavy curtains. Memories of last night drifted back with startling clarity. Her scent still seemed to cling to him, light and fresh, mingled with the memory of strawberries and almonds.

He closed his eyes, recalling the delicate constellation of freckles where her neck sloped down to meet her shoulder—each mark a tiny blessing on her pale skin. Their kiss had revealed the delight that her very essence was infused with a trace of strawberries. It was as if summer itself had caressed her and left its fragrance behind.

Barclay exhaled, running a hand over his face. He was still uncertain what was right, but he could not shake the compelling need to see her again. To feel that rush of vitality, that spark of joy that had been missing since Natalya's departure. It was as if Jane had unlocked something within him—something that had long been dormant. Perhaps his desire to spend time in her company was overriding his good sense, but he could not think of a single reason why he should not seek her out.

What harm could it possibly do?

Inhaling deeply, he assured himself that he was not too old for her—not by society's standards, at least. And they seemed well-matched intellectually, with shared interests and pursuits that set her apart from the ladies of the *ton* with their simpering smiles and empty conversations. Jane was different. She thought, she reasoned, and she expressed herself with a candor that was both refreshing and disarming.

And now that the Earl of Saunton had acknowledged him, surely the Thompsons' standing would be improved once society learned of it? Saunton had even suggested hosting a dinner to introduce Aurora and Barclay to well-placed members of society, pledging his support to the endeavor. The duke's endorsement would lend weight, smoothing the path for his family to enter circles they might have otherwise found closed. A rise in status might mean no diminishing of Jane's own in the event that their relationship progressed to its natural outcome.

The notion stirred something within him—an unfamiliar flicker of hope. *Perhaps ...*

He pondered the idea of spending time with Jane today,

imagining the possibility of discovering more of what lay beneath her poised exterior. She had already expressed an openness to courtship, so why should he not explore it? He could not be expected to make such a decision without properly understanding her character, could he? It seemed only logical that they should come to know each other better—to test the boundaries of compatibility.

Barclay stretched, the tension in his muscles easing as he rose from the bed. Sunlight streamed through the crack in the drapes, casting warm streaks of light across the polished wood floor. He thought of how he might discreetly arrange to be with her—some opportunity for conversation and connection without revealing their mutual attraction. He longed for an activity that would not lead to firm expectations but would allow them to learn more about each other, to discover if theirs might be an advisable partnership.

He knew he did not wish to participate in the typical activities arranged for guests, which seemed a bit too public for his liking. No, he would need to find something away from prying eyes, away from the gossip and inquisitiveness of those with too much interest and too little discretion.

A thought flitted through his mind. *Would Tatiana be sufficient as a chaperone?* They were vaguely related, after all, and these matters tended to be more relaxed in the country. His lips quirked in a half-smile. How fortunate it would be if Tatiana's presence smoothed the way for his time with Jane. But he would need to be certain. Whom could he ask without revealing the true motivation for his question?

His mind wandered to Lady Saunton. Would she find the inquiry odd? Or would her sharp eyes perceive the truth? He needed to tread carefully. The countryside had ears—whispers carried faster than a winter chill, and any misstep could place Jane in a compromising light. He would find a way. He must.

JANE WOKE at her usual hour, sunlight just beginning to creep through the lace curtains of her bedchamber. The kiss she had shared with Barclay had done nothing to restore her former ability to rest peacefully. She had lain awake until dawn, her mind replaying the touch of his lips on hers, the warmth of his breath, and the feel of his strong body pressed against hers. Each memory was vivid, imprinted on her senses as if it had only just happened.

She sighed deeply, her gaze drifting to the window where the first blush of morning light touched the horizon. What would happen now that he had revealed his esteem? Would he pretend it had not happened when she saw him next? Retreat from the unmistakable spark between them? Or would he acknowledge their growing affinity, even in the light of day?

It was unclear, based on his final words before departing the library. His expression had been conflicted, as if he were holding back a tide of emotion.

Groaning softly, she rolled out of bed, her feet touching the cool surface of the floorboards. *Best to dress quickly,* she thought. The sooner she readied herself, the sooner she could find her tray of coffee waiting for her in the library—a small comfort in the chaos of her thoughts.

An hour later, she took her usual seat in the library, the scent of freshly brewed coffee wafting through the room as she poured herself a cup. Sunlight streamed through the tall windows, casting warm patterns on the polished wood floor. In the corner, Ethan and Richard were engaged in an early game of chess. The earl's green eyes glinted with concentration, mirroring his son's own emerald gaze as they both bent over the board, studying each move with fierce determination.

"Checkmate."

"No, Papa! How did you do it?"

Richard grinned, leaning back with evident satisfaction. "I retreated to draw you in, and you followed, thinking I was defending myself."

Ethan frowned at the pieces, his eyes narrowing in thought. His hand drifted to his collar, tugging at it absently—a perfect imitation of what Jane had often seen the earl do during moments of stress. Richard, his expression bright with the thrill of victory, began to move the pieces back, demonstrating the final sequence of moves.

"Papa, Daisy told me we have a *gra-ta* in the woods?"

Ethan blinked, his brows lifting. "You mean the grotto?"

"Yes. She said she heard it was very *boo-tee-fill*, but she does not know where it is. Could you take me there?"

The earl's face softened, then fell with regret. "I wish I could, but I have meetings with my steward and tenants today."

Before Richard could voice his disappointment, a familiar voice resonated from the doorway, low and husky. "I could take him."

Jane's breath caught, her hands stilling over her coffee cup. She had not noticed Barclay's entry, but there he stood, framed in the doorway, dressed in his customary black coat and buckskins. His posture was confident, his expression calm, and Tatiana stood beside him, her small hand clasped in his.

Richard's eyes lit up with hope. "Do you know where it is?"

"Of course. I have studied the plans for Saunton Park many times over the years. It was the project that made Tsar's reputation."

The earl nodded appreciatively. "Then I would be grateful if you would accompany my boy to the grotto. Jane, would you like to join them? Tsar outdid himself when he designed it, and it is especially lovely in the summer."

Jane could not help herself—she beamed. "I would be delighted to escort Ethan there." *And his uncle!* The thought of spending time with Barclay in such a secluded, beautiful spot sent a thrill through her.

Barclay approached, his long stride unhurried as he took a seat nearby while Tatiana and Ethan chattered at the chessboard. He settled into the chair with ease, his dark eyes resting on Jane. "Please, Jane. Take your time." He gestured to the cup in her hand, his gaze warm and steady as he studied her with undisguised interest.

Jane returned his look with a shy smile, her cheeks tinged with color. She noted the earl excusing himself with a nod, leaving the four of them alone. Spending time with Barclay was precisely what she wanted to do today. Had he made up his mind about the possibility of a courtship? His manner seemed more than amenable to her joining him. Hope flared within her chest, and she quickly turned her attention back to her coffee, sipping hurriedly.

The last thing she wanted was for any of the other guests to stumble upon them and insist on joining their party to the grotto. She could easily imagine Mr. Dunsford or Mrs. Gordon attaching themselves to the excursion, and she would not allow that if she could help it. Clinking her cup down on the tray with a bit more force than she intended, she stood briskly. "Shall we?"

Ethan grinned up at her as she took his hand, his small fingers curling around hers with the trust only children could muster. She led him toward the entrance hall, her stride purposeful, and glanced back over her shoulder to see Barclay following behind with Tatiana, the girl chattering happily as she skipped alongside him. A spark of happiness bloomed in Jane's heart—time alone with people she truly liked, away from the pressures of the house party.

Ethan chattered beside her, his small voice animated as he spoke of the grotto, of what he imagined it might look like, and of the tales he had heard from Daisy. Jane responded with appropriate nods and smiles, but her heart was light, and her mind was elsewhere—on the gentleman trailing just behind her.

They exited the manor, stepping out onto the gravel path that wound through the gardens. Manicured hedges flanked their walk, the scent of roses and freshly cut grass heavy in the summer air. Jane kept her pace brisk, eager to reach the shelter of the trees where prying eyes would be left behind.

"Jane, I cannot keep up with you!" Ethan complained suddenly, his little legs working double-time to match her stride. Jane stopped abruptly, turning to look down at him. His cheeks were flushed, and he panted slightly, his small chest rising and falling. "You are *or-ful-lee* eager to see the *gra-ta!*" he exclaimed, his brow furrowing with both curiosity and exhaustion.

Jane paused, blinking in surprise before glancing back at Barclay and Tatiana, who had stopped a few paces behind. She had not realized she had been moving so quickly. Her gaze swept the garden path, noting with satisfaction that they were well away from the manor now. The hedges had grown thicker, and the path had narrowed, winding toward the distant tree line. There should be no danger of Mr. Dunsford or Mrs. Gordon intruding on their privacy.

Barclay's eyes sparkled with humor as he regarded her. "Perhaps Jane is simply eager to spend time with you," he suggested, his voice rich with amusement.

Jane bit her lip, blushing as she accepted that Barclay was not fooled. He must have seen through her efforts to escape the other guests. But then she brightened, realizing that he must have had similar intentions if he knew what she was up to.

"Have you been to the grotto, Jane?" Tatiana asked, her eyes sparkling with unrestrained enthusiasm. Jane noted the child's silver-blonde hair glimmering in the sunlight, bare to the elements. A ripple of surprise ran through her as she lifted a hand to her own head, realizing she had left the manor without her bonnet. Her cheeks flushed at the breach of propriety, but she could not find it within herself to regret it. In her eagerness to spend time with Barclay, she had forgotten entirely.

Barclay's lips twitched as if he fought a smile, his gaze drifting to her uncovered hair. He, too, was bareheaded, his dark hair catching the sunlight in streaks of copper as they walked. "It seems we are all a bit unprepared for this outing," he remarked with a grin.

"I have not," Jane replied, returning Tatiana's eager gaze.

"Do you know anything about the grotto? About what is there?" Barclay asked, his tone unusually light-hearted. He looked nothing like the somber widower who had arrived only days ago. His shoulders were relaxed, his expression open, and Jane found herself captivated by this change in him.

She shook her head. "It is the company that has me engrossed," she admitted softly, her voice barely above a whisper.

Barclay's expression softened. A smile played at the corners of his mouth, fleeting but warm. "It is a rather unusual folly. From all accounts, Tsar did magnificent work, and I am intrigued to see it for the first time."

"What is it, exactly?" she asked, tilting her head with curiosity.

He only shrugged, his broad shoulders flexing beneath his linen shirt.

Remember to breathe, Jane! she chided herself silently, forcing her lingering gaze back to the path.

"You will all have to see it for yourselves," Barclay said, his tone carrying a note of teasing. "I shall not ruin the surprise."

Barclay was pleased with the current turn of events. He had desired time with Jane far from curious eyes, and here he was, entering the woods with only Tatiana and his nephew to witness their interlude. Lifting Ethan onto his shoulders, Barclay was well aware of what had enticed her to hurry so. He shared her enthusiasm to spend time together and anticipated the delight of both Jane and the children when they reached their destination.

Herding their little party along a path winding through the trees, Barclay led the way. The path, well-maintained and clear of obstacles, allowed for easy passage, and there was no danger of Ethan colliding with branches despite his exaggerated height perched on Barclay's shoulders. The boy giggled with each step, his small hands clutching Barclay's head for balance as they ambled along.

The sound of birdcalls echoed through the canopy, a melodic accompaniment to the gentle rustling of leaves stirred by the breeze. Barclay felt oddly at peace, the quiet serenity of the woods soothing his mind. When they reached a fork in the path, he veered left without hesitation. The woods grew cooler, the thick branches overhead weaving a protective canopy that shielded them from the midday sun. He noted with approval the relief on Jane's face as the harsh rays were replaced with soft, dappled light. Her cheeks had been flushed from the heat, but now the color seemed to settle, blending prettily with her complexion. Tatiana, too, seemed relaxed, her curls bobbing as she chattered happily at Jane's side.

Before long, they emerged into a clearing, and Ethan gasped with delight. "Look!" he cried, pointing across the water.

Jane's gaze followed his outstretched finger. A pond stretched before them, its surface green and still, reflecting the pale light that trickled through the trees. And there, on the opposite bank, stood a statue of Persephone, gazing back at them from the entrance of a grand grotto.

Barclay led them carefully around the perimeter of the water, his hands steadying Tatiana as they navigated the narrow path. Moss and slippery green algae clung to the edges, and he kept a firm grip on her hand to ensure she did not stray too close. Ethan remained high on his shoulders, craning his neck to catch every glimpse of the statue as they approached.

They reached the base of the statue, and Barclay's

breath caught. It was an exquisite representation of the goddess of spring, far different from the customary depictions he had seen. Her marble features were turned longingly toward the entrance of the first cave, her expression wistful and full of longing. Rather than the typical sheaf of grain or regal scepter, this Persephone was scantily robed, her draped fabric so thin it seemed almost translucent, as though made of gossamer. She stood upon a bed of marble flowers, each petal lovingly carved to evoke the spring she brought forth each year upon reuniting with Demeter. The tilt of her head spoke of joy and yearning, as if the sculptor had captured her very soul in that fleeting moment of reunion.

Jane stood at the base, her jaw agape, eyes wide with wonder. Tatiana reached out a small hand, her fingertips grazing the smooth, cool surface of the marble. "It is beautiful," she whispered in reverence, her voice hushed as if afraid to disturb the sanctity of the place.

Indeed, Tsar had outdone himself. The roof of the grotto, entirely man-made, reached out over the water, adding to the magic of the quiet space. The goddess stood forever reaching toward the entrance, as if yearning to return to the world above. Within the cavern, the sounds of the woods were muted, replaced by the gentle tinkling of water. A stream flowed gracefully from the bed of flowers at Persephone's feet, winding its way through a carved channel before rejoining the pond outside. It was a water feature for which his grandfather had been exceedingly proud, evoking the melting of winter snow and the renewal of spring when Persephone returned to her mother.

"Grandpapa designed this?" Tatiana asked, her eyes wide with wonder as she gazed up at the statue, her small fingers still resting on its smooth marble surface.

Barclay smiled, surprised and pleased by her curiosity. Perhaps the architectural blood that ran through their veins had just awakened in her. For a brief moment, he imagined her growing up to be a great artist or even working alongside the elder Thompsons in their business. He instinctively knew that such a path would not offend Jane if she were to join their family. It was one of the many things that set her apart from the other ladies of society.

"There is more," Barclay announced as he lowered Ethan to the ground. The roof dipped down as the path wound deeper, and it was no longer safe for the boy to ride so high on his shoulders. Taking the lead, he herded their little party farther along the stone path. Shadows deepened as they moved, the light filtering through with a dim, otherworldly glow.

Barclay led them to the back of the cavern, where a wall extended halfway, concealing a narrow entrance to the second cave. He guided them through, the coolness of the stone walls brushing against their fingertips as they walked. The surface was engraved with a frieze depicting the underworld—chiseled with such skill that the shadows seemed to move and dance across the carved figures.

It was a revelation of design, the stone shaped to mimic the folds of rock, the carvings so intricate they seemed almost lifelike. Yet, it did not escape Barclay's notice that his ... *sire* ... had chosen to commission an underworld theme—a peculiar choice unless one took the dead man's tendencies into account. Of course, the Earl of Satan had bonded with this harsh chapter of classic mythology. How fitting a subject for such a cruel and lecherous man.

But today was not for pondering the failings of his lineage. Today was for learning more about the woman who had captivated him from the first moment they met, and for assessing their compatibility, with Tatiana by their side. He brushed aside his bitter thoughts, unwilling to allow the specter of his father to taint this experience.

The path widened, leading them into a cavernous space where Jane suddenly stopped, her breath catching in her throat. Ethan and Tatiana gasped beside her, their eyes wide with wonder. A circular hole had been cut into the roof above, allowing sunlight to pour down in a concentrated beam that illuminated the statue before them. Barclay had to admit, his grandfather had orchestrated such drama that it fairly took one's breath away.

Hades himself towered above them, carved from gleaming stone, much larger than Persephone. His long bident was clasped in one hand, while the other gripped a chain that tethered the ferocious Cerberus, the three-headed guard dog of the underworld. The beast was captured mid-snarl, each head snarling in a different direction, its muscles rippling with tension as if ready to lunge. On Hades' head rested his helm, the smooth stone polished to a shine, and his gaze was fixed toward the first statue, hidden from view, yet with the same sense of longing.

But this god did not long for the world above. He longed for his wife. Barclay understood the sentiment all too well. He had once shared that same unyielding ache for Natalya. Yet, for the first time since she had departed, his thoughts did not settle upon her this afternoon. Instead, they lingered on Jane—on her bright eyes, her ready smile, and her unguarded wonder.

"Who is it?" Ethan breathed, his small face reflecting his awe as he stood at the base and gazed up at the towering dog. Cerberus stood taller than the boy, its marble teeth bared in a fearsome snarl. Barclay had to confess his own admiration for the scope and perfection of the statue.

One could almost imagine the fetid breath of the beast as it guarded its master's realm.

"It is Hades, the king of the underworld," Barclay explained, his voice low and reverent. He pointed up at the statue's helm, which gleamed in the dappled sunlight filtering through the carved opening above. "That is his cap of invisibility. It allows him to travel undetected by other gods, similar to a cloud of mist."

Jane circled the massive statue, her footsteps light against the cool stone floor as she examined it from every angle. Her gaze traveled over the intricate carvings, lingering on the folds of Hades' robes, which seemed to ripple with movement, and the fine etchings on his helm. "The detail is so intricate," she murmured, awe threading through her voice. She paused by his feet, her eyes widening. "See his sandals?" She pointed at them, marveling at the leather straps depicted with such precision that the texture of the bindings seemed almost touchable. Hades looked as though he might step off his pedestal at any moment, striding forth to search for Persephone.

Tatiana leaned closer, inspecting Cerberus with wide, fascinated eyes. She squinted at the sharp teeth jutting from each of the creature's snarling mouths, her small hands clasped behind her back as if to restrain herself from reaching out. "It is ... magical," she sighed dreamily. "Like *Ladin* in his cave of treasures!"

Barclay beamed, the warmth of it reaching his eyes. He could not remember the last time he had experienced such a moment of unfiltered joy—four special people together, united in wonder as they beheld one of his grandfather's greatest works. His heart swelled with unexpected emotion, and he committed every detail to memory. The soft murmurs of admiration, the sunlight catching in Jane's hair, the echo of Ethan's footsteps as he circled the statue in fascination. It was, quite simply, perfect.

Eventually, they began their journey back to the manor, retracing their steps along the winding path. Tatiana and Ethan clamored ahead of them, their laughter ringing out like bells as they weaved through the trees. Their cheerful voices floated back, punctuated by giggles as they chased one another along the trail.

Barclay watched them for a moment before his gaze slid to Jane. Her eyes were fixed on the path, but her expression was serene, her lips curved in a soft smile. The sunlight filtered through the canopy, casting patterns of light and shadow across her features. Taking the opportunity, Barclay reached out discreetly, his hand closing over hers.

Her fingers curled against his palm, and though her gaze remained forward, he did not miss the smile of bliss that crossed her face. It was a small, secret smile, but it held more warmth than the afternoon sun. A sigh of contentment escaped his lips, a quiet exhalation of happiness. For the first time in longer than he could remember, he felt ... whole.

They walked like that, hand in hand, their steps in perfect sync, the woods around them silent save for the rustling of leaves and the distant calls of birds. He knew that soon they would return to reality—the manor, the watchful eyes of the house party, the ever-present scrutiny of society. But here, hidden beneath the shade of towering oaks and dappled sunlight, there was only them.

No matter what happened after this walk, the wondrous visit to the grotto with Jane and the children would forever remain in his heart, etched there as one perfect afternoon of happiness.

CHAPTER NINE

"You pierce my soul. I am half agony, half hope."

Jane Austen

As they approached the manor, Barclay reluctantly let go of Jane's hand and moved ahead to take Tatiana's small fingers in his grasp. Jane slowed her pace, allowing Ethan to catch up so she might walk beside him. Barclay sighed quietly, the weight of reality settling back onto his shoulders. Their glorious jaunt was over, the guests now coming into view on the terrace, and he longed to turn back to the cool shadows of the woods where everything had seemed so simple—so pure—in the solitude of the grotto.

Climbing the sloping stone steps, Jane discreetly ventured over to where the countess, the Duchess of Halmesbury, and his mother sat drinking tea around a lace-covered table. Barclay watched her departure with deep regret, unwilling to let the afternoon slip away. Yet, at the same time, he recognized the sense in allowing their time together to end before the prying eyes of society interfered. If he was to explore this unspoken bond between them, it would have to be away from the inquisitive glances of those too eager to pass judgment.

The children hurried over to the refreshment table nearby, Ethan clamoring to know what was set upon it, bouncing on his toes in an attempt to peer over the edge. Tatiana giggled and tugged him forward, the two of them barely able to see the array of cakes and finger sandwiches laid out in abundance. Their laughter drifted back to him, and for a moment, he allowed himself to simply enjoy the sound.

His reverie was abruptly interrupted when Mrs. Gordon appeared at his side, her gloved hand resting lightly on his forearm. Her touch was gentle, her expression warm, but his heart sank. Mrs. Gordon was a lovely woman—elegant, refined, and pleasant in conversation—but now her presence felt intrusive, as if she were encroaching upon something sacred. He wracked his mind, wondering if he had, at any point, indicated that he might pursue her. It would be beyond uncomfortable to explore future possibilities with Jane while engaging with the widow if she was forming expectations.

"Mr. Thompson, I have missed you this afternoon." Her voice was smooth, her smile polished. "Were you taking a walk with the children?" She gestured subtly toward Jane, who was now seated beside the countess, with an elegant arch of her blonde brow. Anxiety stirred uncomfortably in his gut. Was that how people would see him and Jane? That he was courting a child?

Barclay cleared his throat, his voice coming out a bit

rougher than intended. "Miss Davis and I took Ethan and my daughter to visit the grotto."

"Oh! I have heard from the countess that it is wondrous." Mrs. Gordon's eyes sparkled with interest, and she stepped a fraction closer. "I was hoping to see it, but I have never learned the route to reach it. I am hopeless with directions." Her expression turned expectant, and Barclay felt the implication settle heavily between them. She was prompting him to take her there.

The idea of sharing it—*their* special place—with anyone but Jane made his hands clench with unease. No matter what the future held, whether Jane and he overcame the many obstacles that lay before them or not, he would always treasure introducing her to that magical place. He could not bring himself to impose on that memory by taking another there. Especially not on the same afternoon.

He straightened slightly, forcing a polite smile. "Perhaps one of the guests will accompany you. Mr. Ridley, I believe, is familiar with the way."

Her expression faltered, disappointment clear in the downward curve of her lips. Guilt prickled at him, but it was not enough to make him intrude upon what had been a perfect memory with Jane. Casting about for a way to soften the rejection, he inclined his head politely. "Shall we take a turn around the gardens?"

Mrs. Gordon's smile returned, faint but genuine. "That would be lovely." She glanced around the terrace, her gaze flitting briefly over the gathering before she leaned in conspiratorially, lowering her voice. "I had a matter I would like to discuss in private."

He hesitated, then held out his arm. Mrs. Gordon accepted it immediately, grasping him a little more tightly than was comfortable. Her gloved fingers pressed into his forearm with surprising strength, but he did not comment. With practiced civility, he led her down the stone steps, their footsteps soft against the gravel walkway that meandered toward the formal gardens. From the terrace above, guests would have a clear view of their stroll, but he suspected that was precisely what Mrs. Gordon intended. He could not deny that he was curious to hear what she wished to say.

"Mr. Thompson, I do not wish to be forward," she began as soon as they were out of earshot of the other guests, her voice lowering conspiratorially. "I would like to make my feelings clear."

Barclay glanced at her, his expression politely guarded. "On what subject, Mrs. Gordon?"

She inhaled deeply, her gaze drifting to the hedgerows and the sculpted topiaries before snapping back to him. "May I be frank, sir?"

He inclined his head, a flicker of wariness settling in his chest. "Of course."

Her hand tightened almost imperceptibly on his arm, and Barclay suppressed the urge to shift away. *What is this about?* A niggling suspicion crept into his thoughts—had he unintentionally created expectations? Had he overstepped in some way? The very notion set his teeth on edge.

"I am aware of your family circumstances ... of your mother and the late Earl of Saunton."

Barclay halted mid-step, turning to face the petite widow fully. She stood several inches shorter than Jane, her stature dainty and precise, her golden curls perfectly arranged beneath her bonnet. He could not help but compare the two women—Jane, willowy and full of life, her laughter as unrestrained as her opinions, and Mrs. Gordon, polished and practiced, with every gesture measured. His thoughts flickered back to the library, to the way Jane's freckles had dotted her creamy skin like a constellation—a perfect imperfection that had nearly undone him.

He blinked to clear his thoughts, realizing belatedly that Mrs. Gordon had raised the question of his illegitimacy. It was shockingly forward—especially in such an open setting where prying eyes could easily witness their exchange.

Mrs. Gordon noted his blink and, misinterpreting its cause, hurried to press her case. "I wanted to assure you that, as a good Christian woman, I would never blame the child for the behavior of the parents." She tilted her chin up with a proud sort of magnanimity. "I think it is lamentable that society treats upstanding men like you poorly for something that is entirely beyond your control."

Barclay's brow furrowed, and he took a moment to digest her words. It was abundantly clear that Mrs. Gordon wished to convey her receptiveness to courtship, but the manner in which she had chosen to express it unsettled him. There was something in her tone, a faint sense of condescension that he could not entirely ignore.

He cocked his head, carefully choosing his words to remain polite but firm. "I appreciate your sentiment, Mrs. Gordon. I assure you, however, that my mother, Aurora Thompson, was but a child when she met the Earl of Saunton. He took advantage of a young girl who had not yet achieved her majority, and there was naught she or my grandfather could do to set it right." His voice remained steady, though there was a sharpness beneath the surface. "She has paid the price dearly, while the late earl dealt with none of the consequences of their association."

His gaze held hers, unflinching, waiting for her reaction. The wind rustled through the hedges, carrying the scent of summer blooms, but the moment between them felt strangely brittle.

The widow's face fell in alarm, her eyes widening. "I did not wish to offend. It is ... admirable that Miss Thompson kept her child and raised him. Very commendable. Of course, as you say, she was merely a child herself when the incident happened."

Barely a year or two year younger than Jane.

Barclay's discomfort rose, the muscles in his shoulders tightening. "My mother is a fine woman of quiet distinguishment," he replied, his tone firm.

"Of course she is. The whole situation is quite lamentable. It is deplorable how some members of the nobility behave, blithely aware of their own superiority." Mrs. Gordon shook her head with a disapproving cluck of her tongue. "I shall ensure I make your mother's acquaintance forthwith. I am ... hoping that our own ... companionship will continue to blossom, and your mother is an important aspect of your life. I am certain that a connection with the widow of a respected vicar will assist her to claim ... an increased element of respectability."

Barclay stiffened at the implication, but he kept his expression smooth. He had had similar thoughts of his own, but it was his situation to consider and the widow was overstepping by pointing it out. "That would be appreciated, Mrs. Gordon," he said, inclining his head with a politeness that was more reflex than sincerity.

They completed their walk in near silence, the cheerful birdcalls and rustling hedgerows doing little to alleviate the tension that coiled within him. The feeling of contentment he had enjoyed in the woods—his first taste of genuine happiness since Natalya's death—now scattered like so many ashes upon the wind.

A knot persisted in his stomach, twisting tighter as he considered the consequences. How could he proceed with a courtship of Jane without becoming an irredeemable cad in the eyes of decent society? The age difference alone gave him pause, and whispers of his illegitimacy would undoubtedly follow. If he were to witness a man of his circumstances pursuing a Jane, would he not have similar thoughts? *How much simpler it would all be if Mrs. Gordon were the one I could not stop thinking of.*

Barclay's jaw tightened with frustration as he led the widow back up the steep stairs to the terrace. Mrs. Gordon's smile remained bright, her posture graceful, as if she were entirely unaware of his inner turmoil. When they reached the top, she curtsied with practiced elegance and stepped away, her gaze flickering across the terrace until it settled on Aurora, who stood near the balustrade with her hands clasped before her.

Mrs. Gordon wasted no time in approaching, her smile widening as she dipped into another curtsy. Though the widow technically outranked his mother, it seemed she was intent on gaining favor with this show of deference. "Mrs. Thompson," she gushed, "it would be my utmost pleasure if you would join me for breakfast tomorrow morning. I do so wish to become better acquainted."

Aurora regarded her with serene composure, her expression unflinching. "That would be lovely, Mrs. Gordon," she replied in her lightly accented voice. Her mother, Barclay's grandmama, had been a lively Italian woman, and Aurora had never fully lost the intonations of her youth. The gentle lilt of her speech, softened with age, lent her words a grace that was distinctly hers.

Mrs. Gordon, visibly pleased, gave another polite curtsy before moving off, her skirts swishing elegantly as she went. Aurora watched her departure with mild curiosity before turning back to Barclay, her expression smoothing into relief. She stepped toward him, her gaze softening. "Barclay, I must admit, I am pleased that you are taking our discussion to court seriously."

Barclay inclined his head, his expression carefully neutral.

Aurora's gaze lingered on his face, her voice dropping to a more intimate tone. "Son, there is no reason to hurry the process. Please assure me you will be certain before you offer to make a young woman your wife." She paused, her eyes searching his. "What you had with Natalya was special, and our family enjoys ... a pleasant dynamic. It would be ill-advised to disrupt your grandfather's household with the wrong companion."

Barclay's lips curved into a faint smile at Aurora's transparent attempt to meddle. "Are you saying that Mrs. Gordon is a poor choice?"

"Not at all. Just ... be certain. There is no reversing that decision." Her voice was gentle, but the underlying firmness was unmistakable.

He regarded her thoughtfully, his gaze tracing the delicate lines of her face. "Why did you never marry, Mother? You are a beautiful woman, and I have to think there were some opportunities over the years?"

Aurora shook her head, her black hair gleaming even in the shade of the terrace, twisted into an elegant knot at the nape of her neck. "It is not a son's place to ask such a question." Her tone was mild, but he detected the hint of rebuke beneath it.

He shrugged, unbothered. "This has been an unusual trip we have taken. We have spoken on other matters we would not ordinarily broach in London, and I have always wondered."

Aurora moved to the balustrade, her hands resting lightly on its stone surface as she leaned forward to gaze upon the manicured gardens stretching out below. Afternoon light spilled across the hedgerows, casting shadows over the gravel pathways that wound between rose bushes and flowering shrubs. "Marriage is irreversible, and I never met the right gentleman," she replied finally, her voice softened with reflection. "One who could accept my situation ... accept you ... and make me feel like taking the risk was worthwhile." She paused, her fingers brushing absently over the smooth stone. "Watching you with Natalya over the years—you were exceptionally fortunate to find someone who was your perfect counterpart."

Barclay felt a touch of melancholy at this reminder. "It was difficult knowing that it had a time limit, but I would never erase my time with Natalya for all the riches in the world."

Aurora turned back to him, her gaze searching his with a tenderness that was rarely so openly expressed. "I believe you are destined to find such a connection again, Barclay. You have always been fortunate, and it is my dearest hope to see you happy as you once were." She straightened, smoothing the fabric of her gown. "Assure me you will not settle ... that you will be sure before you choose a bride?"

Barclay's eyes flickered to where Jane sat talking with the countess on the far side of the terrace. The two ladies leaned in close, their heads bent together as Sophia whispered something in Jane's ear. Jane reached out with gentle familiarity, tucking an errant curl of Sophia's distinctive red-blonde hair back behind her ear. The countess laughed aloud, her cheeks flushed with good health as she exclaimed that Miss Toussaint would scold her for neglecting her coiffure if her lady's maid were present to see her in such a state.

Sophia's hand settled over her rounded belly, and Barclay's gaze lingered there for a moment, thoughtful. *An heir for the earl. A safeguard for the family holdings.* His mind drifted, unbidden, to the image of Jane in a similar state—her hand resting protectively over the swell of her stomach, her expression alight with joy. The thought took him by surprise, slipping past his guard and settling deep within him.

Her love of children was evident. He had seen it countless times in her tender interactions with Ethan and Tatiana. Jane would make a wonderful mother; he was certain of it. His heart clenched at the thought of her with a babe in her arms, her laughter ringing through their household. And though he tried to banish it, he could not help but imagine himself at her side—her husband and partner, watching their family grow.

But would it be fair to expect her to mother a child of Tatiana's age? He felt a pang of uncertainty twist in his chest. Jane was so young, barely older than his mother had been when she found herself in trouble with the Earl of Saunton. How would Aurora react if and when he revealed that he might have found a true affinity with a young woman of such tender years?

He exhaled slowly, resolving his thoughts with careful deliberation. "I shall endeavor to think the matter through thoroughly before making my decision." His tone was even, though the words carried more weight than Aurora could know.

Aurora nodded approvingly, her smile soft and relieved. "That is all I ask, my dear."

MISS DAVIS AND THE ARCHITECT

JANE WROTE FURIOUSLY, her quill racing across the page in the dim light of the library. The scratch of the nib against the paper filled the quiet room, punctuated only by her shallow breaths and the soft crackle of the fire burning low in the grate. She paused, her hand stilling, and frowned at the dull edge of her quill. *Not now,* she thought with a surge of impatience. Grabbing her penknife, she sharpened it swiftly, brushing the stray bits of feather from her lap before dipping it into the inkwell. The interruption grated at her nerves. She needed to get the lines out of her head before they evaporated like mist in the morning sun.

Bending over her notebook, she scribbled as her inspiration spilled across the page in looping script. Her hand moved swiftly, the ink flowing freely as if driven by the urgency of her thoughts.

The afternoon had been an utter delight. Time with Barclay—having him show her the magic of the grotto, existing in that bubble of time and space far from the real world—had been nothing short of a revelation. Her cheeks still flushed with the memory of it, the laughter of the children, the cool shadows of the cavern, and Barclay's presence beside her, steady and unyielding.

But she was uncertain where matters stood. Barclay had stated no intentions—yet she hoped. Oh, how she hoped that their connection would blossom into something more. There had never been such an attraction with any other gentleman of her acquaintance, and her heart was in jeopardy of tumbling head over heels before she even understood what this was ... or where it might lead.

Could Barclay be my Darcy?

The thought sent a thrill through her, and she bit her lip

to suppress the smile that threatened to bloom. Jane could now understand the troubles Emma had faced during her strange courtship with Perry. She had encouraged her sister to pursue the relationship, but Emma had balked. At the time, Jane had not grasped her hesitation. But now, now that her own affections were at risk, she knew what it was to want a man, to yearn for him, yet be uncertain of his regard.

Barclay had raised concerns about the possibility of a courtship. Their difference in age, his lamentable status within society as a by-blow—these were not small matters. But Jane wanted to brush them aside, to leap into his arms and declare that none of it mattered. Yet Emma's voice lingered in her thoughts. Her sister had pointed out that marriage was a commitment that could not be undone and had advised her to be cautious.

Jane now acknowledged that Emma's advice had been wise. She could not simply race headlong into her emotions, not knowing the gentleman's thoughts on the matter. Though her heart clamored for action, her mind, tempered by her sister's warnings, urged restraint.

As she finished the last line with a flourish, the ink pooling neatly at the end of her sentence, she heard footsteps behind her. Her breath caught, and she straightened in her chair, smoothing her skirts with trembling hands.

"Do you have new verses to read to me?"

Barclay's husky voice was low, intimate, and it wrapped around her like the softest velvet. A shiver traced its way down her spine, settling low in her heart, warm and fluttering. She did not turn right away, savoring the sensation of him behind her, his presence undeniable, his voice still lingering in the air.

"These are private verses," she whispered back,

surprised at how coy she sounded in the silence of the library. Her voice was barely more than a breath, yet it lingered between them, heavy with unspoken meaning.

"This is a private moment," he responded. His tone was low and intimate, wrapping around her like the brush of velvet. He had come up behind her, his presence warm and solid as he leaned over the back of her chair. Jane's breath hitched as she felt his lips graze the shell of her ear—a fleeting kiss, barely there, but enough to send a ripple of warmth coursing through her veins. His breath lingered hot against her skin, and her eyes fluttered shut, savoring the exquisite tension that hung between them.

But too soon, he withdrew, stepping around her to take the opposite seat. Her eyes opened, her gaze following his movement, and her heart lifted at the soft affection reflected in his eyes.

"I admit I was quite inspired ... by our visit to the grotto." Her cheeks pinkened, and she bit her lip, a wave of shyness stealing over her. For all the years that gentlemen had gathered around her at social events, displaying their regard with practiced compliments and lingering glances, she had never encountered one who intrigued her as Barclay did.

Perry certainly had his charms, but from the very first moment, it had been clear that Emma was the one he desired. Jane had never envied her sister for it; she and Perry did not share the meeting of minds that he and Emma enjoyed. Their connection had been instant and obvious, as natural as breathing. But what she felt with Barclay ... it was something different.

A slow smile spread across Barclay's face in response to her admission, his eyes bright with understanding. The electricity between them fairly crackled, the air alive with a charged energy that made her skin tingle. It reminded her of the way rubbing wool could make one's hair stand on end, sparking with tiny shocks. Even now, she felt as though her hair might crackle from the force of his gaze alone.

Barclay was different from other prospective suitors. He seemed genuinely intrigued by her thoughts, her mind, and not merely her appearance. Jane knew she was considered lovely—gentlemen had made no secret of it. Her willowy height, the wave of ebony curls that framed her face, her high cheekbones, and the symmetry of her features were often compared to the portraits of English beauties. She took pride in her fashion sense and her understanding of color; caring for her appearance had always been something of a pastime.

But with Barclay, there was something else. *Something new.*

Jane had become aware of herself not just as a woman to be admired, but as a person with thoughts worth hearing. Barclay had listened to her poetry with an intensity she had never known from any other, his eyes fixed upon her with genuine interest. When he spoke, it was with the assumption that her words mattered. For the first time, Jane saw herself as more than a pretty face. She was an intellectual. An artist. Someone who composed lines to capture the marvels she observed in the world around her —and Barclay had treated her thoughts as if they held value.

This was the meeting of minds Emma had spoken of before her departure from Saunton Park. An indefinable kinship, a synchronization of thought that made the world sharper and more beautiful when shared. It was exhilarating, and terrifying, and she found herself yearning for more.

At least, she thought with a flutter of anxiety, *I hope he is sharing the sentiment. That it is not mere wishful infatuation on my side.*

Yet ... his presence in the library for the third night in a row suggested otherwise. He would not seek her out, night after night, if he did not feel it too. Would he?

"What do you compose tonight?" Barclay asked, his voice warm and inviting as his gaze flickered to the quill in her hand. Jane blinked, realizing she had been frozen in place, her quill poised above the page since the moment she had heard his footsteps behind her.

"I was inspired by the statue of Hades," Jane replied, her eyes brightening with enthusiasm. "That such a hard and intimidating god should be so obsessed with a beautiful woman that he abducts her to his dark lair. I like to think he tricked her into eating the pomegranate seeds because he could not ... not do it. That perhaps he truly loved her so much that he could not bear the thought of a future without her, so he granted her freedom while ensuring he could remain a part of her life."

Barclay huffed slightly, his expression bemused. "That is a romantic view of the story," he replied, leaning back in his chair. "And I admit there are aspects of him for which I have empathy. His world is dark, and he is surrounded by the dead. She must have represented the very light and life which he was no longer part of." His eyes grew distant, as if picturing the myth in his mind. "But I confess I have difficulty reconciling that statue with the fact that it was the late earl who commissioned the work, considering the misdeeds that surely inspired him to select such an odd subject." He paused, his lips curving into a wry smile.

Jane chuckled. "Yes, a story can be viewed from many

angles depending on the emphasis one places, and I chose to emphasize the love for tonight."

Barclay's brows lifted, his gaze thoughtful. "That is insightful to consider."

Jane's cheeks warmed under his praise. It struck her again, as it had so many times before, that Barclay spoke to her with genuine interest in her thoughts. Not as if she were a child amusing herself with romantic notions, but as though her perspective mattered. It made her feel mature in his presence—a woman with valuable thoughts and opinions.

Barclay's hands came up to rest on the table before him, his gaze dropping to study them intently. Jane found herself riveted. She had been fascinated by those hands since the first time she saw them—large, strong palms and long, blunt fingers, the kind that spoke of both power and restraint. She remembered the brush of his calloused fingertips the evening before and had to repress the shiver that rippled through her. The feel of his lips on hers still haunted her at the oddest moments, unbidden and undeniable.

His fingers flexed, and he drew in a breath. "I would ..."

Jane leaned forward, her heart skipping a beat as she waited for him to continue. But Barclay merely stared down at his hands, as if the words had caught in his throat. Her pulse thrummed in her ears, and before she could stop herself, she spoke. "Like to court me?"

Barclay chuckled, the sound low and rough, his gaze still fixed on his hands. "When did young women become so direct?"

Jane drew her lips inward, chewing them slightly as she considered her reply. The silence stretched between them, delicate and fragile, until at last she released the breath she had been holding. "I am not usually so forward," she admitted quietly, her voice softening. "But I find myself ..." She trailed off, the words tangled with her thoughts, unspoken yet palpable between them.

The silence fell heavy once more, pressing down upon them until Barclay cleared his throat, his eyes still not meeting hers. "I simply do not know how this new connection with the earl will affect my social standing." His voice was hushed, almost as though he were confessing a sin. "And you are so young."

Jane lifted her hand to chew on a nail in agitation, her gaze fixed on his bowed head. "I would like to try," she whispered, her voice barely above a breath. "I have ... met no one like you before."

His gaze rose to meet hers across the table, his eyes dark and searching. "Nor I you, Jane." His voice was hushed, almost reverent. "If my wife were still alive ... I am convinced you would have been the best of friends."

A tentative smile touched her lips, but it was edged with uncertainty. She found it difficult to breathe, thinking about it. It was, at once, both a deep honor and a profoundly depressing thought. If his wife were here, and they were the best of friends, would Jane have found herself in the agonizing position of coveting the woman's husband?

She hoped not. She hoped she would have had the fortitude and honor to simply view him as a man who was unavailable—appreciated, yes, but untouchable. Fortunately, it was a theoretical situation she would never have to experience.

The gentleman's regard for his late wife was what first attracted you so!

The recollection of the conversation she had overheard

in the library that night drifted back to her—the one where Barclay and Aurora had spoken quietly of his circumstances. The memory served as a consolation. Without that glimpse into his character, he would have been merely an inordinately handsome gentleman attending the house party. Handsome in the same manner as his two brothers—Richard and Peregrine—both of whom she found pleasant enough, but who had never stirred her heart as Barclay did.

"So, what do we do?" she asked softly, her hands clasped together in her lap.

Barclay's head dropped and his shoulders slumped slightly, tension rippling through his posture. "I do not know," he confessed, his voice strained. "I need to think on it. This whole situation is so unexpected." He paused, swallowing hard as if to collect his thoughts. "Just four days ago, I was still in deep mourning for my wife, and now ..." His voice cracked slightly, and he stopped, unable to continue.

Jane felt tears prick at the corners of her eyes, her heart aching in sympathy. The enigmatic gentleman had endured a loss so profound that she could scarcely comprehend it. She had only known him for a few days, yet the mere idea of his death was too devastating to consider. Barclay carried a substantial burden, and she would not be the cause of further strain. He needed time—time to reach his conclusions about how to proceed with this unexpected affinity of theirs. She would not rush him. Not now.

"Take your time, Barclay," she murmured, her voice gentle and sincere.

He looked up, his eyes searching her face. "I appreciate your patience ... Jane."

The sound of her name, spoken in that low, husky tone, sent warmth skittering through her veins. She smiled back, though it was tempered with longing. She wished—*oh, how she wished*—that she could rise from her chair and step around the table to him. That she could slip her arms around his waist, press her cheek to his chest, and breathe in that familiar scent of spice, leather, and ink.

But she did not. Barclay needed time to reconcile the past with the future, and she would not press him. So she remained seated, her hands folded neatly in her lap, and listened as his footsteps receded down the hall, growing fainter with each step.

Her hand flew to her chest, pressing over her pounding heart. *Drat!* He was so fascinating, so compelling, that she nearly wanted to chase him down the corridor and fling herself into his arms lest he slip away entirely.

CHAPTER TEN

"There is, I believe, in every disposition a tendency to some particular evil—a natural defect, which not even the best education can overcome."

Jane Austen

Barclay knocked firmly on the earl's study door early the next morning. From within, he heard his brother's voice call out for him to enter. Squaring his shoulders, he opened the door and stepped inside, hesitating on the threshold. He was not entirely certain what he wanted to say, but he knew he needed to talk to someone about his predicament. It was imperative he obtain a man's perspective on this minor crisis, and with Tsar at least two days away in London, Richard seemed the logical choice.

"Barclay, please come in." Richard's voice was warm, and he gestured to the seating area overlooking the sprawling park. "Would you like some coffee? I just had some delivered a few moments ago."

Barclay nodded gratefully, closing the door behind him with a soft click. He noted the quirk of Richard's eyebrow as he secured the latch—a subtle indication of curiosity. Barclay crossed the room to join him, lowering himself into the chair opposite his brother. The scent of fresh coffee mingled with the faint aroma of leather and old parchment, and he accepted the cup Richard poured for him with a murmur of thanks.

Richard leaned back, cradling his own cup in his hands. "Did you have something to discuss?" he asked, his tone careful, almost apprehensive, as if steeling himself for bad news.

Barclay took a steadying breath, his gaze dropping to his hands, which were clasped in his lap. "I need some advice," he admitted, his voice a touch rougher than usual. "I find myself without a confidant."

Richard straightened in his chair, his expression sharpening with interest. There was something almost boyish about the way his eyes lit up—clearly flattered that Barclay had sought him out. It was rather endearing, this eagerness to be included as a valued family member.

Barclay stared down at his hands, the tips of his fingers pressed tightly together. *This is deuced awkward,* he thought, but with Tsar in London, he was at a loss. He supposed he could confide in Aurora, but somehow, the idea did not sit well with him. What he needed was the perspective of a steady man—someone who understood the responsibilities of being a husband, a father, and a protector within the framework of their society.

Moreover, perhaps this was an opportunity to strengthen his bond with Richard. After all, the earl had shown him vulnerability concerning Ethan's future. It seemed only fair to reciprocate. And there was a certain comfort in knowing that the duke was out riding, leaving him with only one newly acquired relative to reveal his thoughts to this morning.

Barclay took another breath and squared his shoulders. "My mother impressed upon me the importance of moving on. It has been two years ... since my wife died." His voice roughened, the words heavy with memory. "We were very close."

Richard's gaze remained steady, his hands resting comfortably on his knees as he leaned forward slightly, giving Barclay his full attention. The room fell silent save for the faint ticking of the mantel clock.

"I regret I shall never meet Tatiana's mother." Richard's voice was soft with sincerity. "She must have been an exceptional woman to have captured the heart of such an intelligent artiste."

Barclay nodded, his expression reflective. "You would have liked her very much. And she was breathtaking."

Richard pulled a face of sympathy, his gaze dropping briefly to his hands. "I cannot imagine how I would cope if anything ever happened to Sophia."

A grimace twisted Barclay's features as he smoothed his hands over his breeches, the fabric soft beneath his palms. The mere thought of such a loss was enough to make his chest tighten. He would never wish that sort of anguish upon another man.

"Tatiana has made a request," he continued, his voice softening. "She wishes to have a new mother, something Natalya made me promise I would take care of once she was gone. Tatiana is to grow up loved by two parents, and I am afraid …" He paused, drawing in a steadying breath. "I allowed my grief to prevent my fulfillment of that promise."

Richard leaned forward, his brow knitting with understanding. He reached for the coffeepot, pouring a fresh cup and handing it to Barclay before filling his own. "It seems a topic that requires some fortitude," he remarked by way of explanation when Barclay raised a quizzical brow at the gesture.

Barclay accepted the cup with a nod of thanks, sipping slowly before leaning back in his chair. His gaze drifted upwards to the ornate ceiling, tracing the delicate cornices and floral plasterwork with the eyes of a practiced architect. He had been doing this often since arriving at Saunton Park—studying the ceilings and moldings as if seeking answers hidden in their designs. It was a habit he had developed when under pressure, a means of grounding himself amid uncertainty.

"I am attempting to move on," he admitted at last, his voice a touch hoarse. "To notice the women in my surroundings and determine if there are any who appear to be suitable." He paused, swirling the coffee in his cup absently. "However, there are complications."

"Complications?" Richard echoed, his brow lifting in curiosity.

"First, there is my parentage." Barclay's gaze dropped from the ceiling, settling back on his brother. "As we discussed, it is difficult to be a man in my position. It is even more so for my mother and daughter. Natalya knew she only had a short time to spend with me, so she forwent such concerns to follow her heart. But a new wife …" He sighed, his fingers drumming lightly against the porcelain of his cup. "She may have to deal with the same issues for decades, and I do not wish to inflict that upon a respectable woman."

Richard cocked his head, his expression thoughtful. "You do not think that matters will be improved ... because of us?"

"Perhaps. Only time will tell. Even if matters improve, there will still be certain doors that remain shut." Barclay's jaw tightened almost imperceptibly. "Some souls are ... self-righteous."

Richard barked out a laugh, the sound rich and full of disbelief. "I find they are usually the ones up to no good themselves."

A smile broke over Barclay's face, genuine and unguarded. He savored the fleeting sense of unity with his younger brother. Richard had made every effort to build a brotherly relationship between them, and for the first time, Barclay felt a flicker of genuine kinship. "Just so. The guilty seem to speak loudest in accusation."

"Agreed." Richard leaned back, his eyes glimmering with mirth. "When I acknowledged Ethan as my son, I had at least three peers snub me within the halls of Westminster. Men I happen to know have fathered secret children the length and breadth of London." He snorted in disbelief. "They dared to disdain me for taking the honorable path, while they failed to take acknowledge their own progeny. It was all I could do not to ask after their sons and daughters with solicitous concern."

Barclay chuckled, leaning forward with interest. "What did you do?"

"I disdained them in return," Richard replied, his tone dry. He leaned back in his chair, stretching his legs out before him. "If they possess so little integrity, they are not worthwhile connections. They are riffraff, despite the blue blood flowing through their hypocritical veins." His eyes gleamed with satisfaction. "But then, I have the advantage of more powerful connections than they. The duke alone makes for a powerful ally in most matters."

Barclay chuckled, swirling the coffee in his cup. "What of Sophia? Were there consequences for her when you acknowledged Ethan?"

"Some." Richard's expression softened, and his gaze grew distant. "None that perturb her. She is an unusual woman—not overly fond of polite society." He smiled faintly. "That, I believe, has been our salvation. She is entirely unbothered by their censure."

Barclay's eyes returned to the ornate cornices above them, his mind turning over this revelation. It struck him how much more freedom Richard must have found in his marriage than many of their peers. An unconventional wife, one who did not require the validation of London society—perhaps that was the key. His mind lingered on Jane, her willingness to discuss poetry, art, and even mythology with him as if it were the most natural thing in the world. She was not shackled by the expectations of the *ton* in the way so many young ladies were.

"There are two candidates who might lead somewhere interesting," Barclay began, his voice thoughtful. "One is eminently suitable …"

"And the other?" Richard prompted, leaning forward, his eyes sharp with curiosity.

Barclay hesitated, his hands clasped around the warm porcelain of his coffee cup. "The other …" He paused, drawing in a breath as if to steady himself. "I do not know that it would be appropriate." He looked up, his gaze meeting Richard's directly. "But we share something. An affinity that runs deep. Something I have only experienced one time before."

Richard's expression turned solemn, his voice dropping. "With Natalya?"

Barclay nodded. "With Natalya."

Silence settled between them, the mantel clock ticking softly in the background. Richard was the first to break it, exhaling slowly. "I once thought to marry someone suitable," he admitted, his voice quiet with reflection. "I spent several Seasons searching for the right choice. My plan was to have the sort of marriage favored by the nobility—a dutiful union where we would barely spend time together, and I would continue my pleasurable pursuits discreetly on the side."

Barclay raised an eyebrow, intrigued. "You considered that arrangement?"

Richard chuckled ruefully. "I did. It seemed … sensible. Efficient, even." He leaned back, crossing his arms over his chest. "Then one night, I overheard a young lady lambasting my character to her cousin, and I …" He trailed off, his expression softening with the memory. "Please, do not scorn me when I say this, but I simply lost my heart. It made little sense to pursue her, but I could not imagine an existence without her by my side to disparage my prior roguish pastimes with her cutting wit."

Barclay's mouth curved into a smile. "The countess?"

"Indeed. Sometimes your heart knows what you need far better than your mind does." Richard's gaze softened, his expression reflective. "I needed someone strong, opinionated, who would not accept things as others expect them to be. Someone who would confront me about my worthless behavior." He leaned back, his eyes fixed on the distant horizon beyond the window. "My heart recognized the void she would fill in my immoral existence, and my mind simply caught up."

Barclay lifted a hand to smooth his beard, his fingers brushing over the coarse hair as he mulled over what the earl had revealed. "The second woman is ... exquisite. In very way," he admitted, his voice thick with sincerity. "I just hope I would do right by her if I pursued the affinity we share."

Richard regarded him thoughtfully. "I cannot say, but I will tell you this—it is far easier to contend with life's challenges when one has the right partner at one's side."

The truth of those words struck Barclay with surprising force. That was what he missed most, wasn't it? A wife and partner who always had his best interests at heart. Someone who stood by him even when he faltered, someone whose loyalty was unwavering.

Clearing his throat, Barclay broached the most awkward of questions. "As you are a man of experience ... if I were to pursue he ... how does one go about courting?"

The earl, who had just taken another sip of coffee, was suddenly seized with a paroxysm of coughing. He hastily set his cup down and fidgeted with his cravat, his face turning an alarming shade of red. Barclay narrowed his eyes as his brother squirmed, embarrassment flickering across his expression. "I do not really know all that well," Richard finally admitted, his voice subdued.

Barclay raised an eyebrow, entirely unconvinced. "I do not understand."

Richard rose from his chair, pacing over to the window to gaze out over the park. His hands clasped behind his back, shoulders squared in that slightly rigid stance he adopted when uncomfortable. "I am more familiar with the art of seduction than with courtship, I am afraid," he confessed, his voice dropping to just above a whisper. "Perry could recite every rule, every nuance of courtship with perfect recollection, but I ... can merely give you a rough outline."

Barclay leaned back in his chair, crossing one leg over the other. "Such as?"

Richard turned from the window, his gaze steady. "Two dances imply a sincere interest. A third is practically a public proposal. Hothouse flowers are considered an appropriate gift, but not a piece of jewelry or anything too personal or expensive." He shrugged helplessly. "I always assumed I would gather the details when I actually found a young lady worth courting."

Barclay's eyebrows shot up. "I thought you hunted for a wife for several Seasons?"

"Yes, but I never went past a single dance." Richard's mouth quirked with wry amusement. "None of the young misses captured my interest, so I only knew what was expected in broad strokes. Or rather, defensive strokes. Like never being caught alone with a young lady if one did not wish to be led to the parson's noose ... and to be mindful of that dancing rule of two and three."

Barclay huffed a laugh. "Even I know that."

"I am mortified to reveal this to you of all men." Richard's voice grew softer, almost confessional. He clasped his hands behind his back, his gaze still fixed on the window's view of Saunton Park. "I was so afraid of becoming like our father. I changed my entire life around when I realized how perilously close I was to following in his footsteps." He paused, his shoulders straightening as if bracing himself. "Fortunately, my conscience is eased because the moment I learned of Ethan, I knew I would acknowledge him." His voice grew firmer, edged with pride.

"After meeting my boy, I learned of your existence—it is incredible to me that my father did not marry your mother, or at least acknowledge you. He should have been proud to bestow his name on you or, at the very least, pledge his support for such a talented man."

Barclay straightened, his heart squeezing at the sincerity in Richard's voice. He rose from his chair and joined his brother at the window, gazing out over the park where the morning mist still clung to the grass in delicate wisps. It mitigated his guilt to discover that Richard, too, had wrestled with the shadow of their mutual parent. "You are a good man, Richard," he said quietly. "And I must confess, hearing that you considered similarities between you and the late earl is a bit of a relief. I have been doing the same since I was told he was my father, and it has worried me to notice possible elements of him in me."

Richard turned from the window, his brow furrowing in disbelief. "You?" he asked, his voice laced with incredulity. "You are a bastion of honor and integrity, who is still faithful to his wife two years after her death. What could you possibly have in common with our father?"

Barclay's gaze did not waver as he responded. "I think any discussion of women inevitably stirs thoughts of the actions that led to our existence, does it not?"

Richard winced, his expression twisting with distaste. "Well, that is a repugnant thought to consider." He hesitated, his gaze dropping momentarily before he looked back at Barclay with conviction. "However, I feel compelled to tell you I have not noticed a single trait in you that reminds me of our father. He was the worst kind of libertine."

Barclay's brows knitted. "To what extent?"

Richard's mouth pressed into a hard line, his hands

clenching behind his back. "If you knew ..." He shuddered visibly, a shadow flitting across his expression. "There are no words to describe the hell that my younger brother lived in under his roof." His eyes flicked back to Barclay, heavy with the weight of memory. "Suffice it to say that when I see how you are with your mother and your daughter, I can assure you that you have not inherited even the tiniest fraction of character from the Earl of Satan. He was an irredeemable monster."

Barclay's gaze dropped to the patterned carpet, tracing the floral swirls absently with his eyes as the silence stretched between them. Finally, he spoke, his voice low and thick with emotion. "I am constantly reminded since I arrived here that he seduced my mother when she was just seventeen years old. Somewhere in this house ... or the grounds." His fists tightened at his sides. "It does not bear thinking."

Richard leaned a hand against the window frame, his posture relaxed as both men gazed out over the expanse of Saunton Park. Barclay's eyes tracked a group of gentlemen striding in the direction of the lake, their fishing poles slung over their shoulders and hampers dangling from their hands. Their laughter carried faintly on the breeze, punctuated by the occasional shout as they jostled one another in good spirits.

On the distant horizon, two riders appeared, crossing the open field at an easy canter. Barclay squinted, trying to distinguish their figures. One was clearly a man of considerable size, and he wondered if it might be the Duke of Halmesbury. The second rider was smaller by comparison, though whether that was due to stature or distance, he could not quite tell. It might have been the duchess, though he could not yet make out the distinctive silhouette of a sidesaddle. Then again, considering the duke's formidable size, even a fully grown gentleman might appear diminutive at his side.

"I wish I could do more for your mother," Richard said suddenly, his gaze still fixed on the scene below. "Sophia and the duchess have pledged to introduce Aurora to the very best of society—the worthwhile best, that is. Not the judgmental biddies beneath our notice."

Barclay turned, meeting the earl's gaze. His chest tightened at the sincerity in Richard's expression. "I appreciate that ... brother."

The earl's head came up at that, surprise lighting his features. His eyes widened with clear delight. "Brother?"

Barclay nodded, his lips curving into a tentative smile. "Just assure me your door will remain open in case I decide to blunder through a courtship during my stay in your home?"

Richard's eyes softened with warmth, and he stepped forward to clasp Barclay's shoulder with a firm grip. "You have my support always. You are my blood, Barclay."

Barclay could only hope that the earl's sentiment extended to a potential courtship of Jane. Richard was fiercely protective of his family, and the young woman was his sister-in-law.

Faith! Did I need to think of a further complication?

How had he failed to realize sooner that he was contemplating courting Perry's sister-in-law? Emma Davis's recent marriage to his new brother only deepened the complications. Barclay suppressed the urge to hang his head in dismay. Instead, he kept his gaze fixed on the trees outside the window, the gentle sway of the branches in the breeze doing little to settle the turmoil in his chest. He took a steadying breath, forcing his composure before Richard could detect any trace of his inner conflict.

This was an impossible situation. He could only be grateful that Richard had not pressed him for the identities of the women he was considering. How on earth would he reveal to his new brother that it was Jane who had captured his interest?

When he left the study a few minutes later, his thoughts churned relentlessly. If he were to truly consider this courtship of Jane, he would need to speak with Aurora first. His mother was typically engaged in lively conversation with their hostess at this time of the morning, her laughter often drifting through the corridors of the manor. Yet, today, he had not caught so much as a glimpse of her among the guests who meandered through the grand rooms.

Setting off to look for her, Barclay traversed the spacious halls, his footsteps echoing softly against the polished marble. He soon confirmed she was nowhere to be found in the main house; the drawing room, the conservatory, and even the library were vacant.

As he walked back toward the family wing, his professional eye drifted to the architectural details of Saunton Park. Tsar's hand was evident in every line and curve of the manor—the arching windows that framed endless views of the parkland, the delicate cornices that traced the ceilings, the balance of light and shadow in the vast hallways. Barclay found himself admiring how Tsar had incorporated the natural landscape into the very design of the estate, as though the walls and windows merely framed what the land already offered.

Yet his appreciation was quickly overshadowed when he reached the family wing and approached Aurora's door.

It was slightly ajar, and from within, he heard the unmistakable sound of a woman weeping. His heart clenched painfully in his chest. Striding forward, he pressed the door open, his gaze sweeping the room to confirm it was his mother seated in a plump armchair by the window.

But she was not admiring the view. Her face was buried in the crook of her elbow, propped on the ledge, her shoulders shuddering with the force of her sobs.

Barclay's breath caught. His mother was always composed and unyielding—a model of quiet dignity. She had withstood decades of slights, barbs, and outright insults with unflinching grace. To see her now, alone in her room, weeping so openly, shook him to his core.

Without hesitation, he stepped inside, closing the door softly behind him to keep the rest of the household from witnessing her vulnerability. He crossed the room with deliberate care, lowering himself into the chair beside her and reaching out to lay a gentle hand on her trembling shoulder.

"Mother?" His voice was tender, threaded with concern. "What is it? What has happened? Is it Tsar?"

Her voice was muffled, barely rising above the soft rustle of the curtains stirred by the morning breeze. "No! It is not anything of import. Please, leave me and do not be distressed by my ridiculous behavior."

"Mother, I cannot." Barclay's voice was firm but gentle, his hand still resting on her trembling shoulder. "Please, tell me what has happened?"

Aurora shook her head, wiping her cheeks with the back of her hand. "I do not wish to speak of it, Barclay."

"Mother, please." His tone softened, edged with concern. "I cannot bear to see you so distressed."

For a moment, she remained still, her eyes cast downward, but finally, with a shuddering breath, she held up a letter he had not noticed before, her hand shaking as she offered it to him. "I received a response from the London Virtuous Committee of Charitable Endeavors."

Barclay's heart clenched painfully. Without hesitation, he pulled his mother up from the chair and enveloped her in his arms, his hold gentle but unyielding. Aurora collapsed into his embrace, her slender frame shaking as fresh sobs wracked her body. Her tears soaked through his linen shirt, but he scarcely noticed, his focus entirely on the weight of her grief.

He smoothed his hand over her back in soothing circles, his chin resting atop her head as she wept into his shoulder. It was rare—almost unheard of—for Aurora to display such vulnerability. She had always been a pillar of fortitude, unyielding in the face of whispered insults and exclusion from polite society. To see her now, utterly undone, tore at his very soul.

As her sobs subsided to soft sniffles, Barclay gently pried the crumpled letter from her hand. Holding it behind her back, he unfolded the page, scanning the lines while his jaw tightened, and fury began to burn hot in his chest.

"I was so sure ..." she whispered brokenly against his shoulder. "I allowed my hopes to become engaged, thinking that this new connection to the earl would sway the ladies to allow me entry ... Oh, Barclay!"

A fresh wave of sobbing overtook her, and he tightened his embrace, his arms strong and steady around her slight frame. His heart broke at the sight of his strong, dignified mother reduced to such despair. But mingled with his sorrow was the creeping rise of fury—righteous and unyielding—at the self-righteous matrons who had inflicted this pain upon her.

He raised the letter again, his eyes scanning the florid script, noting each carefully chosen word designed to wound under the guise of propriety. His fingers tightened on the parchment, the edges crumpling slightly as he read:

My Dear Miss Thompson,

In respect to your recent application to join the London Virtuous Committee of Charitable Endeavors, and in light of your connection to the Earl of Saunton, Lord Richard Balfour, it falls to me to convey the committee's decision regarding your request. I regret to inform you that the committee has rejected your application.

Corruption is, as we all must acknowledge, the scourge of our age. It is a blight that festers even within the ranks of those who outwardly display the ornamentation of excellent social conduct. I must, with great delicacy, express that there are members of the fairer sex who present a mask of propriety, affectations of virtue, and yet harbor inappropriate passions— passions that tempt our gentlemen into base behaviors and contribute, most grievously, to the moral decline of society.

Notwithstanding your unwedded status, you have shown no inclination to amend your situation, thus leaving unaddressed what some would call inherent moral turpitude. After so many years, you have yet to demonstrate the piety that might counterbalance such impropriety, instead continuing to bear the ornament of lewdness by remaining unwed—a state which some might interpret as evidence that your innate passions have not abated.

The committee has tasked me with notifying you that no further applications shall be considered. This decision was reached with unanimity and is, I must stress, final. There is no avenue by which the committee shall be persuaded to amend its position. We would, however, direct you to consider taking advantage of our charitable endeavors as a recipient, rather than as a member.

I remain,
Ever yours,
Mrs. Iona Campbell

Secretary to the London Virtuous Committee of Charitable Endeavors

Barclay was not a man given to emotional outbursts, but at that moment, he was sorely tempted to rip the letter in two. Or perhaps tear the drapes from the fittings. Or throw something—anything—through the window to assuage the fury that simmered beneath his skin. His hands clenched at his sides, the letter crumpling slightly in his grasp as he fought to restrain the urge. The unkindness—the sheer cruelty—of the words written by that sanctimonious shrew ignited a fire in his chest that threatened to consume him entirely.

When Aurora had first expressed her desire to reapply to the London Virtuous Committee of Charitable Endeavors, he had wanted to dissuade her. He had seen the way those spiteful women had treated her before, the judgmental glances, the snide remarks couched in false pleasantries. He feared she would be disappointed yet again. But she had been so confident that her connection to a powerful and wealthy earl would sway the minds of those harpies, so he had not the heart to crush her hopes. Now, seeing her reduced to tears, he could hardly contain his rage.

"These women are worthless, Mother!" he burst out, his voice harsh with indignation. "You must cast them from your mind and speak of them no more!"

Aurora's sobs had subsided, though she still rested her

head against his shoulder, her breathing uneven. "I should have paid you heed when you said not to write," she whispered, her voice trembling. "But I was so sure ..." Her voice cracked, and for a moment, he feared she would dissolve into fresh tears.

Carefully, he eased her back into the chair, his movements gentle yet firm. He knelt before her, resting his hand atop hers, which she was twisting together in her lap. Her fingers were icy beneath his touch, and he covered them with both hands as if to lend her some of his own warmth. He struggled to find words of comfort, but guilt coiled within his belly, heavy and unyielding. It was a familiar ache—one he had carried for years. A guilt that, like a narcotic, threatened to drag him into oblivion if he let it consume him.

"This is my fault," he murmured, his voice barely above a whisper.

Aurora's tear-streaked face tilted up to meet his gaze, her eyes glistening with confusion. "Why?"

"If you had given me up, you would have been able to lead a full life," he replied, his voice thick with regret. "Free of scorn and derision. No one would ever have been the wiser that I even existed." His words trembled on the edge of bitterness, a blade of truth he had never spoken aloud.

"Never, Barclay!" Her hands flew to clasp his, gripping them tightly. Her voice, though weary, was resolute. "That was never an option. I would receive a thousand cruel rejection letters and never, for a single moment, regret that you are in my life." Her gaze softened, and she reached up to brush his cheek with trembling fingers. "This is just a silly dream that has been dashed for the last time. I am disappointed, yes, but I shall dry my eyes, and life will continue."

Barclay's heart clenched painfully at her words, the

strength in her gaze momentarily stealing his breath. But the injustice of the letter burned hot and unyielding in his chest.

His voice was softer when he finally spoke. "I have never understood why this particular society was so important to you."

Aurora sighed, the sound heavy with the weight of years. Her gaze dropped to her hands, which she still wrung together, the pale knuckles standing stark against the delicate skin. She did not answer right away, and Barclay waited in silence, his hand resting atop hers as if willing her to draw strength from his touch.

CHAPTER
ELEVEN

"To wish was to hope, and to hope was to expect."

Jane Austen

When Jane opened her eyes to the morning light, the elation of the afternoon before had not worn off. She lay still for a moment, savoring the warmth of the sunlight streaming through the curtains, her heart brimming with the memory of their magical outing. Barclay was considering a courtship. The thought made her smile as she stretched luxuriously beneath the covers, recalling how his eyes had lingered on hers, how his hand had clasped hers in that fleeting, secretive touch.

She wished she could have shared more kisses with him last night, but she had promised him patience, and she would honor that promise—no matter how her heart ached to feel his lips on hers again.

Optimism swelled within her, stubborn and bright. She could not shake the feeling that it would all work out. Jane had known from the very first that her sister Emma and Perry belonged together, that Perry was destined to be Emma's Darcy. Despite a few setbacks, it had proven true, which meant that her intuition in such matters was, if nothing else, rather reliable. Which meant Barclay could very well be her Darcy ...

No, that did not seem quite right. Barclay was not a Fitzwilliam Darcy in character—he lacked the brooding reserve, the icy pride that had hidden Darcy's better nature. But he could be her ... Colonel Brandon? Perhaps ... but not entirely. Mr. Knightley? No, that was not right either.

He was her ... her ... Jane gave up with a huff of amusement. There was no one to compare him to. He was simply Barclay. And after the promising events of yesterday, she felt sure that soon he would be *her* Barclay if she just gave him the time he needed.

Weary from the persistent insomnia that plagued her, but alight with excitement to see the gentleman, she threw back the covers and rose swiftly, the chill of the morning air forgotten in her haste. Outside her door, she found the breakfast tray waiting, as it did each morning, and she carried it inside with a smile.

Her breakfast was eaten in record time, and she immediately set to work with her mortar and pestle, crushing the strawberries to make her beauty water. She had been prepared to forego the new ritual this morning in her eagerness to begin the day, but the memory of Barclay's breath, warm against her neck as he murmured his delight that she tasted of strawberries and almonds, made her pause. If there were the possibility of stolen kisses this evening, she wished to be prepared—to bewitch him if she could.

His own scent had imprinted itself on her senses. It had intoxicated her, drawing her back to memories of their walk to the grotto, the way his hands had clasped hers. It made her heart sing and her mind awaken to new possibilities.

As she mashed the strawberries, she recalled Tatiana's sweet voice as the child had spoken of her life when her mother had still been with them. How they had traveled with Barclay to various building sites, learning about architecture and playing in the gardens of grand estates. Jane's heart quickened at the idea of such a life. She could almost see it: penning poetry beneath the shade of ancient trees, Tatiana by her side, while Barclay worked nearby with his plans and measurements. A life of travel, of discovery, of sharing each moment with family she loved.

It sounded idyllic—like the words Emma had spoken to her the day she departed Saunton Park. Her sister had reminded her of her longing to travel, her desire to write, and the way she had always dreamed of having children. With Barclay, it seemed that all those dreams could converge in the most beautiful way. She would gain a sweet daughter—a young girl whose company she already adored.

But was she truly mature enough to assume such a role? To be a mother to a nine-year-old?

Jane bit her lip as she poured the crushed strawberries into a basin, assuring herself that she could muddle her way through. Tatiana herself had announced her willingness for such a relationship, and Aurora had given no indication that her granddaughter's affections were fleeting.

Barclay might be at a different stage in the journey of

life, but Jane was determined to catch up. Whatever it took, she would do it. For the first time in her life, she could imagine her future with one specific man, and she knew with every fiber of her being that he would be worth any troubles they might encounter. What relationship did not have its obstacles to overcome?

Her heart light with anticipation, Jane finished her preparations, smoothing her hair and donning a day dress of pale blue muslin. She hurriedly gathered her things, casting one final glance at her reflection before nodding in satisfaction.

She needed to find her morning coffee in the library. And then—she needed to find Barclay.

AURORA CONTINUED to twist her fingers in her lap while Barclay waited for his mother to speak. Eventually, she sighed as if accepting a dark fate and spoke.

"I told you that Grandmama—my mother—was a member of the committee, which is why I so desperately wanted to be accepted?"

"You did."

"I did not tell you about the day Grandmama was expelled from the society."

Barclay frowned. Indeed, that fact had never been mentioned. He had always assumed that she had remained part of the group. By the time he was old enough to be aware of his mother and grandmother as individuals with their own hopes and dreams, the topic of the committee had faded into the past.

"It was a few weeks after you were born. I had returned

to London with Mama, and we were settling into life with a new babe in the house."

"What happened?"

"Word was slow to spread at first, but then overnight, it seemed as if everyone knew about that Thompson girl with the illegitimate child."

Barclay sank back into his chair. His mother had never told him what it was like when he was born. She never complained about the situation, and all he knew were the accumulated observations since he had reached an age to be included in adult conversations.

His gaze found the ceiling, and he scowled harder than he ever had at the cornices to quell the disquiet he felt to hear Aurora's anguish as she recalled the past.

"One night, I was returning from your room. We had my old nanny to assist me, but I spent as much time as I could with you, and so I was passing the drawing room. The door had not latched properly when I had left them earlier, so I could overhear their conversation. I ... I had never heard ... my mother cry before that night."

Barclay's gut roiled in protest. He squeezed his eyes shut, fighting against the surge of anguish that rose within him as Aurora continued to tell her story.

"Mama was crying, and Tsar was comforting her," she whispered, her voice trembling with the weight of memory. "She wept because they had abruptly severed their ties with her. That night, I learned how hard she had worked to be accepted when she first arrived in England, how joining the committee had been one of her greatest triumphs, and how the day they accepted her had been a victory for her—a symbol that she had carved a place for herself in Britain. She had worked diligently as a member of the society, so proud of the charitable work she had done ... I could not believe it."

Barclay leaned forward, his brow furrowing with concern. "Could not believe what?"

"That I had been so foolish with the earl. That I had allowed him to seduce me into hurting my family." Aurora's voice cracked, but she straightened her back, a flicker of pride glimmering despite her sorrow. "She was such a good mama, and I caused her pain with my selfish, foolhardy choices."

Barclay clenched his fists at his sides, fighting back the anguish that clawed at his heart. He was the cause of four generations of Thompson pain. His grandmother had always been so steadfast, so joyful despite the whispers. To think of her weeping as she lost her place in society—how his mother had suffered, how Tatiana might suffer in the future—made him ache with longing for Natalya more than he had in years.

He remembered his fumbling attempts to court young Englishwomen in his youth, only to have fathers slam their doors in his face. The memory still burned, raw and unhealed. Meeting Natalya's father in St. Petersburg and being so warmly welcomed into his home, then meeting Natalya herself and experiencing that same warmth and acceptance—it had been one of the best days of his life.

That a beautiful young woman like her had willingly accepted his proposal and waved away the snubs she experienced when she arrived in England had been nothing short of a miracle to him. Natalya had brushed it all aside with a laugh and a wave of her hand, as though the cruelty of society meant nothing. *"They would have snubbed me for being Russian regardless. There is no harm, Barclay,"* she would assure him, her accent curling around the words with confidence and grace.

His mind snapped back to the present when Aurora continued speaking, her voice steady though laced with regret. "I vowed, no matter what it took, I would gain a place on the committee in order to honor my mother." She gestured at the crumpled letter, her fingers brushing the edge as though its mere touch stung. "Obviously, that vow will never be fulfilled. I know it is inconsequential in the grand scope of life, but I feel I have let my mother down all over again."

Barclay felt his heart crack in his chest, for he had let his own mother down. This connection to the earl had been about opening doors for Aurora. For Tatiana. And this letter proved that nothing had changed.

He imagined the impossible—that he might one day come home to find Jane weeping from the rejections of the day, her heart bruised by society's cruelty, with no hope of him being able to fix it for her. He could picture the shimmer of tears on her cheeks, her lovely face marred by sadness, and the thought hollowed him. What advice could he offer her, other than to ignore those who behaved with such unkindness? How could he ask her to endure that pain? A young woman at the prime of her life, with her entire future ahead of her, and he knew there was only one decision he could make.

But his own troubles aside, first he needed to attend to his mother.

It was some time later when he escorted Aurora to the public rooms. She had composed herself, the evidence of her tears having subsided, and her good cheer restored once more. Her chin was held high, her eyes bright with determination, as if she had resolved to shut away that painful chapter for good. It would seem she had simply needed a moment to grieve her disappointment, but now, the charitable society was firmly behind her. That door had closed, and she would not knock upon it again.

Barclay deposited Aurora with the countess and the duchess for tea in one of the drawing rooms, exchanging nods of greeting with the elegant ladies before he steeled his nerve and went to search for Mrs. Gordon.

He donned his beaver, smoothing a hand over its brim as he scanned the terrace. Spotting her amid a group of guests, he made his way outside, the cool breeze tugging at the coattails of his jacket. "Mrs. Gordon?"

The widow turned, her face lighting up with obvious delight. "Mr. Thompson! I was hoping to invite you to play ninepins!"

Barclay ignored the fissure of irritation that crept up his spine. Here was a mature woman with a solid reputation who was well aware of the challenges she would face by his side. A woman who understood the pain of losing a spouse, whose presence in society had remained untouched by scandal. As a woman of nearly thirty years of age, it was possible that the widow did not wish for any more children, which would be a balm to his conscience. He could not, in good faith, bring another child into the world only to endure the burden of his bastardy.

Perhaps the widow could grant Tatiana increased respectability. Perhaps she would be a mother figure who understood discretion and grace. If playing ninepins every day for the rest of his life would protect his mother and his child from further derision, then so be it.

Surely he would grow to enjoy it, given time?

He proffered his arm, and the widow gratefully took hold of it, her hand curling around his arm a little more tightly than he was accustomed to. But he was a man of strength, and surely he would grow to like that, too.

Resolutely, he plastered an affable smile on his face and escorted the widow toward the gardens, ignoring the dull ache in his heart as hopes for a future with Jane Davis withered away.

When Jane reached the library to drink her morning coffee, she found Tatiana waiting for her, perched upon the edge of an armchair with her legs swinging idly.

One of the maids assigned to the nursery for the house party had recently confided to her that the servants responsible for the children had all but given up trying to keep track of the little girl. Apparently, Tatiana would occasionally visit the nursery to play with Ethan and the other children, but she left without a trace when she grew bored. Radcliffe had informed the countess, who had told them to leave the child to her own devices unless Barclay instructed otherwise, as it did not seem to be causing any difficulties and Tatiana was clearly independent.

"Have you seen my papa?" the little girl queried, her silver-blonde curls bouncing slightly as she tilted her head. She waited patiently while Jane poured her coffee, her blue eyes wide with anticipation.

"I have not, but I just left my bedroom."

"Oh." The little girl twirled a lock of her pale hair around her forefinger, her expression thoughtful. "Would you play chess with me? Ethan beat me again. It is quite embarrassing. I am five years older than him!"

Jane smiled warmly. "Of course. I will drink my coffee and then we can play." The scent of the freshly brewed coffee was beckoning vigorously this morning, its rich aroma curling invitingly around her senses.

Tatiana grinned, then skipped past the window to join her, her slippers barely making a sound on the polished wooden floor. Jane watched as the girl came to an abrupt stop, pressing her face to the glass as if trying to see something more clearly. Her breath fogged the windowpane, and when she turned around, her cheeks were flushed with color.

"Are you all right, Tatiana?" Jane asked, setting her cup back on its saucer with a soft clink.

"Uh ... I will have to play with you later. There is something I must do." With that, the little girl spun on her heel and raced from the room, her skirts fluttering like silken wings as her legs pumped across the distance.

Jane stared after her, the suddenness of Tatiana's departure unsettling. A flicker of worry creased her brow, and she walked over to the window to see who or what had distracted the child. She pressed her hand to the glass, scanning the gardens, but whoever it was had disappeared from view by the time she reached the window.

Biting her lip, she felt a ripple of anxiety for Tatiana. Should she follow the girl to find out what had upset her?

BARCLAY VIEWED THE PINS, which truly were set far too close to make for a challenging game, but it was how the ladies played, and so he must engineer some method of enjoying it. Perhaps he could practice knocking down specific pins to hone his aim. His aim in—*drat*—ninepins. He swallowed, assuring himself there was a way to make it a passable pastime, even if it felt like an exercise in futility.

Lifting a ball from the table, he made a show of preparing to bowl. He reached back, his arm swinging forward—

"Papa!"

The cry was practically a shriek. Barclay halted mid-swing, the weight of the ball knocking against his chest with a dull thud. He composed himself for a moment, his brow smoothing as he turned to find his daughter standing just a few feet away, her expression stricken and outraged. Her tiny fists were clenched at her sides, and her face was flushed with emotion.

Turning back to Mrs. Gordon, he forced a polite smile. "Mrs. Gordon, if you would not mind, I need to speak to my daughter for a moment."

The widow's smile faltered, her fingers tightening on the handle of her parasol before she gave a slow nod. Without a word, she opened the parasol with a soft snap and strolled away, her skirts sweeping elegantly along the grass. Barclay watched her departure for a beat, then turned to Tatiana. Taking her small hand in his, he walked her over to the shade of the great oak tree that dominated the lawn. He settled himself on the bench and gently lifted his daughter to sit beside him, her legs swinging slightly as they dangled above the grass.

"What is it, little one?" he asked, his voice softening.

Tatiana fixated on her toes, her leather slippers scuffing lightly against each other. When she finally raised her face, he saw tears shimmering on her lashes, her large blue eyes brimming with sadness. The sight of it stabbed him in the chest like a thousand tiny daggers. *Lud*, he was bungling his family duties. First, he had failed to help Aurora fulfill her lifelong dream of joining that society she so cherished, and now Tatiana looked as though her heart were breaking.

"Why are you with Mrs. Gordon, Papa?" she asked, her voice so small and fragile that it nearly undid him.

Barclay's shoulders stiffened slightly. "Our situation is ... difficult, little one. Mrs. Gordon might help us," he replied, choosing his words with care.

Tatiana's lip quivered. "But I like Jane. I want her to be my mother."

Barclay braced himself. He could not bear the thought of another woman in his care being broken by their association with him. Mrs. Gordon might help both Aurora and Tatiana overcome this ... this ... wretched notoriety. He was not afraid of ruining the widow's life with his situation, for she was rusticating in the country and seemed more than willing to contend with the challenges that came with his name. They enjoyed a companionable relationship, but no deep feelings were engaged on either side. A marriage to her would be ... safe. And he must do what was right for his family, no matter how much he might wish for something different.

"Jane is a young girl," he began gently. "You need a proper mother. One who can help you grow up to be a great lady one day."

"Mrs. Gordon does not like children."

Barclay stiffened. "How can you know that? Did she say something to you?"

"No, but I can tell." Tatiana's voice was small but resolute, her eyes sharp with the clarity of a child's intuition. "And I know Jane makes you happy. You smile when you are with her. Please do not do this. You like her too. I know it. It is not too late. I left Jane in the library, and we can go join her there."

Barclay relaxed somewhat at the news that Mrs. Gordon had not spoken unkindly to his daughter. He reached out his hand and clasped Tatiana's gently, his large hand nearly engulfing her tiny one. "You must trust me, Tatiana. I am doing this for you. One day you will understand."

But instead of calming her, his words seemed to kindle a fire. Tatiana's eyes grew glassy with tears, and then she began to sob in earnest. For the second time that day, Barclay found himself attempting to comfort one of the women he was honor-bound to protect while they wept. He reached out to embrace her, but Tatiana pulled away from him, slipping from his grasp.

There she stood, glaring up at him with her arms akimbo and her face flushed with anger, looking for all the world like a little warrior princess. Her chin jutted out defiantly, and her blue eyes blazed with unshed tears.

"You know nothing," she declared, her voice trembling with emotion. "I know Jane is the one, but you will not listen!"

And with that, she spun on her heel and ran, her skirts flaring behind her as she disappeared from view. Barclay remained where he stood, his hands falling uselessly to his sides as he watched her go.

He needed to set this right, and this was the only way he knew how. Tatiana would be upset at first, but he was certain it would all work out in the end—because it had to. He could not be the cause of any more disappointment for their little family, not when it was breaking him in two. Tatiana would be disappointed for a little while, but she would eventually forget the young woman. *They* would forget her ... in time.

He should never have encouraged Jane or Tatiana with foolish hopes.

Jane spent the afternoon searching for Tatiana and Barclay, but they were nowhere to be found. She had wandered through the gardens, peeked into the nursery, and even made discreet inquiries with the household staff, but no one had seen them. Eventually, she surrendered to the inevitable and played chess with her cousin Ethan before returning to her bedroom to prepare for dinner.

Later, she ventured eagerly to the drawing room where the guests were gathering, her eyes scanning the room with anticipation. But Barclay was not there.

At last, he walked in, dressed in immaculate black trousers, a black coat, and snowy white linen that gleamed against the richness of his attire. The sight of him fairly took Jane's breath away, as it did each evening. Barclay was especially fine in evening finery—his tall form graceful and confident, his broad shoulders cut to perfection by the tailored lines of his coat.

Caught in conversation with Mr. Dunsford, she could not help but watch as Barclay made his way over to his brother, his strides long and assured. Before she could make her excuses to leave Mr. Dunsford's side, dinner was called, and Jane's heart clenched when she saw Barclay hold out his arm to the widow, Mrs. Gordon, to escort her to the dining room.

Once they entered the lavish dining area, where crystal, silver, and fine china glinted in the soft candlelight and the austere Balfour ancestors observed them from ornate gilt frames, Barclay took his seat with the widow while Jane found herself seated next to Mr. Dunsford. The gentleman was solicitous and charming in his self-deprecating manner, his smile easy and his conversation smooth, but Jane's attention drifted. Her eyes flickered down the table, catching glimpses of Barclay in conversation with Mrs.

Gordon, his head inclined toward her as she laughed softly, her golden hair shimmering beneath the candlelight.

Who had made these seating arrangements? Jane wondered, her fingers gripping the edge of her napkin. She was customarily seated with the family at the far end of the table, near Barclay and Aurora—but not tonight. Tonight, Mrs. Gordon had somehow claimed her usual seat.

Forcing herself to focus, Jane dipped her spoon into her soup, engaging in conversation with Mr. Dunsford as propriety demanded. But she could hardly remember what was being discussed. Her mouth spoke the appropriate pleasantries, but her mind raced, swirling with thoughts of the widow sitting where Jane was meant to be.

I will ask Barclay about it when he comes to visit me in the library!

The thought restored her spirits, and Jane felt her tension ease. Her fingers relaxed on the napkin, and she even managed a genuine smile when Mr. Dunsford recounted an amusing anecdote from his last hunt.

Still, she could not help but notice that Mr. Dunsford's gaze lingered on her face with a soft sort of admiration. It stirred a small flicker of worry in her belly. She had not intended to encourage him, and she hoped he would not make an attempt at courtship. Her hopes regarding the young man had been before. *Before* the visit to the grotto. *Before* the kiss in the library. Just ... *before*.

She could not possibly consider accepting his courtship now. Her affections were engaged with the darkly handsome man sitting near the earl. Even now, Barclay was leaning over to say something to Mrs. Gordon, who laughed in response, her face radiant and her golden curls glimmering in the warm candlelight.

He would never pursue the widow. You promised him time to

reconcile his grief with the idea of courting you, she reminded herself.

Assuring herself of this helped somewhat, but she still longed for dinner to end and the midnight hour to arrive, when Barclay would visit her once more.

After dinner, she laughed and chatted with the countess and Aurora in the drawing room over tea, the warm glow of candlelight flickering off the polished surfaces of the room. But her eyes kept wandering to the ormolu clock on the mantelpiece, its gilded hands inching forward with agonizing slowness. Time seemed to tick by at a crawl, each chime of the pendulum stretching longer than the last.

A short while later, she joined in the parlor games, Mr. Dunsford at her side with his usual good humor. His cheerful chatter made the minutes pass more swiftly, and she managed a few genuine laughs, but her gaze still drifted to the clock at regular intervals. Where was Barclay? He had remained conspicuously absent since dinner, and the thought tugged uncomfortably at her heart.

When the evening drew to a close, she excused herself with as much grace as she could muster and ascended to her room. She undressed with uncharacteristic haste, her fingers fumbling slightly with the buttons and ties. Tossing her gown over the back of a chair, she slipped into her night rail and tied on her wrap, the silk whispering against her skin. She picked up her journal and quill, then quietly opened her door and slipped into the corridor. The house was silent at this late hour, and the only sound was the soft rustle of her skirts as she strode down the family hall to the main manor.

The library was dark and still when she entered, save for the soft glow of oil lamps. Jane took up her usual seat and found the inkstand where it was stored, the glass bottle cool and smooth beneath her fingertips.

A quick glance at the clock on the wall told her the midnight hour had begun. Lowering her head, she dipped her quill into the ink and began to write the verses she had been composing in her mind throughout the evening.

Thirty minutes later, she checked the time again. *He always comes near the end of the hour,* she reassured herself, *so there is time to finish the verses that he inspired.*

Sharpening her quill and dipping it back into the ink, she bent once more over the page, her brow furrowed in concentration. She imagined reading the lines to Barclay, her heart lifting at the thought of his reaction. It had been mortifying to reveal her inner thoughts when she had recited her poetry before, but Barclay had listened with such aplomb. His steady gaze and quiet encouragement had bolstered her confidence, making her believe her words held weight and meaning. Ever since that night, her faith in her poetry had grown.

The lengthy poem she had composed stretched across several pages, and when she finally reached the last line, she sprinkled pounce over the ink to dry it, blowing gently across the surface. Satisfied, she raised her head to glance at the clock once more. Her heart sank. It was ten minutes past one o'clock. Barclay should have been there by now.

Pushing her chair back, she stood and walked out into the hall, her slippered feet making barely a whisper on the polished floors. The corridor was empty, stretching long and dark, illuminated only by the occasional sconce flickering with candlelight. She ventured farther, peering around the corner that linked the family wing to the main house. *Nothing.*

Confused, she walked back into the library, her hands

clasped tightly together as she began to pace up and down the length of the room. Surely he would come to explain his absence? He must have been delayed. Or perhaps he was attending to something urgent and would arrive any moment.

Another ten minutes passed, and Jane's heart began to beat like a drum in her chest, her stomach twisting itself into anxious knots. Her fingers traced the edge of the mantel as she wandered restlessly, her eyes darting to the clock with every lap she made.

After another twenty minutes of assuring herself that he was merely running late, or had been delayed by correspondence, or perhaps had not yet noticed the time, she finally slowed her steps. Her feet carried her to the armchair by the fireplace, where she slumped into its cushions, the opposite armchair the only companion for her disappointment.

Her eyes drifted to the empty doorway, and the truth she had been dreading since dinner settled heavily in her heart, squeezing it tight.

He is not coming.

In all her years on this earth, Jane had never felt so despondent. Barclay was rejecting her. He had reached a decision and had not even bothered to visit to explain himself.

For the first time, true loneliness descended like a fog rolling in from the coast—cold, damp, and heavy, settling over her shoulders and pressing down on her heart. The weight of it made it hard to breathe, as though the very air had thickened with sorrow.

She did not want to pursue another gentleman. Barclay made her feel special. Not merely for her appearance, as so many others did, but for her mind and character. He listened to her with sincerity, as though her thoughts mattered, as though her words were worth something. Perhaps when the house party was over, she would lift her spirits by visiting Emma at her new home. Her sister's cheerful disposition and steadfast companionship might be just the balm she needed.

This adventure—joining the earl in his home for a Season, attending this grand house party to be introduced to prospective suitors—had seemed so exciting just a few weeks ago. She had imagined herself swept into the whirl of society, admired, and courted, perhaps even falling in love. Now, Jane simply felt homesick. It was not turning out to be how she had hoped.

To make matters worse, it seemed even Tatiana was avoiding her now. She had yet to see the girl since she had run off before their game earlier that day. Jane had searched the grounds, hoping to catch sight of her silver-blonde curls flashing in the sunlight, but the girl was nowhere to be found.

Jane recalled the trouble she had gone to with the strawberry water that morning—the careful crushing of the berries, the sweet aroma that lingered on her hands. There was no denying it: she was a fool. A hopeless fool. Fortunately, no one was aware of her attraction to Barclay, so her foolish hopes were private to her ... and the gentleman.

Her teeth worried her lower lip as she tried to think of something to settle her despair. It would be even more foolish to grieve over a passion that had never truly begun. *Stop being maudlin, Jane.* It was a whispered command she could not quite obey.

Perhaps she should give Mr. Dunsford another try?

Discover if he could accept the fact that she favored coffee? Learn what he thought of her poetry, even?

No. Sharing her lines with another was too much to bear. It was a reminder of her magical evenings with Barclay, of the way he had listened with such rapt attention, his dark eyes fixed on hers as though her words held the power to transport him. Even now, the memory was enough to make her chest tighten with longing, the tears she had been holding back threatening to escape once more.

If only Emma were here to talk to. Emma, who always knew what to say to lift her spirits, who would listen and understand, and never judge her for falling in love with the wrong man.

I will have to begin with revealing my coffee habit, she resolved, thinking of Mr. Dunsford's surprised expression the last time she had poured a cup. *Then learn if he and I share anything in common.* Perhaps she had been too quick to dismiss him. Perhaps if she tried ...

Raising her hand, she wiped the tears from her lashes and took a long, steadying breath. Rising from her chair, she smoothed her skirts and forced her shoulders back. There was nothing more to be done tonight. Tomorrow would be another day, and she would meet it with as much grace as she could muster.

CHAPTER
TWELVE

"We live at home, quiet, confined, and our feelings prey upon us."

Jane Austen

The following morning, Jane sat alone in the library with her cup in hand, gazing out the tall windows to where clouds were banked heavily in the sky. They sprawled across the horizon like billowing waves of smoke, casting a gray pall over the grounds below. It was a perfect reflection of her current mood. Dark. Melancholy. Silent.

She had never needed her coffee as much as she did this morning. Its warmth seeped through the delicate porcelain into her palms, offering the only comfort she had found since Barclay had failed to appear the night before. Fortunately, the tray beside her held a full pot, its silver lid gleaming softly in the morning light, ready to keep her company until she could rouse herself to leave the library.

After tossing and turning all night, sleep had remained stubbornly out of reach, leaving her mind tangled with restless thoughts and her body aching from fatigue. She had not yet eaten; her appetite had failed her entirely, shriveled by disappointment and a heavy sense of longing she could not quite shake.

No book had brought any solace. She had tried to read —to lose herself in stories of adventure or romance—but the words had swum before her eyes, refusing to arrange themselves into anything meaningful. Even the dawn had failed to bring the drowsiness she usually felt after a sleepless night. She was restless, heartsick, and thoroughly exhausted.

Perhaps I should return to Rose Ash? she wondered, her gaze still fixed on the dreary landscape beyond the window. *I slept fine there.*

The thought was a bitter one. She had come to Saunton Park full of dreams and ambitions, determined to begin the next chapter of her life. Now she contemplated returning to the comfort of home, retreating with her tail between her legs. Perhaps she was too young to know her own mind. Perhaps she had rushed into the idea of a Season, believing herself prepared for the rigors of society when, in truth, she was still just a girl with romantic ideals.

Perhaps I should speak to the earl about returning for a Season next year and take some time to mature a little more, she mused, brushing her fingertips over the rim of her cup. Emma had returned home, and things had worked out beautifully for her.

But even as she entertained the notion, she knew it was different. Emma had gone home to Rose Ash, and Perry had followed her there. *Would Barclay follow me if I left?* But no. He would not. Barclay was not Perry, and she was not Emma.

Returning home would simply be a temporary retreat so she might lick her wounds, think about what she wanted from her future, and then return to the Balfour household for another attempt.

Lud, it all sounds like such an effort, she thought, stifling a weary sigh as she took another sip of her coffee, the bitterness a welcome distraction from the ache in her chest.

She sipped her coffee again. If she could just get a full night's sleep, perhaps she could reach a decision about how she wanted to proceed. Trying to make a life decision when she had not slept a wink was probably ill-advised, she mused, pressing her lips together in thought.

Perhaps it is time to visit a herbalist and tackle this insomnia. She had been convinced it was merely the excitement of the unexpected Season that had ruined her sleep, but last night had been the worst yet—and she certainly could not blame that on excitement. She had never felt less enthusiasm than she had in the past twelve hours.

Jane finished her coffee, the last drop pooling in the bottom of her cup. She reached for the pot to pour another, her hand pausing mid-air as she flinched in surprise. Tatiana had taken a seat in the chair across the table without her noticing. How long had the little girl been sitting there, so silent and still? Seeing her was a comfort despite the ache in Jane's heart. At least one Thompson was not avoiding her.

The child was staring down at her slippers, her shoulders slumped, and the usual bright light in her eyes dimmed.

"Tatiana, are you all right?" Jane asked gently, setting the coffee pot down with careful precision.

"I came to tell you I am sorry."

Jane tilted her head, dismayed. "Whatever are you sorry for?"

"I am sorry that Papa is courting Mrs. Gordon."

The words struck like a blow, a sharp and unexpected pang that tightened Jane's throat. It was true, then. Barclay had reached a decision regarding her. She had told herself it was merely his grief that held him back, that he simply needed time to make peace with the idea of a future. But it would seem he had decided she was not the right woman for him.

Jane's hands trembled as she poured her coffee, the liquid swirling into the cup with a soft, delicate splash. She took a steadying breath, forcing her voice to remain calm. "I did tell you that your papa had to find his own wife. He is a good man, and whatever he decides, I am certain that you are an important part of his decision."

Tatiana's face crumpled with sorrow as she continued to study her slippers, her little hands twisting in her lap. "It is not right. I do not like that woman. I like you."

Jane's heart squeezed painfully at the girl's sincerity. She reached across the table to take Tatiana's hand, her fingers warm and soft in her own. "Oh, sweet girl. I like you, too. Whatever happens in the future, we shall remain friends."

Tatiana turned her gaze to Jane, her deep blue eyes brimming with emotion that was far too raw for someone so young. "The afternoon at the grotto, I thought ..." She shook her head, her little face twisting with the effort of holding back tears. "I was so ... sure."

Jane fought back her own tears, determined to be

strong for the little girl who had known far too much pain in her short life. Her smile trembled but held firm. "Every moment with you has been a gift. I am certain that everything will work out for the best for you. Your papa loves you —" She paused, swallowing hard to steady her voice before continuing, "—and he will do what is best for you. I know it. Please do not worry about me. You should put your attention on getting to know Mrs. Gordon if Bar—your papa is courting her."

Tatiana's eyes searched Jane's face, her expression earnest and unguarded. "Would you have courted him? If he had asked?"

Jane bit her lip, her mind racing to find the right words that would neither betray her own emotions nor sound critical of Barclay's choice. At last, she replied gently, "It would be a great honor to be considered for the position of your new mother. I considered it a great honor the first time you asked me, and nothing will ever change how I feel about you."

Tatiana's eyes grew wide and bright with emotion before she flung herself off the chair and into Jane's arms. Jane barely had time to set her cup down before she caught the little girl, Tatiana's small arms wrapping tightly around her neck. Jane's heart clenched with tenderness as she hugged the child back, squeezing her to her bosom and breathing in the sweet scent of lavender and innocence. She held her there for a long moment, allowing herself to imagine what it might be like to truly be Tatiana's mother, if only for this brief, stolen instant.

"We are part of the same family now, Tatiana. We shall see each other often, and I can read you *Aladdin* anytime you like." Jane's voice was soft with the promise, but then she hesitated, wincing slightly over the girl's shoulder. Had she overstepped? Would Barclay disapprove of her making such an offer? She swallowed and quickly amended, "Although I am sure that Mrs. Gordon has read stories to her husband's parish and will make a fine storyteller in my place."

Tatiana pulled back, her little face full of sincerity as she looked up into Jane's eyes. "Thank you, Jane."

"You are, and always will be, very welcome, Tatiana." Jane stroked the girl's hair, her heart aching with love and loss all at once.

After their embrace, Tatiana dashed off before Jane could even suggest a game of chess. She watched the girl go, feeling slightly cheered to know that, at the very least, Tatiana did not reject her. The child's acceptance, small though it was, soothed the edges of her wounded pride and heartache.

Realizing she had not yet eaten, Jane went to find some food to break her fast. To her own surprise, her appetite had returned. Perhaps the child's acceptance had been enough to ease her melancholy.

Entering the breakfast room reserved for the Balfour family, she found Aurora seated at the table, reading over a plate of eggs and fruit. The morning light streamed through the tall windows, casting soft rays upon the polished mahogany and silver platters that adorned the sideboard. Jane quietly filled her own plate, selecting fruit and a delicate slice of toast before seating herself across from Barclay's mother.

"How are you this morning, Aurora?"

Aurora looked up from her reading, her smile warm and inviting. "I am quite enjoying this visit. It has been a long time since Barclay has taken any time for himself. He appears happier since we arrived, and I must admit that, as a mother, it gladdens my heart to see my boy smiling again."

Jane paused, her fork suspended in midair as she absorbed this unexpected news. "I am ... happy to hear that. He seems a good man."

Aurora's eyes softened with motherly pride, her expression serene and wistful. "The very best of men."

Yearning pierced Jane's chest like a dagger. She struggled to control her breathing as she looked away. "Indeed," she mumbled, her voice barely above a whisper. Her appetite deserted her once more, leaving her with only a hollow ache that no amount of fine breakfast fare could fill. Perhaps she was nothing more than a silly young chit who did not yet understand enough about life to make a suitable wife for a man like him. Barclay seemed to think that the widow was a far more qualified choice, and he was an intelligent, professional man. Certainly, he must have insight into matters such as marriage. Who was she to think she knew better?

With a sigh of resignation, Jane pushed her plate aside and rose to fetch a pot of coffee from the sideboard. The silver gleamed in the morning light, polished to perfection, and the rich aroma of the brew teased her senses with the promise of comfort. Returning to her seat, Jane poured a cup with unrestrained relish. She added cream and a spoonful of sugar, stirring slowly as she watched the swirl of white soften the dark liquid.

Food be damned today. She would drink coffee until Barclay faded from her thoughts. It was the only thing that seemed to lift her spirits these days, and she cradled the cup in both hands as if it were a lifeline.

Jane raised the cup to her lips, taking a fortifying sip, but as she glanced across the table, she noticed Aurora's eyes fixed upon the cup, her expression pinched with concern.

Blazes. Was the woman going to judge her for drinking the gentlemen's beverage? Jane steeled herself, already bracing for a lecture on decorum, reluctant to complete her list of inadequacies for the day.

"Jane, I know it is not my place ..." Aurora's voice was gentle, her eyes scanning the room to confirm that there were no footmen lingering nearby.

Here it comes. Jane forced a smile, keeping her fingers steady around the delicate handle of the cup.

"But I feel I must inform you of the troubles associated with drinking coffee."

Jane took another sip to fortify herself, then set the cup down, forcing her smile to remain fixed. "You refer to the fact that it is a gentlemen's beverage and not considered acceptable in social circles for a woman to drink it?"

"Well ... no. That is too fine a point of etiquette for me to comment on with any knowledge. I was referring to the other issues."

Jane frowned, her eyes narrowing as she tried to make sense of Aurora's words.

Aurora sighed, setting her fork down with a soft clink against the china. "It is just that Tatiana mentioned you have trouble sleeping at night."

Jane blinked, surprise flickering across her features. "That is correct."

"Did the trouble start around the same time as ..." Aurora gestured delicately to the cup on the table. "Perhaps when you began to drink coffee?"

Jane folded her arms, leaning back in her chair as she contemplated the timeline. "I arrived in London. Then I tried coffee the following morning for the first time." She narrowed her eyes, tracing her memories with weary difficulty. "Yes. That was the first night I could not sleep. Why?"

Aurora leaned forward slightly, her expression turning wistful. "When Barclay was a young man doing his studies, there would be nights he needed to ... not sleep. To stay awake to study or complete a design overnight. When that happened, he would drink coffee. Pots of it." She smiled gently. "He told me that the coffee kept his mind and body alert and allowed him to work through the night."

Jane glared down at the cup, her thoughts racing as she pieced together the chain of events. She recalled when the trouble had begun—how she had started having difficulty sleeping, waking restless and unrefreshed. Then came the habit of drinking coffee in the afternoon to lift her spirits and stave off the weariness. That small comfort soon transformed into an evening ritual, the dark brew her salvation when her eyelids threatened to seal shut of their own accord during dinner.

"Blast!" The word burst from her lips before she could catch it. Jane gasped, clapping a hand over her mouth, her cheeks flushing with embarrassment. Her twin brothers, Oliver and Max, were little terrors with a colorful vocabulary of uncouth words they liked to parade about when their parents were safely out of earshot. Jane knew all manner of expressions that were unfit for polite company, but she rarely used them. It seemed her lack of sleep had chipped away at her restraint.

Aurora's eyes danced with amusement, and she waved a hand in dismissal. "It is all right, my dear. We are all family here."

Jane expelled a breath she had not realized she had been holding. "I think you are right! The coffee is causing me to stay awake. I have never had trouble sleeping before.

In fact, my family always expressed their envy that I could sleep anytime and anywhere!"

"What do you plan to do?" Aurora asked, arching one elegant brow as she sipped her tea.

Jane hesitated, then looked earnestly at the older woman. "What would you suggest?" she asked, genuinely eager for her input. How she missed having Emma or her mother to confide in. Aurora made her feel at ease—a steadying presence amidst the chaos of emotions she had been battling. More than that, she admired Aurora's forbearance in weathering years of censure to protect her family. How many women in her position would have simply handed their child over to strangers for the sake of reputation? Jane respected her deeply for it.

Aurora set her teacup down with a soft clink of china. "I would recommend you stop drinking it if your sleep is so poor."

Jane bit her lip. Of course, it was the most sensible course of action. How else was she to confirm that coffee was the culprit unless she abandoned it entirely? The very thought filled her with dread—her beloved brew had been the only comfort she had found this gloomy day. But she nodded resolutely. "I shall do that, then. I thank you for advising me."

Aurora's expression softened with understanding. "I must warn you, when Barclay stopped drinking coffee, there was some trouble."

Jane's eyes widened. "What kind of trouble?" she asked, already feeling a flutter of anxiety at the idea. Her hand reflexively tightened around the handle of her cup, as if it might disappear at any moment. Giving up coffee was already a daunting prospect—must there be more to endure? She shivered slightly, the unease settling in her bones.

"Barclay complained of experiencing the most dreadful cravings when he stopped drinking it," Aurora confessed, her eyes softening with the memory. "He also suffered headaches for several days, which only improved with a small amount of coffee. To hear him speak of it ... it put me in mind of the troubles some people have with laudanum—though, of course, to a much lesser degree. I felt it worth mentioning, in case you notice any effects."

Jane dropped her head into her hands, groaning softly. "What have I done?"

Aurora reached out to pat her hand. "Do not trouble yourself. My mother was from Florence, and she told me it was commonplace for young men there to become reliant on coffee. It is a potent brew, after all."

Jane raised her head, eyes wide. "How long will it take to recover?"

Aurora considered this, her gaze thoughtful. "Only a few days after you stop drinking it. But do expect some headaches and perhaps a touch of ill-temper as a result."

Jane's shoulders slumped in resignation. "Thank you for telling me."

"It is nothing. I felt you ought to know," Aurora said gently.

Looking down at her cup, Jane steeled her nerves and pushed it away, the porcelain scraping slightly against the table. Then, she pulled her plate back toward her with determination and forced herself to take a bite of the eggs that had grown cold in her distraction.

"How have you been enjoying your stay so far?" Jane asked, eager to shift the conversation to less troubling topics.

Aurora's face brightened, her features softening with genuine pleasure. "Excellently! The earl and the countess are so gracious. It has been wonderful to enjoy such exalted company."

"I am so happy to hear that." Jane hesitated, her hands nervously smoothing over her napkin. "I do not wish to be indelicate, but I think it is quite unfair for a lovely lady such as yourself to …" She paused, struggling to find the right words.

Aurora's expression remained gentle. "To be cast out of good society because of a mistake I made as a child?"

"Um … yes. I apologize. It is just that my cousin Kitty—Ethan's mother—was in your position. There are barely any consequences for the father, yet the mother is never allowed to forget she erred."

Aurora sighed, the sound weary yet resolute. "I am fortunate that my family supported me, just as your family supported Ethan and his mother. It is difficult for me, but it is Barclay who has had to live under that cloud of shame his entire life. He is blameless, yet it still affects him—and Tatiana. He has struggled with it, and I would do anything to ease his burden."

Jane leaned forward, her brow creased in concern. "He has struggled?"

"Very much so," Aurora continued, her voice softening with maternal pride. "He blames himself for so much that was never his fault. I was overjoyed when the earl came to find him to acknowledge him as his brother. It will balance out over time—that he is a brother of a powerful earl cannot be ignored. My father is very pleased about the improvement in Barclay's situation."

Jane forced a smile, nodding along. "I am so happy to hear that."

"More than that, I want to see Barclay make a suitable match." Aurora leaned back in her chair, her gaze distant with memory. "My son relied on his late wife more than he cares to admit. It has been difficult for him, and this new connection to the earl will open up new possibilities for courtship."

Jane's hand faltered around her fork. The thought of Barclay with a new wife sent a pang through her chest that was sharper than she anticipated. She swallowed back the ache and speared a piece of egg, chewing mechanically while she tried to imagine Barclay with another woman. Of course, she had always known he would marry again, but she had not imagined it would happen so swiftly. Nor had she considered that, once he made his match, she would continue to see him with the new Mrs. Thompson because they were relations now.

When she found her voice, she responded with as much composure as she could muster. "He is a good man ... and he deserves any happiness he can find." Her voice only wavered a touch, but she despised herself for it.

Aurora regarded her with a tilted head, a glimmer of curiosity crossing her face. Jane's cheeks warmed, and she dropped her gaze to her plate, determined not to reveal her emotions. Heaven help her if she let Barclay's mother become privy to her unrequited affections. Was it not mortifying enough that both Barclay and Tatiana were already aware of his rejection? Now she was about to alert his mother to her feelings, which she had been so desperately trying to suppress.

I suppose it should flatter me that he thought I would work it out for myself.

But she was not flattered. She was hurt. Despite her

best efforts to be understanding of his situation, the sting of his absence lingered.

Jane quickly finished her breakfast, her resolve hardening with each bite. She set her napkin aside, forcing a cheerful expression. "If you will excuse me, I think I shall go find Mr. Dunsford and see if he is available for a game. I have not played lawn bowls in some time."

Aurora's smile was warm but laced with something Jane could not quite place. "Of course, my dear. Enjoy your game."

With a polite nod, Jane rose from her seat, her hands trembling ever so slightly as she smoothed her skirts. Anything—anything—to stop thinking about Barclay and remind herself that there were other men. Other possibilities. She might be young, but Mr. Dunsford seemed to appreciate her youth, so it was time to stop ruminating over her infatuation with an unattainable widower and explore her other options.

Perhaps it would ease this relentless ache in her chest.

BARCLAY HAD JUST RETURNED to the manor from the stables. He did not frequently have the pleasure of riding, so before he could be recruited into another game of ninepins or shuttlecock—or any other of the inane amusements favored by many of the female guests—he had seized the opportunity to ride with the earl.

Jane was never to be seen at those frivolous games, and his prior observations suggested she occupied herself with more worthwhile activities, such as chess. Perhaps she had played bowls that day he had tried to persuade Mrs.

Gordon to join him. She certainly had not made an appearance for ninepins.

He and his brother had toured the park, the estate's grandeur revealing itself at every turn. Barclay had the opportunity to appreciate Tsar's brilliance in selecting the location of the manor. Of course, the late Earl of Saunton would have agreed to the advice from his architect, but he knew Tsar was excellent at persuasion and would have steered and cajoled the earl into making the right decision.

After the brisk ride, Barclay's inner thighs ached in the pleasurable manner of a man who had exerted himself. Days of idle revelry at a nobleman's house party were far outside his usual daily activities. It had indeed been an escape to feel the power of the beast beneath him, the reins taut in his hands, and the wind sweeping through his hair as they galloped across the estate. For those precious hours, he could forget about ninepins and polite conversation and simply exist.

As he entered the hall, Jane appeared in the doorway of the family breakfast room, and the sight of her stopped him mid-stride. He could not help himself—his eyes swept over her form with a hunger that bordered on desperation. She was loveliness incarnate, her dark hair framing her delicate features, her eyes brightening with what he dared to imagine was joy at the sight of him.

But then, as swiftly as it had arrived, the light in her eyes faded, as if a shadow had been cast across her spirit. Her gaze dropped, her lashes sweeping down to conceal the expression in her eyes, and she turned away, her skirts whispering around her ankles as she walked down the hall, each step taking her farther from him.

Barclay stood rooted to the spot, every fiber of his being

urging him to follow her. *Talk to her. Explain. Apologize.* Anything to stop the desolate expression that had crossed her lovely face. But if he were alone with her—if they were to share even a single moment of solitude—he feared all his best intentions would fly out the window like birds escaping a cage, desperate for freedom. He would haul her into his arms, crush her to his chest, and sip from her strawberry-sweet lips until neither of them could remember why it was forbidden.

But he did not move. He watched her turn a corner in the corridor, disappearing from view, and the spell finally broke. He blinked slowly, exhaling a breath he had not known he was holding. It was only then that he realized Aurora had taken Jane's place in the doorway. She was watching him intently, her brow creased with inquisitive concern.

Barclay squared his shoulders, praying she had not witnessed him mooning after Jane like a green boy fresh out of school. "Mother," he greeted her, his voice steady.

"Barclay," she acknowledged, but the curiosity etched into her features did not fade. Barclay's spine stiffened under her scrutiny, and he worried he had given himself away. He dipped his head in a hasty nod before striding off, eager to escape his mother's perceptive gaze before she pressed him with questions he could not—would not—answer.

Mrs. Gordon was on the terrace, engaged in that infernal game of shuttlecock—or battledore—or was it *jeu de volant*? He could not keep track of the ridiculous names they gave to the child's game. Feathered corks flitted back and forth in the air, propelled by delicate wooden rackets, and the ladies tittered with delight each time one fell to the ground.

Zounds, it would be far more entertaining if the feathered device were used for its intended purpose—falconry, with a hawk diving from the heavens to snatch it midair. At least then, there would be some sense of purpose to it, rather than this insipid flapping about with rackets, as if they were little children amusing themselves.

As predicted, the day passed at a glacial pace once he joined Mrs. Gordon. The ladies she played with chattered ceaselessly, their giggles punctuating every light volley. When the shuttlecock fell to the ground, they squealed and swatted at it as if it might come to life and fly off of its own accord. Barclay forced a smile, nodding politely, while his thoughts wandered far afield.

Once again, Lord Trafford was there, pretending the dreary game was delightful. Barclay was not fooled; he saw the way the man's gaze wandered restlessly, his smiles a touch too strained. But Trafford's motive was clear—he was wooing a widow considerably older than himself. Barclay assumed it was not marriage that Trafford had in mind, but rather ...other, less noble pursuits.

And yet, here Barclay stood—pretending as Trafford did—enduring this nonsense for the sake of politeness. For the sake of duty. For the sake of Tatiana, Aurora, and all those who depended on him to make the proper choice.

The hours crept by, each one stretching interminably, and then it was time for dinner. As arranged, he once again sat beside Mrs. Gordon, the seating order having been quietly adjusted at his request. His conscience pricked him with the knowledge that Jane had been pushed farther down the table. He had caught sight of her, seated next to Mr. Dunsford, laughing and chatting animatedly, her eyes sparkling with mirth.

Barclay swallowed hard and forced himself to look away. At least she seemed happy, he told himself. Perhaps she had found a man more appropriate for her age, a man who could give her the future she deserved. It was better this way. Safer. She could grow fond of Dunsford and forget all about those stolen moments in the library. Forget *him*.

But the thought grated against his heart like jagged glass. Had she forgotten him so quickly? Was it that simple for her?

He squashed the notion with ruthless determination. If he would not pursue her, the young lady had every right to seek her happiness elsewhere. It was proper. It was right. And still, the sight of Dunsford's gaze dipping to her bodice sent jealousy coiling through his gut with a fierceness that left him breathless.

When the evening finally ended, Barclay trudged back to his room, the weight of his choices pressing on his shoulders. He settled on the ledge of the window, the chill of the glass seeping through his shirt as he stared unseeingly into the darkness. The stars blinked back at him indifferently, their cold light a mockery of the warmth he had found in Jane's company.

Natalya would no longer visit him in his dreams—he knew that now. She had faded, her spectral presence dissipating since he had met Jane. But there was no solace to be found in that revelation. He could no longer visit the library at midnight to share whispers and stolen kisses.

He had hoped, foolishly, that his newfound ability to sleep had returned for good, but the truth was undeniable. He had paced his room the night before, back and forth over the same creaking floorboards, longing to see Jane. The yearning had barred him from slumber, and it would continue to do so.

When the first light touched the horizon, stretching pale fingers of dawn over the estate, Barclay finally surrendered to his bed. He stared at the cornices, memorizing the whorls and carvings as if they might grant him peace. And at long last, when the room began to fade into shadow, sleep claimed him—not as a comfort, but as a reluctant captor.

He was in the library, but he did not know how he had arrived there. This was not supposed to be! He was meant to stay in his bedroom, no matter how tempting it was to walk the corridor to the main manor to find Jane. Yet here he was, and the firelight flickered warmly over the familiar spines of books, casting shadows that danced along the walls.

Before him, a woman sat at the table, her head bent over a page as she wrote, the feather of her quill catching the light with each graceful stroke. She did not stir as he approached, though his footsteps sounded loudly in the silence, his breath unsteady with anticipation. As he drew nearer, his heart quickened, and the world seemed to narrow until it was only her—Jane—with her ebony curls tumbling loosely down her back.

Reaching out, he took a silky lock between his fingers. The strands slipped through his hand like liquid midnight, and he brought it to his face, inhaling the scent of strawberries and almonds. His heart twisted with longing, his entire soul aching with the need to simply be near her.

Jane turned in her chair, her face lighting up when she saw it was him. "You came!" she exclaimed, her voice soft and warm, threaded with joy.

"How could I stay away?" he murmured, his own voice thick with longing.

Her lashes lowered as she blushed prettily, and Barclay's hands itched to trace the path of that blush, to feel the warmth of her skin beneath his fingertips. He offered his hand, and she accepted it without hesitation, rising to her feet with a grace that made his breath catch. He pulled her close, his arms circling her as if she belonged there, as if she had always belonged there.

"Jane," he whispered. Her eyes glimmered with trust and something deeper that he dared not name.

He dipped his head and captured her mouth with his own, and it was like coming home. Her lips were soft, yielding to him with a tenderness that made his heart lurch painfully. She tasted of strawberries and sunshine, and he was lost. He traced the curve of her cheek with his fingertips, memorizing the sensation of her satin skin beneath his touch.

"You are so soft," he whispered, brushing a kiss against her brow.

Her hands came up to cup his face, and she smiled up at him, her eyes shining with unspoken emotion. "And you are so gentle," she whispered back.

They stood like that, wrapped in each other's arms, the fire crackling gently in the hearth. Barclay's heart swelled with a joy he had not known in years, a peace that settled over him as he held her close. He imagined more of this—many more moments stolen away in the quiet corners of libraries or sun-drenched gardens, the two of them laughing and talking as if the world had shrunk to just the two of them.

He imagined Tatiana running up to join them, her silver-blonde curls bouncing as she demanded Jane read to her again from Aladdin, and Jane laughing as she pulled the girl onto her lap to do just that. He imagined evenings spent by the fire, Jane's head resting on his shoulder as he read aloud to her, the feeling of family and peace wrapping around him like a long-forgotten comfort.

Jane tilted her face up to his, drawing him from his thoughts. "What are you thinking about?" she asked, her eyes searching his.

"That I would like to spend every evening like this," he replied without hesitation. *"Here, with you."*

Her smile widened, and she leaned up to kiss him again, her lips soft and warm, and full of promise. Barclay gathered her closer, holding her as if she were the most precious thing in the world, and for him, she was.

And when she rested her head against his chest, he closed his eyes and simply breathed her in, his heart filled with the hope that perhaps dreams like this did come true after all.

Barclay started awake to find morning light streaming through the curtains, the soft glow spilling across the room. His heart pounded, his breathing uneven as he tried to gather his scattered thoughts. He ran a hand through his hair, blinking away the remnants of sleep, and sighed heavily. Dreams of Jane had filled his slumber—visions of her smile, her laughter, the gentle touch of her hand in his. It had been so vivid, so achingly real that waking up alone left a hollow ache in his chest.

It is merely a reflection of your desires reawakening, he told himself sternly. *It does not mean you are meant to be with Jane.*

Still, the dreams lingered. The way she had looked at him in the library, her eyes warm with trust and affection. The sensation of holding her close, her hair soft against his cheek, her laughter ringing out like music. He had not dreamt of such tenderness since Natalya, and the depth of it shook him to his core.

Barclay sat up, rubbing his face with his hands as he tried to steady himself. *What was happening to him?* For ten years, his heart had been bound up in memories of his late wife, and he had assumed it would remain so. He had not entertained the notion of feeling anything for another woman—certainly not with such intensity.

He stood and crossed the room to the basin, splashing

cool water on his face as if to cleanse away the thoughts that clung stubbornly to his mind. It would not do to dwell on what could not be. He must press forward and decide whether he could tolerate Mrs. Gordon as a wife to aid their family respectability.

It would be better if he did not engage his heart in his second marriage. He had already found and lost the love of his life, and a man did not get a second chance to love so deeply. It was foolishness to imagine otherwise. He was fortunate to have loved at all, and it would be greedy—reckless—to think he could feel that again. Deep down, he knew that if he allowed himself to love and lose once more, it might be more than his heart could bear.

CHAPTER
THIRTEEN

"Selfishness must always be forgiven, you know, because there is no hope of a cure."

Jane Austen

By the time Jane went to bed that night, she knew Aurora had been right about the coffee.

She had skipped her afternoon cup, then her customary cup before dinner. Now it was midnight, and she paced her room with restless energy, her mind fixated on the notion that she should find a servant and demand a pot of coffee be brought to her immediately. The urge clawed at her insides with a desperation that astonished her.

Aurora's warning regarding the cravings had proved true, which could only mean that this truly was the cause of her insomnia.

Her body was utterly worn out, but she could not relax. She had thought about going to the library to write her poetry, but it was inconceivable. For one, she could not summon the patience to sharpen her quill and dip it in ink—the mere thought of the effort it would take was enough to make her want to scream in frustration. Secondly, the library would remind her of how Barclay had so cruelly snubbed her.

The mere thought of it sent a wave of melancholy washing over her. Was this the foul temperament Aurora had warned her about? She had expected irritability, but this ... this hollow, aching sadness was entirely unexpected. Perhaps it was the combination of Barclay's rejection and deprivation of the demon brew that was causing this newfound despair.

It was all she could do to drag herself to the bed and fall in, her limbs heavy as stone.

To her surprise, she drifted off almost instantly, only to jolt awake not long after. Checking the time, she estimated she had slept for barely half an hour. Groaning, she returned to her pillow, squeezing her eyes shut and willing sleep to come again.

Eventually, she dozed in that strange half-sleep, half-waking state, where feverish dreams blurred with reality. Images danced before her eyes—Barclay at the altar with Mrs. Gordon at his side, Jane sitting alone in the family pew as his sister-in-law, forced to pretend joy while carrying the weight of sorrow like lead in her chest.

Her eyes flew open, the image searing her mind. She stared up at the ceiling in the darkness, too afraid to close her eyes again for fear the vision would return. It felt so real, the agony of it sharp and vivid.

But eventually, the fatigue in her limbs became too heavy to bear, and sleep dragged her back under.

When she awoke next, it was to find that morning had

arrived, sunlight creeping between the drapes and spilling onto the carpet in warm golden pools. Sitting up, she moaned in agony. Her head pounded so fiercely, she could swear there was an entire orchestra tuning its instruments inside her skull. The light seemed to stab her eyes with every flicker.

She took hold of the coverlet and threw herself back onto the bed, yanking the fabric over her head to block the light until the throbbing in her temples receded to a tolerable hum. Was this what men felt like when they imbibed too much brandy at their clubs? If so, she was inclined to pity them.

Weary, she decided that drinking some tea and eating breakfast might assuage her physical torment. Groaning, she rose from the bed.

Bah to the strawberry water! There was not an ounce of energy in her for beauty treatments. This morning, she would do the bare minimum. Walking to the door, she found the cart waiting in the hall and pulled it into her room with more effort than she thought should be necessary.

After sipping a small amount of tea and consuming a few bites of eggs and fruit, her headache abated to a tolerable level—tolerable in that she thought she might conduct a conversation without embarrassing herself. But when she heard a light tapping at the door, she realized she had overestimated her capabilities in this fragile state. She wanted to shriek at whomever stood behind it to simply go away and leave her in peace. Raising a trembling hand to her temple, she massaged in slow, steady circles to calm herself.

"Who is it?" she called, her voice just above a whisper.

"Tatiana. May I enter?"

Jane gritted her teeth, massaging her temples where the dull ache of her megrim persisted. The last thing she wanted this morning was a delicate negotiation with an inquisitive nine-year-old. Tatiana would require a measure of diplomacy, and Jane was not sure she had any to spare.

"Of course," she replied, her voice carefully modulated.

The door creaked open, and Tatiana stepped quietly into the room. At least, Jane assumed she did, because her eyes remained squeezed shut as she continued to rub her temples, attempting to alleviate the relentless throbbing.

"Are you all right?" the little girl asked, her voice soft with concern.

"Yes, yes. I am suffering from a megrim, is all."

"Oh." There was a brief pause before Tatiana continued with cautious optimism, "I was wondering if I could ask you to join me and Papa for a walk?"

Jane stilled, her hands dropping to her lap as she stared at the child. A walk? With Barclay? After everything?

She clenched her jaw to prevent herself from groaning aloud. It would be mortifying. She was the silly young woman he had rejected, and worse, he was entirely aware of her feelings. Their last encounter in the hall had confirmed it, when she had greeted him with a beaming smile before recalling his abrupt decision and watching the joy drain from her own face like ink spilled in water.

No, a walk would be far too humiliating.

"Did your father agree to that?" she asked, striving to keep her tone neutral.

Tatiana hesitated, twisting the hem of her skirt between her fingers. "I have not asked him yet, but I am sure I could convince him."

Jane's stomach twisted. She did not wish to disappoint the child, but neither could she bear Barclay's polite indifference—not today. Not when her heart was still tender, and her mind felt scattered from her restless sleep.

"I am sorry, Tatiana," she replied gently, forcing her voice to remain steady. "I cannot. I already made plans for the day."

It was not true, but she would find something to occupy her time, even if it meant wandering the gardens alone with her thoughts.

Tatiana's little face fell, her lower lip quivering slightly. "Please, Jane. I ... miss you. It felt like when Mama was alive and we would do things as a family. I want ..."

Jane's heart clenched painfully, but she forced herself to remain firm. "I am sorry. I cannot. I already promised my time to Mr. Dunsford, and I must hurry if I am to meet him."

The child's eyes shimmered, and Jane had to look away lest she be swayed by those imploring blue eyes.

"What about *Ladin*? Could you read to me this evening?"

Jane closed her eyes, willing herself not to break. The memory of reading *Aladdin* to the girl and seeing her enchanted expression was enough to bring fresh tears to her eyes. But if she agreed to read to her this evening, Barclay might be present as he had been the first time, and Jane could not endure his cool civility—not when her emotions were still so raw. She needed time to recover from the coffee ordeal and this heartbreak before she could manage any pleasantries with Tatiana's father.

"Perhaps in a couple of days. There is no telling if this headache will recede by this evening."

Maybe by then her battered spirits would have time to mend. Perhaps she could muster the strength to sit in the same room with him without her heart shattering all over again.

Tatiana's expression fell, her shoulders sagging in resignation. "I am sorry you do not feel well," she murmured.

Jane managed a small smile. The child was so sweet and earnest, her belief unshaken despite the barriers that seemed insurmountable. It truly would have been an idyllic life—to spend her days with Tatiana, sharing books and adventures, while traveling at Barclay's side as he designed magnificent buildings across England. Jane quickly squashed the errant musing, forcing herself to remember that it was not to be. She needed to focus on her health, particularly conquering this ordeal with the cursed coffee.

"Thank you," she replied gently, her voice thick with emotion.

To her surprise, Tatiana stepped forward and threw her little arms around Jane's neck, hugging her tightly. Jane instinctively wrapped her arms around the child, drawing comfort from the unexpected embrace.

"Please do not give up," Tatiana whispered fiercely against Jane's hair, her small voice trembling with conviction.

Jane pulled back slightly, her brows drawn in confusion. "Give up?"

"On Papa. Promise me you will not give up. We can be a family, I know it! I will make him see, I swear it."

Jane's mouth opened to respond, to offer some gentle, reasonable explanation of why such a dream was impossible—but before she could form the words, Tatiana released her and darted from the room, her skirts fluttering behind her like the wings of a determined little bird.

～

BARCLAY STRODE down the family hall, his boots tapping against the polished wood as he made his way to meet the earl for a spot of fishing. He was just passing Jane's door when it opened unexpectedly, and Tatiana stepped out, shutting it quietly behind her.

Drawing to a halt, Barclay rubbed his temples, a nagging sense of unease settling in his mind. Why did this not sit right? He realized with a pang that he needed to gently dissuade the connection between his daughter and the young woman before Tatiana's hopes grew even more entrenched. The thought of it left a sour taste in his mouth, but it was necessary. He could not allow her to build dreams upon a foundation that would never come to be.

Dropping his hand, he straightened up, his expression hardening as he fixed his gaze on his daughter. But Tatiana, unyielding and unafraid, narrowed her eyes and glared right back.

"Tatiana, are you bothering Miss Davis?"

Tatiana's little chin lifted with defiance. "Miss Davis? I thought you called her by her given name?"

Barclay's jaw clenched. "That was before."

"Before what?"

"Before I started spending time with Mrs. Gordon." His voice was firm, but his heart twinged with regret.

Tatiana shook her head, her silver-blonde curls bouncing with the motion. "No. That is not true. You spent time with Mrs. Gordon playing ninepins. Then we all went to the grotto, and you called her Jane several times. Jane is family, and she invited us to call her ... Jane."

Barclay's frown deepened as he gazed down at his daughter from his not inconsiderable height. But Tatiana, resolute as a tiny warrior, folded her arms and glowered right back up at him, her eyes blazing with fierce determination. If he did not feel so deeply conflicted, he might have even been proud of her audacity. She would go far in life if she maintained that inner fire.

But not on this subject. Barclay exhaled slowly and reached out to clasp her small arm gently. "Come, Tatiana."

He guided her down the hall toward Aurora's chambers. They needed privacy for this conversation—somewhere quiet where the walls did not have ears and there would be no interruption. Tatiana walked beside him, stiff with defiance, her little feet almost stomping with each step.

When they reached Aurora's room, Barclay closed the door behind them and turned to face his daughter. Kneeling so they were at eye level, he spoke gently but firmly. "Tatiana, it is not proper to impose on Jane. She has her own life to live, her own path to follow, and you must allow her to do so."

"Jane enjoys spending time with me. She told me so. It is your fault that there is trouble, and I refuse to turn my back on her."

Barclay walked away, raking his hands through his long hair, to stand by the window while he tried to think how to explain this to his child. Good grief, when had he last had his hair trimmed? Tatiana was not wrong about his need for a wife, it would seem.

"It is not possible for me to court Jane, and it would be inappropriate to spend time in her company, little one."

"Why? She is family. Her sister is married to your brother, Uncle Perry. If I want to spend time with her, I can."

"Tatiana, perhaps in the future. But not now. We must allow Jane her time. She is seeking a husband, and she needs to be allowed to do so."

His daughter growled at him, causing Barclay to blink.

It sounded more like a mewling because she was such a little girl, but it was unprecedented. He spun back to face her, discovering that her face had turned red with anger.

"You are a selfish man! Jane was to be my new mother! Mama would have approved. Now you are ruining it! Not only that, now you are trying to ruin my time with her!"

Barclay shook his head. "There are things—adult matters—which you do not understand. I am doing this for you. And your grandmama, and I need you to trust me."

"Why? I see what Jane did, but you will not listen. You changed. You were smiling and happy like you were when Mama was still here. Now you are back to your sadness. I am worried about you, but you will not listen to me. I know Jane is the one!"

Barclay hung his head, too ashamed to look at her while he tried to find the words to explain once more. "It is not right, Tatiana. Jane could marry anyone. She is the sister-in-law to an earl, from a good family, and there will be problems for her if she were to marry me."

"We are a good family! We look after each other. We spend time together. We try to make each other happy. That is what Jane would do if she were part of our family."

Barclay drew a deep breath. Usually, he was so talented with negotiations, but there was something complicated about dealing with one's own child. He knew he was trying to do what was best for her, and for Jane, but how did he tell Tatiana without ruining her childhood? She did not need to know about the troubles surrounding his parentage. The troubles she would deal with in the future. Nay, that must wait until she was much older. It was his duty to protect her innocence and allow her this time of ignorance for as long as he possibly could.

"You must give Mrs. Gordon a chance, little one."

"She does not like children!"

"How do you know that?"

"I ... just know. I can tell. Ethan agrees with me."

Barclay shook his head. He did not know why Tatiana was convinced the widow did not like children. There had been no evidence of that. "Ethan is four years old and not an expert on women. She is very pleasant, and she can teach you many things."

"Like what?"

He was not prepared for the question. *Lud*, he was quickly learning during this house party that his daughter might look like her mother, but she had inherited all the stubborn traits of the Thompson family. Tsar was going to howl with mirth about all of this when they returned to London in a week or so.

Barclay would laugh himself if this was not so terribly disheartening. Perhaps that was a good sign. A sign that his mourning truly was over if he even considered laughing. He could not recall when he had last laughed about anything —not truly, without forcing it politely—but since arriving at this house party, it seemed he had recovered his sense of humor.

"She can teach you to behave like a proper young lady."

"Jane can teach me that."

"Yes, but ..."

"But what?"

"Mrs. Gordon was the wife of a vicar. She can teach you all about ..." Barclay sought for something to say. "Charity!" he announced, proud of himself for thinking of it.

Tatiana considered this, and Barclay realized neither of them knew enough about Jane to know if she was involved in charitable work. After a lengthy pause, her face lit up, and she responded, "Grandmama can teach me that."

That was true. Aurora involved herself in charity work with their church.

"Mrs. Gordon has a lovely voice, and she must know how to sing. She could teach you to sing lovely hymns."

His daughter narrowed her blue eyes in a menacing manner. "Are you saying I cannot sing?"

Barclay coughed into his hand. If Natalya were here, she would do a much better job of handling their daughter. But if Natalya were here, they would not be arguing over who would be her new mother, so that was a moot point.

"You have a lively singing voice, little one."

Thankfully, she appeared mollified. Barclay straightened his shoulders and endeavored to return to his original point before Tatiana had debated him into a corner.

"I need you to leave Jane alone and allow her to seek a young man to marry. We cannot stand in her way, or cause complications."

She shook her head. "I do not agree to this. I have already asked Jane to read me *Ladin*, and she said when she is feeling better, she will do so."

Barclay frowned, worried despite his vow to steer clear of the young woman. "Is Jane unwell?"

"She said she has a headache."

He exhaled. "Then I need you to listen to me. I am the parent."

"I should listen to you, even if you are wrong?"

Scowling, Barclay tried to think how to respond to that. "I am the parent, and you must listen."

Tatiana drew herself up to her full height. It was not much, but she was as regal as a queen when she replied, "I shall not. Jane is my friend, and you cannot stop me from spending time with her."

Before he could respond, she turned and ran from the

room in a blur of skirts and stockings before he even had time to think. *Bosh!* He should have stood between her and the door, knowing she might bolt. Now he would have to wait to find her and start this discussion all over again. Natalya had always been so talented at dealing with Tatiana. He was a brute compared to her finesse with the child.

Dash it, if his nine-year-old daughter besting him in debate was not a sign of his advanced years! This was precisely why this age gap between him and Jane would not work. If he did not know better, he would swear he had aged a hundred years based on how he had felt since he had found Aurora crying in her room.

JANE LEFT her bedroom at about two in the afternoon, once the pounding in her head had receded sufficiently to paste a smile on her face and feign some social pleasantries.

While preparing for the day, she had reached a decision. It was time to seriously consider a match with Mr. Dunsford. With him, she would access a path to the familiar. As the daughter of a landowner, she would marry the heir to a similar situation. This was a world which she could understand and navigate. Her sister was the wife of a landowner. Her father was a landowner himself, and her mother was the wife of a landowner. It would be perfect because she would have plenty of help to make such a situation a success.

It had been the original plan she had had for this Season, before Emma had meddled with her ideas of a meeting of the minds. She had tried following Emma's advice, which had led to bitter disappointment. Her sister's success with bringing Perry up to scratch had been a fluke, a once-in-a-lifetime stroke of luck not to be repeated.

All that remained was to confirm that she and Mr. Dunsford had enough in common to make a marriage work. Anything to leave this miserable situation in the past.

Jane stopped in the hall to rub her weary hands over her face. She was having trouble maintaining the appearance of conviviality. Fatigue was setting in once more, and she cursed the coffee that had put her in this infernal mood, while craving a cup of the demon brew, which would release her from this current agony.

Be strong! Aurora said this will only last a few days before it wears off.

Inhaling deeply, she pasted the jovial expression back on her face and continued her walk to the library. She would rest there for a moment while she regathered her wits, then set off to find Mr. Dunsford. Hopefully, his attentions had not wandered to another female guest while she had been occupied with Barclay.

When she reached the library, she scowled at the coffeepot with loathing. And longing. It was hard not to recall the blissful sense of tranquility after drinking a cup. Shaking her head, then groaning when it caused the thudding to echo against her skull, Jane squared her shoulders as if preparing for battle.

Resolutely, she headed down to the main level in search of the other guests. She soon found the countess drinking tea in one of the drawing rooms with an accompaniment of women of all ages. The Duchess of Halmesbury gestured for her to come join them, so Jane walked across to take a seat.

The moment she sat, the babe in the duchess's arms turned to watch her. Reaching up two chubby arms, Jasper mewled loudly. The duchess laughed. "Jane, my dear son has grown weary of his mother. Would you like to hold him?"

Jane immediately reached for the boy. As soon as he was in her arms, gazing up at her with enormous eyes, she leaned forward to sniff his sweet scent and was hit with a wave of yearning. If she could find a beau to marry, she could start her new life. Perhaps have her own babe by this time next year. She nearly wept with the sheer desire to begin on this path. This Season was turning out to be a bitter experience, and there was no need to prolong the agony.

Faith! These symptoms from the coffee are turning me into a dreary mess!

As Jasper grabbed one of her fingers with his tiny fist, Jane thought once again about how she might be betrothed before the house party ended. She was ready, and she did not want to meet more men who would lead to more disappointment. All she needed was one suitable gentleman to propose. Her impatience was not to do with her throbbing head, she assured herself, nor the architect she wished she had never met. This was about stepping into her future.

When Jasper grew weary, his little eyelids drooping, she handed him back to his mother, who summoned their nanny to take him for a rest. Then Jane left to find Mr. Dunsford. Exiting the manor, she found him engaged in a discussion with several young gentlemen and ladies. He grinned broadly when he spotted her. Completing the anecdote he was telling, he quickly excused himself to join her.

Bowing, with a tip of his hat, he straightened and held out an arm. "Miss Davis, would you do me the honor of taking a turn in the gardens? There are several guests here to maintain propriety." He gestured back to the table. Jane accepted his arm, and they descended the stairs to walk the pathways of the formal garden.

"Tell me about your home, Mr. Dunsford. Is it far from here?"

"Not at all. About two hours at most, to the northeast of Saunton."

"And do you have a large family?"

"Alas, no. There are my father and my little sister. My mother died a few years ago. What about you, Miss Davis?"

"I have three brothers, all younger than me. And two sisters. You might have met Emma the day you arrived?"

"Ah, yes. The young lady who married Mr. Peregrine Balfour. I was most surprised when he mentioned he plans to remain at Shepton Abbey throughout the year. I always thought the gentleman loved the sophistication of London too much to rusticate."

"Do you visit London?"

"As frequently as family obligations permit. Now that I hear you will be there with the earl's family for the rest of the Season, I am quite inspired to follow you!" Mr. Dunsford smiled, revealing pearly teeth. He was the epitome of the gentry. Fine-looking, charming, and modest for the most part—having made her smile many times with his dry and self-deprecating wit.

Jane smiled in acknowledgment, thinking about how she had enjoyed their interactions. There was every reason to believe that they would enjoy the companionship of a good marriage and to believe she would eventually forget the architect who had awakened her to passion.

CHAPTER
FOURTEEN

"Friendship is certainly the finest balm for the pangs of disappointed love."

Jane Austen

Barclay had not seen Jane except for dinner last evening, which was a small mercy. Instead, he had spent his time with Mrs. Gordon, even mildly enjoying their game of nine-pins under the afternoon sun. He had been regaling the widow with various anecdotes about his clients across the realm, and she had giggled and laughed in a gratifying manner for most of their game.

He had not been aware that he could be so amusing, but clearly, he had unplumbed depths of humor to share with a new wife.

As the afternoon progressed, they completed their game and walked with the other players back to the terrace. There they found refreshments awaiting them and took a seat at one of the tables. In the distance, he noted Jane arm in arm with the young Mr. Dunsford, and for a moment, he was distracted, before dutifully pulling his attention away to laugh at an anecdote Mrs. Gordon now told him about visiting one of the tenants' homes at Saunton Park.

Apparently, the widow made a habit of visiting the various homes, seeing it as her duty, since until recently there had been no mistress at Saunton Park in many years.

Swallowing a dainty biscuit, Barclay reflected on how much he had changed since his arrival there. Here he was laughing and enjoying pleasant conversation instead of pursuing his wife's ghost. Soon he might bring a new wife home with him. Tatiana would have a mother once more, who could sit with her and play the pianoforte on a Sunday afternoon, as Natalya had done.

He could well imagine this woman bending her head over his daughter as they learned a new piece of music together, and he watched from the comfort of his armchair. It was the small moments he missed the most. The joy of sharing a lazy afternoon with Aurora sewing, Tsar reading his news sheets, and him ... just watching his wonderful family in a moment of quietude. He missed it like the blazes.

Mrs. Gordon was a mature woman who understood the implications of marrying someone like him. She believed her reputation would further improve his credibility, and her fascination with him had not flagged.

Aurora had confirmed that the widow had taken pains to join her for breakfast, so Mrs. Gordon was willing to do the work required to make their family whole.

Several times during their conversations, he had clarified that he lived with Tsar and Aurora in their family home, to ensure that the widow found this acceptable.

"Have you traveled much, Mrs. Gordon?"

"I have a little. I used to live in Canterbury, which is where I met Mr. Gordon. When he learned of his new post here in the village, he asked my father for my hand in marriage. So I am well familiar with Kent, as well as Surrey, where I attended a ladies' seminary."

Barclay blinked. "Surrey? So far from home? What age were you when you were sent away to school?"

"I first left home when I was seven years old. I personally think it was a little too young, but it all turned out for the best."

He hesitated briefly before replying. The thought of sending Tatiana away two years ago would have been inconceivable to him as her father. More so because she had just suffered the loss of her mother, but even so, he could not imagine sending his daughter away at such a young age. Tatiana suffered from night terrors, and he was sure there would be no one to comfort her in the dormitories of a ladies' seminary in a different county from their family home.

"You say it was for the best?" he ventured.

"Certainly. I learned all my accomplishments there. Sewing, watercolors, dancing. They had a talented French teacher, so I speak fluently. Not to mention, playing ninepins and shuttlecock with the other girls was a pleasant way to pass the time."

Barclay restrained himself from rolling his eyes. He hoped he could convince the widow to bowl in the future by offering her his personal tutelage in the game.

"You have had many opportunities to use your French, then?"

The widow frowned in an effort to recall. Finally, she admitted, "I cannot say that I have. There are few opportunities in such a small village, but it serves well when I attend events here at Saunton Park."

"Because you have met French people here?"

"Well, no. The earl did not entertain prior to his marriage. But now that he has, I am sure I will have an opportunity to use it more! Or if I were to move to London." The last was said in a beguiling tone as she laid a gloved hand over his for a fleeting moment of suggestive impropriety.

Barclay had not the heart to inform her that, outside of his work, he never used any of his French. She seemed quite hopeful on the matter.

If Mrs. Gordon were to take a place as his wife, she would instruct Tatiana on all the skills she had learned at the ladies' seminary. He still had a difficult time understanding why the widow's father had sent her away so young, but he supposed all that learning would be helpful for his own daughter.

He smiled, lifting another dainty biscuit to his lips while he considered the situation. Was he confident that Mrs. Gordon would be a good wife? Should he seek advice from his mother or his brother, or simply propose to the woman? She had shown her eagerness on many occasions. With the amount of time they had spent together, if they were in London, he would be required to propose by this stage of their acquaintanceship. Fortunately, he could think on the matter a little longer because the rules at a house party were considerably less *de rigueur*. He did not wish to marry for love again, and Mrs. Gordon seemed eminently suitable as a choice.

He noticed Tatiana had arrived, peering through the windows of the terrace door at him.

Lifting his watch fob, he recalled that he had promised

her a game of chess. He bade farewell to the widow, who appeared disappointed at his departure. Barclay admitted his own vanity when he realized it was pleasing to have such an attractive woman seeking his company. He missed the feminine influence in his life, and his dream in the early hours suggested he missed other aspects of the marital union.

Brushing those thoughts aside, he strode over to join Tatiana, grasping her small hand in his to make their way to the library. It took a few minutes to reach it, the manor being a very large home to traverse. When they reached the room, he heard Ethan calling out victoriously, "Checkmate!"

Tatiana grimaced. "He practices far too much. I shall never catch up with him. How can a child be beating me so?"

Barclay hid a smile. She was a child herself, but he could recall how much relative ages had mattered to him as a small boy. Even half a year was something to brag about to younger children.

They had entered the doorway when Barclay's smile was wiped from his face. Ethan's opponent was Jane.

ETHAN HAD EASILY OUTPLAYED HER. Her head was thudding something terrible, and the effort to concentrate was more than could be borne. It set off fresh thudding, and she had to prevent herself from groaning from the agony of it. She had left Mr. Dunsford's side earlier when the light had wreaked havoc, and she had been afraid she would reveal her discomposure, so she had joined Ethan for a game of chess.

Her cousin was far more tolerable company when she was this set upon. She could be herself and not behave with rigid propriety. Considering she hoped to make a match with the gentleman, it would not do to show any temper in his vicinity.

"You seem poorly, Jane. Are you not sleeping still?" Her cousin's face twisted with fret.

"My sleep is slowly improving," she admitted, "but I have a headache at the moment."

"I thought you played poorly. It seemed too easy to corner your king."

Jane smiled tremulously. Ethan had only begun playing within the past few months, after Emma had introduced him to the game, yet he sounded like a professional player now. He had really committed to learning its intricate strategies and was maturing before her very eyes, a little virtuoso in the making. When she sat back in her seat, she caught sight of Barclay and Tatiana standing hand in hand by the doorway. Her heart sank.

I shall consider that progress.

The last time she encountered the widower in the hall, she had practically leapt into his arms with joy before recalling he had rejected her. It was little consolation. She felt bereft in his presence. It had appeared to be progressing so well, and she had been certain she had found her Darcy. All that was needed was her patience with the man's grieving, but then it suddenly all ended.

Now she knew there was no Darcy for her, and she needed to find whatever happiness she could. Fortunately, she no longer needed to reveal her coffee-drinking to Mr. Dunsford because she no longer drank the demon brew that was causing these megrims.

Jane slowly rose, while Ethan clamored to his feet and

raced over to the pair at the door. "Uncle *Bar-clee*, I have not seen you since the grotto!" He held up his arms, and his uncle quickly raised him up.

She winced. The grotto was quickly becoming a painful memory, rather than the sheer joy it had been at the time. Picking up her shawl, she pulled it over her arms, jerky in her impatience to leave the library. Her fingers trembled as she hastily prepared the board for play, putting all the pieces in their place. She needed a moment to collect her wits and consider the best method to leave without revealing too much of her angst. One had to have some pride after such a rejection.

Jane had no ideas of how to feign any social graces in this moment. All she could think of was the need to escape as quickly as possible. If she was not battling with this coffee issue, she would collect herself and deal with all of ... this. But she was dealing with the coffee issue, and it was incredibly uncomfortable. Her only solace was that Aurora said it would be over within a few days. Two had passed thus far.

Determinedly, she put the pieces back, but her fingers hesitated as she recalled the magic of being in Barclay's arms.

Truly, she needed to get away from the Balfour homes. She was certain to see the architect regularly unless she married and moved on. Even if she returned home to Rose Ash Manor, her family would visit Ethan and she would have no excuses to not attend with them, and Barclay might attend, too.

She might be forced to attend his wedding to another woman, to watch his family grow, to remember her one kiss with him here in the library of Saunton Park when she thought that anything was possible. That love was possible.

Squaring her shoulders, she made for the door. When she reached the Thompsons, she paused for the briefest instant to acknowledge them for the sake of the children present. "Barclay. Tatiana." She bobbed, then quickly exited before the disappointment in the little girl's face could register on her already fragile state.

She knew not if Barclay had acknowledged her presence as she strode away as fast as her fatigued legs could carry her. Returning Ethan to his nanny was something she should do, but the gentleman was more than capable of doing so. She needed to get away.

Jane had appeared dejected when she had brushed past them. Not only that, she was pale and drawn. Ethan had been talking to her about a headache. And Tatiana had mentioned Jane having a headache earlier that morning. Evidently, it had not improved. Perhaps that was the reason she was disconsolate. That notion assuaged his conscience over disappointing the young woman.

Realizing that he now had possession of Ethan, he asked the boy where he was meant to be. Ethan told them he needed to be returned to the nursery, which was on the upper floor of the family wing. So Barclay and Tatiana accompanied him back.

When they came upon the nursery, Barclay was impressed. It was light and airy, unlike many noble houses. There was evidence of recent work. The drapes looked new, the walls were clad in rich colors, and the schoolroom was well stocked with toys and children's books.

Richard had only discovered his son's existence earlier that year, so he must have immediately ordered the changes in the nursery to have had them ready in time for this house party. Barclay now understood his brother's dismay when Barclay had expressed his feeling of insult that the butler had presumed to take Tatiana to the nursery on their arrival at Saunton Park.

He had pictured something ... gloomier.

Tatiana and he returned to the library in silence to play their game. His daughter was obsessed with improving her chess so she might beat her little cousin, and Barclay was amused at this hitherto unknown spirit of competition in her that had surfaced. With each year that passed, facets of his daughter's personality made themselves known, and he wished her mother could be present to witness her transformation.

Once they were alone in the room of shelves and books, Tatiana sat in her seat across the table with the chessboard between them, but she did not begin playing. Instead, she watched him for long moments, causing Barclay to want to squirm in his own chair like an errant child caught in the act of some wrongdoing.

He knew what she was thinking about. He had been trying not to think about the same issue—a struggle the entire walk to and from the nursery. She was thinking about how Jane had hurried from the room.

When she failed to say something, he got up his nerve. "What is it, little one?"

Tatiana sighed and turned her head to stare out the window, a disappointed look on her face. "I always thought you were brave. I am sad to know ... that you are not."

Startled, he straightened in his chair. "What do you mean?"

"I saw how you were with Jane, and that is when I realized ... that you were afraid. Afraid of her. Afraid to love. Because of what happened to Mama."

"Tatiana, it is not that. There are things you do not understand. Adult ... things."

She shook her head. "I think that is why I have been losing these games with Ethan. I am afraid to take a risk. Then he swoops in and beats me. If I am to win, I shall have to ... be brave." With that, she leaned forward and moved a pawn.

Startled by her perception of the weakness in her chess, Barclay did not know what to make of what she had said. Instead, he studied the board and made his own move, allowing her to drop the subject.

Tatiana stuck to her newfound conviction, attempting offensive moves on the board that earned Barclay's respect. He still won, but she had done much better, and there was a possibility she might corner Ethan the next time they played.

After their match was over, Tatiana joined her grandmother, and Barclay entered the billiard room.

He was to have a reprieve from thought, from debate, from feeling guilty for not being enough. Not doing enough to bring happiness to the women in his life.

And he would play a game that required skill.

Thankfully, there were no women in sight in this masculine retreat of mahogany and green baize. Inspecting the billiard table, he ran his fingertips over the intricately carved strapwork and eyed the well-formed legs. It was such a fine piece, Thomas Chippendale himself could have carved it.

Nodding to the assembled gentlemen in the room, he

stretched his neck. Tension eased from his shoulders as he walked over to find a cue.

Mr. Ridley was at the table, setting the balls in place, while Lord Trafford and Mr. Dunsford selected their own cues. They were engaged in a discussion, which Barclay barely noted until their words caught his attention.

"So you plan to propose to the Davis girl, Dunsford?"

Barclay felt the tension in his shoulders return. He wanted Jane to be happy, only in the deepest recesses of his soul it was him she was to be happy with. Quickly, he reminded himself that this gentleman was an eminently more suitable prospect for the young woman than he was.

"That is the plan," responded the young man with his mop of perfect curls on his head. There was no doubting the skill of the valet who attended him, to Barclay's annoyance. Barclay had never obtained a manservant, although Tsar had offered the privilege. It had seemed an extravagance, although they could afford it. Until Natalya's death, she had performed little tasks such as cutting his hair—an intimacy that he had quite enjoyed.

"So then you shall reside in the country at your father's estate forevermore, like my good friend, Peregrine Balfour, who has made the inexplicable decision to take up estate management and leave the delights of London behind him."

Dunsford chuckled in reproach. "I would not go so far as to say that. I have always enjoyed the ... delights ... of London."

Barclay narrowed his eyes, not appreciating the implication. Jane was to find a good husband who would do right by her. Speaking without turning to look at the young fop, he joined in the conversation. "There are no current ... delights ... awaiting you in London, I trust?"

"What if there were? Proposing to Miss Davis surely does not preclude such a arrangement on the side?"

Ridley straightened up from the baize-covered table to frown across the room. "I would not recommend it, Dunsford. Saunton is protective of his family, especially his womenfolk, since his change of heart earlier this year. If he were to discover you were anything but loyal ..."

"There is no reason for him to learn of my private matters!" interjected Dunsford. "Miss Davis would never learn of it. She will be happy rusticating at my family home with a babe to dote on. If she is anything like my mother, she will barely notice my absence. Tell him, Trafford. It is how things are done in polite society."

Carefully, Barclay chalked the leather-tipped end of his cue. It was that or turn and break it over the young fop's head. He was so angry, his hands trembled with his repressed emotion. Under any circumstances, he would dislike the views the spoiled dandy aired, but the thought of it being Jane in the loveless, societal marriage Dunsford described was too much to comprehend. She deserved the love of a good man.

Trafford threw his hands up in surrender. "I am not the ally you seek. I love women, but when I settle down, I do not plan to continue playing the field. It is difficult and fraught with the threat of disease if one makes a misstep with the wrong paramour."

"What rot!" sputtered Dunsford. "It is practically our duty to sow our wild oats. If we do not, we would bother our wives with an excess of desires. No gentlewoman could handle such appetites."

For the first time, Barclay was grateful the late earl had not married his mother. She might have lost her reputation, but at least she had held on to her independence in Tsar's household.

His mother was a loyal, kind woman, and she would not have fared well with a treacherous lech for a husband. From what Richard had described, their own father was much worse than this little upstart. Aurora might be relatively traditional in her feminine pursuits, but she was single-minded about issues that were important to her. The Earl of Satan might have broken her spirit.

Ridley took his time responding. "I have enjoyed the company of many fine women of the upper classes. My experience is that their ... appetites are the same as any other women."

"You never met my mother, then!" exclaimed Dunsford.

Ridley and Trafford shook their heads, Ridley pressing his earlier argument. "Be that as it may, heed my warning when I say that Saunton will not like it, and he is not a man you should rouse to anger."

Dunsford tensed, his next words demanding and cocksure. "And how will he know? Are you going to tell him?" It would have been amusing because of his medium stature, if Barclay were not seething with restrained anger.

Ridley shrugged. "Saunton need not be informed of such things. He would know. I would wager money that he will see through your ploy and turn down your proposal. The man knows what true love is, after all."

"That is nonsense! This pretense that he is in love with the countess will last as long as it takes to confirm he has an heir before he reverts to his old ways. It is in his nature!"

Trafford frowned, considering this statement as he walked forward to take his place at the billiard table. "I am as cynical as any man who has sampled the delights of London, but I do not believe that is the case. The earl has sought out the women of his past to make amends. His actions are not ones of impermanence. I agree with Ridley. If it is your aim to dally, do not choose Miss Davis as your wife. You will invoke not only the earl's wrath, but that of his younger brother who wed Miss Davis's sister. The Balfour brothers are formidable alone, but paired up, they would wreak havoc on your existence for daring to toy with a relation under their protection."

"The connection to Saunton is the very rationale for making the offer."

Barclay wanted to thrust his cue through the man's chest to stake Dunsford's beating heart.

He restrained himself with an effort. Overreacting could start rumors about Jane, so he needed to temper his reaction lest he create a scandal for the young woman. Of all Jane's fine qualities, her connection to Saunton was the least important. If he could trust himself to speak without flying into a rage, he would set the arrogant little toad right. He assured himself the benefit of staying silent was that he had learned the man's true intentions, so he might take action.

Perhaps he must warn Jane? No, he did not have that right. He would inform Richard, who would refuse the match.

Ridley went to stand near Trafford, inspecting the shot Trafford had taken. "Then trust me, Dunsford. Do not make this decision lightly. If you wish to wed Miss Davis, you need to be fully committed when you approach the earl. Anything less and he will know. Saunton is not a fool."

Dunsford came to stand by the table to await his turn to play. "I shall think on what you have advised."

Barclay placed his cue down. "If you will excuse me,

gentlemen, I find that I have an earlier engagement I forgot to attend to."

Straightening his coat, Barclay departed the room. He would not take a chance on this. Jane was too important. He must find the earl to discuss the matter right away.

When he found Richard, Barclay would demand to know more about the reparations to the women of the earl's past. Richard had failed to mention such, and it was not acceptable that Barclay learned of it in the presence of the sniveling ninny who planned to propose to his Jane—he grimaced—to Jane. *Not his Jane. Just Jane.*

Setting off to find the earl, he learned that both Richard and the duke had left Saunton Park for an undisclosed errand in Chatternwell and were expected back in the morning.

Barclay fumed in frustration, hoping that Dunsford would not approach Jane without the earl's prior approval. He could not allow her to be disappointed if the earl had to veto the match after she had already accepted the proposal. Yet the young cad could not be trusted to submit to propriety if he was so shallow about matters of faithfulness. Dunsford might approach her without the earl's approval.

CHAPTER
FIFTEEN

"Till this moment I never knew myself."

Jane Austen

In the morning, Barclay quickly arose to await the earl's return. From the library windows, he frequently checked the drive for the ducal carriage that had taken his brother and cousin to Chatternwell.

It was essential that he inform the earl of Dunsford's intentions. He could not allow Jane to be tricked into the type of marriage the young dandy planned. She was to have a long and happy marriage, and many children to mother. What Dunsford planned was beyond the pale.

Pacing up and down the library, Barclay had to admit he was worried for the lady's future. Somehow she had come to mean so much to him in a short length of time, and he could not allow her to be manipulated into an unhappy union with the loathsome little cad.

By midmorning, Barclay decided he should go to eat his breakfast. At least it would occupy some of his time while he waited.

Having just taken a seat with a laden plate, Barclay forked baked eggs into his mouth.

"Barclay!" He started in surprise, dropping his fork with a loud clatter as it bounced off his plate, splattering egg across the table. Turning around, he found Aurora, who appeared disheveled and mildly distraught.

"What is it?" Barclay quickly rose to his feet, thoughts of breakfast forgotten.

"Have you seen Tatiana this morning?"

He shook his head. "Why?"

"She was not in her bed when I awoke. I cannot find her anywhere."

Barclay's face twisted into a worried frown. "When did you last see her?"

"I put her to bed after her dinner, and she was sleeping when I returned to the room. At least …" Aurora's brow furrowed as she attempted to recall the evening before. "Yes. She was there when I came back because I saw her plait on the pillow." She looked back up. "What do we do?"

"What happened when you woke up?"

"Her bed was empty. We customarily come down to breakfast together at this time, but she must have risen much earlier. I have been searching for her, but this manor is so large, it took the longest time to check the public rooms!"

Barclay ran a hand through his hair. "I will look for her."

"I already checked the nursery, and the library, and all the rooms on this level. And the terrace."

He tried to think. With a sinking sensation, he realized

there was one place he would have to check. "Did you look in Jane's room?"

"No ... Jane has trouble sleeping, so she has been rising late. I did not want to disturb her too early. Do you think Tatiana could be with Jane?"

Barclay briefly closed his eyes. He could hardly ask his mother to go to Jane's room. Tatiana was his daughter. His responsibility. He was going to have to march himself down that corridor and force himself to knock on Jane's door.

He still felt regret over how he had handled the situation with Jane. Had she waited for him the night he had stayed in his room? She deserved better, but he simply did not trust himself to be alone with her yet.

Yet you do not have a choice.

Barclay grimaced. "I shall learn what I can."

Aurora frowned. "Barclay, what is happening between you and the young lady? I feel as if there is an undercurrent, and now ... you appear quite reluctant to speak to her. Jane is a charming young woman and—"

"There is nothing happening between me and Jane!" He kept a straight face, but he knew his mother would not be fooled. Not after barking as he had just done.

"Barclay—"

He turned and walked to the door. "I must find Tatiana." And prevent this discussion. Aurora would likely blame herself if she knew his motive for ending his connection with Jane. He rushed off before Aurora could press the issue.

As he hurried through the grand hall, Barclay tried to prepare for his imminent conversation with Jane. Should he apologize? The young woman was clearly aware that he had snubbed her. She probably perceived it as a rejection, while he was merely attempting to navigate this awkward situation and ensure he did not take advantage of her passionate—and youthful—nature.

He exhaled deeply to settle his nerves, but the knot in his gut remained where it was. Blurting out a warning about that worm, Dunsford, was ill-advised, considering the circumstances. She was more likely to reject the caution from him than from his brother, and it was vital that she heed it, so he would not risk telling her himself.

Jane was to be happy, and his admonition would be poorly received after his callous handling of her the past few days. If only he could explain that he was doing it to protect her from himself. Reaching the corridor leading to the family wing, he hesitated to compose himself before entering.

JANE'S SLEEP had improved a little, but she was afraid that it was mostly due to sheer exhaustion. She had been struggling with headaches and fatigue since ... She tried to recall. Since a few hours after her last cup of coffee.

She cursed Perry for not warning her of the effects of drinking the devil's brew, which she likened to a marsh now that she was aware of what it did. Drawn in by the pretty scenery, only to find herself sinking into the swamp water, unable to extricate herself from the pull of the mud. She could happily raise her head to howl like a trapped beast—her head ached so much, she felt like a wounded animal herself.

What a fool she had been to meddle with the so-called gentlemen's drink. Her only consolation was that Barclay had been through a similar suffering, so it was not her gender that was the basis of her problem.

Rubbing her temples, Jane attempted to think. Which set off a series of thudding echoes in her skull. She had woken with a headache, and it had only been intensifying through the past hour. Somewhere in the quagmire of pain and regrets, she recollected that Aurora had said something about relieving the symptoms.

There had been something she could do to reduce the intensity.

What had it been?

Hazily, the answer came to her. Aurora had mentioned a small amount of coffee could ease the transition. Jane rose. Resolutely, she made for the library, where there should be a pot waiting for her. She had yet to cancel the request.

Making her way slowly down the hall of arching sash windows, she headed for the main house. As she reached the end of the corridor, she nearly jumped out of her skin when Barclay suddenly appeared in front of her. She considered turning around and heading back to her room, but she could not see if anyone accompanied him to witness her cowardice, so, squaring her shoulders in frustration, she defiantly forged ahead, intending to brush past him.

"Jane?"

She halted. This was not the time to engage her in conversation. She was in no mood to hear anything he had to say. Between contending with the coffee troubles and coping with her feeling of loss over the burgeoning relationship he had severed so abruptly, Jane had no patience for a discussion. She needed to reach that coffeepot.

With determination, she resumed her trajectory. If the gentleman was to force a conversation on her, he would do so while she continued on her quest to alleviate her suffering. Reaching Barclay, she sidestepped him and marched on toward the library.

Behind her, he sighed heavily before turning to fall in step with her.

"Jane, have you seen Tatiana?"

"I have not." Her head hurt too much for pleasantries. That he had not sought her out to apologize for his behavior was disappointing, but she only had thoughts for the coffeepot, so she kept walking.

"Did she attempt to visit you this morning?"

Jane carefully shook her head, noting that she was only steps away.

"Not at all? It is just … She is missing, and Aurora thought she might have …" Barclay trailed off as Jane strode into and across the room. To her great relief, the tray with the coffee was waiting in the usual spot on the table near the chessboard.

"Mr. Thompson, I have not seen your daughter since yesterday. Now, if you do not mind, I wish to be alone."

Barclay had followed her, surprising her when he spoke behind her shoulder. "Jane, I know it is not what you wish to hear, but I assure you I am doing what is best."

"Best for whom, Mr. Thompson?" She could not help herself. Her frustration came rushing out in a tight, angry demand.

The architect blinked before responding. "For you."

"Am I not the best judge of what is best for me?"

"You are so …"

"Young?"

He nodded, devoid of words to say.

"Too young to know my own mind?"

Barclay bit his lip, visibly uncomfortable at the question.

"Tell me, Mr. Thompson, when you were my age—what were you doing?"

His gaze dropped to his boots, which he studied carefully. After a moment, he mumbled a reply. "I was training to be an architect."

"And what did that involve? In that specific year?"

He cocked his head to think. "That would have been the final year of designing and drawing plans."

"You were designing buildings?"

"Elevations, mostly."

"But you were so young. How could you possibly have known your own mind? How could you know you would be an architect? How could you design elevations for buildings? Surely you were too young?"

"It is more complicated than that! There is my social status and ..."

"And?"

"I cannot debate with you. My daughter is missing. Do you know where she might be?"

"Tatiana frequently wanders off on her own. Why are you so anxious?"

"She was gone before Aurora awoke. To our knowledge, she has not had her breakfast."

Jane paused, apprehension washing over her despite her physical discomfort. "How long has she been missing?"

"Since sometime between last night and this morning. Do you know of places she might go?"

Jane rubbed her aching temple. "I cannot think." She reached a trembling hand out to grasp the coffeepot. Aurora's advice to drink a small quantity was now an urgent matter.

"Miss Davis!"

Her heart sank, as did her hand back to her side before

the newest arrival could see what she was about. "Mr. Dunsford."

She saw a grimace flash across Barclay's face as he politely turned toward the gentleman standing in the doorway. Mr. Dunsford was prepared for the outdoors, a beaver tucked under his arm. "I was hoping to talk to you, Miss Davis. Could we have a word alone?" He glanced at her companion, who was glowering at her side.

"That is hardly appropriate," growled Barclay.

Mr. Dunsford frowned slightly at the accusation. "Yet you are alone with Miss Davis?"

"We are related. Miss Davis is my sister-in-law, as you are well aware. I must insist I remain to chaperon if you wish to talk with the young lady."

Jane quelled her irritation. *Sister-in-law? Chaperon?* She could cheerfully punch Barclay in the face. Drawing a deep breath, she feigned a calm voice. "I shall think about your question and get back to you. Mr. Dunsford wishes to speak with me, and I am sure it will be acceptable if we keep the door ajar, so please allow me to have my conversation with the gentleman."

Barclay turned his narrowed eyes on her, and in their depths, she observed concern. What was he concerned about? Mr. Dunsford hardly presented a danger—he was a guest of the earl!

"I shall wait outside."

Jane shook her head. "That is hardly necessary. You should find Tatiana."

Barclay bit his lip, clearly torn. Lowering his voice, he spoke to her privately. "Just do not agree to anything. Tell him you will think about it."

Jane wrinkled her nose, a question hovering on her lips as the architect left her side.

As Barclay left the library, he could not deny his fears on her behalf. Jane was sensible, and he hoped his warning was enough to delay her acceptance of Dunsford's proposal.

Realizing that Tatiana had been missing another thirty minutes in his delayed search, he swiftly returned to the main house to find Aurora and learn if she had subsequently found his daughter.

As he entered the main hall, he looked up to find that the Duke of Halmesbury and the earl had returned. They were headed toward the earl's study, and Barclay considered taking a moment to inform his brother of the trouble with Dunsford as he had intended to do that morning, but the length of time Tatiana had been missing was more than could be borne. If Aurora had not yet found her, Barclay needed to search the grounds.

Raking through his recollections of the past few days, he quickly cataloged places Tatiana had visited in the gardens and park so he might begin his search.

He did not wish to involve the rest of the household in searching for her yet, but if he did not find her soon, he would need to ask for help.

Aurora was in the breakfast room but had not yet seen Tatiana. Barclay strode down the hall, exiting the manor onto the terrace. He peered in every direction but saw no movement in the gardens except for a group of male guests heading to the lake for fishing.

Stepping up onto the balustrade, he used the higher vantage point to scan the park, but still no sign of his daughter. Hopping down, he ran down the steps to search the area around the majestic oak where the ladies played ninepins, but Tatiana was nowhere in sight.

His distress mounted as he accepted that it was time to ask his brother to form a search party. There were several ponds around the property, and his fear increased at the thought of Tatiana slipping into one of the waterways.

Barclay jogged back to the manor. The idea of something happening to Tatiana was too much to bear. He must find her.

CHAPTER
SIXTEEN

"We have all a better guide in ourselves, if we would attend to it, than any other person can be."

Jane Austen

After her conversation with Dunsford, Jane's head was pounding so hard she thought she might faint. Holding a hand to her temple in an attempt to push the pain back, she vaguely remembered her quest—Aurora had said a small amount of coffee could assist with the symptoms. Now that she was alone once more, she quickly headed to the coffee tray. With trembling hands, she poured out an ounce of the black brew, adding a few drops of cream before swirling it in the cup and downing it.

Dropping into a chair, she licked the coffee from her lips and leaned her head back while she waited for it to follow its course.

After several minutes, the pain receded to a dull ache. Raising her head, Jane opened her eyes and gently stretched out her neck. As Aurora had promised, the symptoms had dulled to a tolerable level, and for the first time since she had stopped drinking the evil beverage, Jane recovered the ability to think.

Quietly, she contemplated the situation with Barclay. If Emma were here, her sister would recommend she be honest about what she was feeling. *Zounds.* If their situations were reversed, she would recommend to Emma to confront her feelings. She had told her sister something to that effect during her strange courtship with Perry.

Staring sightlessly out the window, Jane admitted the truth she had been avoiding since the night Barclay had failed to come to the library. She had foolishly fallen in love with the man.

Yet ... had it been foolish? Everything in her being yearned to spend more time with him. More time with Tatiana. They would have had a perfect life together. Her ideal life. But she could not force the gentleman to court her, and only he knew what was right for his little family.

Clearly, he had decided that she was not it. Mrs. Gordon had something to offer, which apparently Jane did not. Which was why she was now making plans for her future. She had no choice—she could hardly sit around in her room and the library lamenting what could have been with the brooding widower. What a pathetic situation.

Nay, she needed to make her future. She did not want to return home unwed.

Rather, she wanted to begin a new chapter in her life, which was why she had made the decision she had while talking to Mr. Dunsford. She did not know why Barclay had cautioned her to think about it, so she had decided on the spot. There was no need to delay her response. The time for hesitation was over because attempting to be thoughtful and procrastinating the other night had lost her a chance at a great love.

She should have demanded her right to be taken seriously then, rather than earlier when they had quarreled. Now Barclay was committed to a path with Mrs. Gordon. For all she knew, they had already come to an understanding and planned to wed.

It might be too late to turn back the clock, but Jane would proceed with more decisiveness so she did not miss out on any more opportunities.

With that, she was reminded that Tatiana was missing. She had grown to know Tatiana well over the past few days —having an inkling of how the little girl thought, Jane could help find her. Straightening up, she thought about places perhaps she could look, her qualms growing now that she had recovered her wits. Tatiana might need her, so Jane was going to find her.

When Barclay returned to the manor, he found several guests had congregated on the terrace. Waving to Mrs. Gordon, he headed over to talk to her. Perhaps she might have encountered Tatiana somewhere.

Drawing the widow away to the corner, he briefly thought of his intention to propose to her. That would have to wait until he located his child, but he admitted to himself he was experiencing a certain reluctance to take the next step with the woman.

Perhaps he was just tired. His sleeplessness had returned, and he was quite bored at night. Natalya never visited anymore, and he could not leave his rooms lest he encounter Jane in the middle of the night, so instead, he had been pacing his bedroom in the moonlight.

Perhaps Mrs. Gordon's presence will ease my sleep?

It seemed probable.

The widow smiled up at him from beneath the brim of her bonnet, and Barclay was reminded of his quest. "Mrs. Gordon, have you perchance seen Tatiana anywhere in the house or grounds?"

She looked confused for a moment, frowning slightly. "Tatiana?"

"My daughter."

Mrs. Gordon's face lit up. "Of course, the little imp with the silver hair."

Barclay suppressed a surge of irritation. He was certain this woman was contemplating taking her place as his wife, but she did not know his child's name? "Yes. Have you seen her this morning?"

The widow's expression did not change, but something about how she spoke next made her cheerful countenance seem feigned. "Is she not in the nursery with the other children?"

Barclay sighed. "Tatiana has not been staying in the nursery."

There was no mistaking it—the widow was appalled. "Why ever not?"

"My daughter is not accustomed to being parted from her family, so she has been staying with her grandmother in her room."

"Well ... that is hardly the way to teach her independence."

"She is nine years old, and she lost her mother only two years ago. We are allowing her to grieve at her own pace."

"Two years is a long time. I would say it is high time the young lady attend a ladies' seminary to master her accomplishments."

It was Barclay's turn to look appalled. "I thought you were telling me how you were sent to school too young?"

"I was seven. Tiana is nine years old. She should have been sent off when she was eight."

"Eight! Her mother had just died."

Mrs. Gordon thought about it for a moment. "You are correct. If one factors in some time for mourning, then she is the perfect age to be sent off to school. Perhaps I could contact the headmistress of my school in Surrey?"

"Surrey!"

"Yes. It is quite lovely. And the weather is mild like here in Somerset."

As his mind tried to follow the shift of conversation, he became aware of the sound of birdcalls and the chattering of the guests behind them. He took it all in while he came to the realization that he had been wrong. Very, very wrong. And Tatiana had been right.

Barclay could not help himself. He raised his hands to rake them through his hair. If only he had listened to Tatiana. She had warned him that the widow did not like children, and now he knew his daughter's instincts had been correct. Who would send such a young child away? A young child who suffered from night terrors and missed her mother like the devil?

He opened his mouth to argue these points, then shut it. He knew, without a doubt, that Mrs. Gordon would brush those issues aside as so much distraction from the main topic.

Composing his thoughts, he prepared to speak again. "Would you like to have children?"

The widow's face was aghast. "Goodness, no! I hoped that you would be done with all that since you already have a child."

"Tatiana."

"Of course, Tiana."

"Tatiana."

"That is what I said. Tiana."

Barclay accepted that he had made a grave error. Tatiana had said that Jane was the new mother she needed. The new wife he needed. He had brushed his daughter's assertions aside and pursued a woman utterly unsuitable while the perfect wife and mother had been before him. Jane had lovingly read *Aladdin* to his daughter. They had partaken in activities together. She had even taught his daughter how to play cricket. With a smile on her face and tireless patience in her heart.

And Barclay had cruelly rejected her affections. Admonished her for her age, for her lack of experience. Effectively given her the cut direct.

Now his daughter was missing, and he knew it was because he would not heed her advice to pursue Jane.

If only the ground would open and swallow him up. His behavior had been horrible. As horrible as this charming but shallow woman who watched him with a quizzical expression on her face, attempting to make sense of the familial bond he shared with his child.

It had been a horrible mistake when he had walked away from Jane. He now knew he had fallen in love with her that night in the library, and fear had driven him to run from her. All the rest had been excuses he could have overcome. But fear had driven him to run. He had been afraid to love, as Tatiana had observed. Afraid to love and lose again, as he had with Natalya.

Barclay could not fathom his behavior. He had uncovered a deep fondness for a woman for the second time in his life, and he had thrown it away, giving in to his fear.

Even now, Jane could be agreeing to marry a disloyal little worm because Barclay had hurt her by denying their closeness. Which was his own fault, and there was nothing he could do to address it until he found Tatiana.

"Mrs. Gordon, I am afraid I must leave you to find my daughter. Who will be staying at my side where she belongs for as long as she so desires."

Her face fell. "I... see."

He brushed any feelings of culpability aside. Mrs. Gordon had a different vision of the future than himself, and there was nothing to be done about it. If there was any possibility of making matters right with Jane, he would, but the widow was not an option now that he knew her philosophy about the rearing of children. Considering he was a single father, he should have been more assiduous in his assessment of her as a prospective match.

Barclay bowed, having said everything he wanted to say, and turned to walk away. He had wasted enough time. He needed to find the earl to request his help in the search.

JANE RACED through the family wing, checking each bedroom before climbing the stairs at the end of the hall. Reaching the nursery, she took a moment to catch her breath before stepping inside. Several children greeted her eagerly, clamoring to tell their stories of the day, their small hands tugging at her skirts to gain her attention.

Ethan held up his arms, his little face beaming with delight. Jane scooped him up, settling him on her hip as she made her way around the nursery. She marveled at how much her young cousin had grown; carrying him now was not as easy as it had been even a year earlier. His weight rested solidly against her side, and she hugged him closer, comforted by his innocent affection.

Only when he became distracted by a game that the other children had started did Jane finally set him down. He wobbled a bit before regaining his balance, then turned back to her with a grin. "You will meet me later for chess, yes?" he asked, eyes wide with expectation.

Jane smiled. "Of course. I promise."

After extracting her word, Ethan dashed off to join his friends, and Jane left the family wing to head up to the attic level. She searched through the maze of storage rooms filled with old furniture, trunks of forgotten clothes, and dusty toys. Her voice rang out as she called for Tatiana, the sound swallowed up by the thick air and stacks of belongings. But there was no reply.

Her steps grew quicker as she weaved through the clutter, dust motes swirling in the sunlight streaming through the small, grimy windows. Tatiana was nowhere to be found.

It was now midday, which meant the child had been missing for some hours, and Jane's anxiety twisted tighter with each passing minute. She descended the stairs, the ache in her head pulsing with her mounting worry. Reaching the landing outside the library, she paused, pressing her fingers to her temples. Where could the girl be?

Her mind drifted back to their last conversation. Tatiana had wanted her to read *Aladdin*, and Jane had vaguely agreed to do so once she was feeling better. Guilt prickled at her memory. She had only promised because it had seemed like the right thing to say—deep down, she had intended to avoid it, unwilling to endure Barclay's presence. But the little girl had been so excited at the idea.

Drat this ache in her head. It had improved, but it still dulled her thoughts. Tatiana had mentioned something about *Aladdin* before that, but Jane could not think what it was. Something that could be a clue to where the girl had gone, if only Jane could remember it.

Barclay had informed Richard of the situation, who called on Radcliffe, his butler, to form a search party using the grooms and footmen. The duke himself had collected two gentlemen they thought could be useful, Ridley and Trafford, and they had gone to saddle their horses to search farther afield while the earl remained at the house to supervise the search parties.

Still worried but feeling infinitesimally better that the men were to search all the waterways as a top priority, he found Aurora in a drawing room to apprise her of what was happening. His mother was drawn with worry, sipping on tea and attempting to still her shaking hands.

"This is my fault," she exclaimed.

"Why would you say that?" Barclay had taken a moment to sit with his mother while he tried to think of places to look. He had a nagging sensation that he knew where Tatiana would have gone based on something she had said. Realizing he had not eaten, he quickly downed some dainty biscuits and a cup of tea to help him collect his thoughts back together. Perhaps it would come to him if he got some food in his body.

"I should have woken up earlier."

"Tatiana has never done this before, so it would have made no sense for you to do so."

Aurora's gaze dropped to her hands, where she was twisting her fingers together in her agitation. "I sensed something was wrong."

"With Tatiana?"

His mother shot him a perplexed glance. "Yes, with Tatiana. Who else?"

Barclay cleared his throat, nervous he had revealed too much. "What about her?"

"She was gloomy last night, talking about her mother and how, if she were here, she would settle this muddle. I did my best to cheer her up, but she seemed fixated on something to do with you and Mrs. Gordon."

Barclay leaned back to stare at the cornices. The ornate cornices that Tsar had especially designed for this manor, as part of his commission from the late earl. Barclay's sire. Four generations of Thompsons had their lives entwined within the walls of this manor, this grand design, and it was time for Barclay to confess his sins.

"This is not your fault, Mother. It is mine."

"Why would you say that?" Aurora asked in an echo of his earlier question.

"I had planned to propose to the widow. Tatiana was adamant I was making a mistake, but I did not listen. She insisted the widow does not like children, and I informed her that was stuff and nonsense. So it is my fault she has run away. Or is hiding. Or is lying somewhere injured."

Barclay lowered his head into his hands, his fear of something happening to his child causing his breath to come out in pants. What was the thing Tatiana had said that nagged at him? If he could just recall ...

"Was she correct?"

He hesitated before answering. "Mrs. Gordon thinks *Tiana* should be sent to a ladies' seminary in Surrey."

"Tiana?"

"That is what she repeatedly called her."

"But ... Tatiana is only nine years old. I know there are families that do such things, but I could never send a child away that young."

"I informed the widow that I, too, would not consider it."

Aurora was silent. Then she cleared her throat and asked the inevitable question. "What did she think of that?"

"It does not signify. Any woman who asks me to send my child away while she still mourns her mother's death can ... get hanged."

Aurora chuckled. "I presume you were not so eloquent with the widow?"

"I was not. I did make it clear that there was no future for us."

"Why were you pursuing her, Barclay? I sensed that there was something between you and Jane Davis. Why would you pursue another woman if your affection is engaged by someone else?"

"I thought ... that given our situation, I should not inflict it on someone so young. Someone with such a promising future ahead of her."

"You mean my recent situation with the charitable committee?"

Barclay's shoulders slumped at the memory of his mother crying earlier that week. "I do."

"Jane Davis strikes me as a sensible young woman with a good head on her shoulders. And her cousin is a by-blow, so she is aware of the difficulties associated with our situation. What were her thoughts on making a match? Is that why she was avoiding you?"

"No. She avoided me because I severed our connection."

"Oh, Barclay." Aurora covered her mouth with her hand, crestfallen.

He straightened up in his chair to defend himself, his gaze averted. "I thought I was doing the right thing. That Mrs. Gordon was the logical choice, given her maturity and social standing."

When he glanced over at his mother, it surprised him to find pity on her face.

"Barclay, it is not about the logic of the match. It is about the person in question. Their integrity, their loyalty. Your loyalty. Natalya was not a match that made sense, but she stood by your side every day of your marriage. She did not care about the scandal in our family; she cared about us. As a family, we are strong. We can face adversity together."

Barclay hesitated for several seconds before admitting the truth of it. "Jane would make a wonderful addition to our family."

"I agree."

"I think it is too late."

Aurora stayed silent, waiting for him to explain.

"I hurt her, and I believe Mr. Dunsford intended to propose to her earlier in the library. Given how things are between us ..."

Barclay let his words trail off. If Jane had accepted a proposal, it would cause a scandal for her to reverse her position.

Unburdening himself to Aurora had helped ease the tension in his mind. In doing so, he turned his attention back to Tatiana to run through their last few conversations so he might seek a clue to where she might be.

Inspiration hit. Jumping to his feet, Barclay hastened out the door for the one place he had not searched. This time he was certain he would find his child, but he hoped she would be safe, recalling the pond's slippery edges covered in green algae that lay nearby to his destination.

CHAPTER
SEVENTEEN

"There are as many forms of love as there are moments in time."

Jane Austen

B arclay darted from the terrace, jogging across the gardens toward the woods. He was aware of drawing curious looks from the other guests, but he did not give a damn. He needed to reach Tatiana and ensure she was safe. Approaching the woods, he stopped to scan for the path they had taken days before.

As he entered the trees, the call of birds and the singing of insects were his only companions as he strode down the path. When he left the manor, he had been certain he would find Tatiana, but doubts had crept in as he kept walking. What if Tatiana was not there? His breath caught at the thought. That would mean she was still unaccounted for.

Why had he agreed to this cursed house party? It had

created nothing but chaos and hesitation. He had been perfectly satisfied with his prior life, working hard and mourning Natalya's absence. Now—swallowing hard, Barclay finally admitted the truth—he was in love with Jane, whom he had wronged, and his daughter was missing.

It was all so ... complicated.

It was with a huge sense of relief that he caught sight of the pond through the trees. Picking up his pace, he jogged the last of the path and, navigating a final bend, the pond came into view. Across its expanse stood Persephone, gazing back at him over the water. Barclay steadied himself on his feet, giddy with joy when he noted the figure of his daughter scrunched near the feet of the statue.

Careful to avoid the banks of the pond, Barclay ran the last forty feet to join her. His fear was assuaged, but his anxiety returned when he saw how her head was bent against her knees, her slender arms wrapped around her shins.

"Tatiana!"

Her head lifted to reveal a tear-streaked face. "Papa?"

Reaching down, he grasped her under her arms and raised her to his chest in a hard embrace. "Oh, little one, I was so worried about you."

She lifted her reed-thin arms around his neck, lowering her face against his chest to hug him tightly. "She did not come," she whispered into his coat.

"Who did not come?"

"Jane did not come. I left her a note, but she did not come." And, for the third time in as many days, Barclay held a sobbing female to his chest. He looked about, then walked over to a bench near the back of the cave to take a seat.

Settling Tatiana on his knee, he pulled out a handkerchief to carefully wipe her cheeks and dry her eyes.

"I do not think that Jane received your note, little one."

Big, blue eyes found his as she leaned her head back from his chest to look up at him. "How do you know that?"

"I asked her if she knew where you were, and she did not."

"Oh." Tatiana hung her head, her expression devastated. "I failed."

"Failed at what? Why are you here?"

Tatiana turned her face away to stare at the cave wall sweeping around the bench. "You will not believe me. You did not believe me when I tried to tell you before."

Barclay raked a hand through his hair while he tried to think. He was afraid he had not been on his best behavior these past few days. In an attempt to be responsible and do his duty, he had hurt Tatiana and Jane. He should have listened to his daughter—to his heart—and in not doing so, he had let both of them down.

"I will listen now. Tell me what this is all about, and I promise to pay attention."

Tatiana bit her lip, evidently considering his words. Eventually, she turned her Baltic-blue eyes back to him. "Mama told me Jane was the one."

Barclay blinked. "Mama?"

"She came to visit me, and she told me it was time for her to leave and that Jane was to be my new mother."

Barclay shook his head and tried to make sense of what she was saying. "Do you ... mean that Mama came to you in your dreams?"

Tatiana shrugged, clearly disinterested in the distinction. "I tried to tell you that Jane was the one, but you did not listen. Mama said I must insist."

He sighed. Tatiana had conjured her mother through her grief, as he had been doing these past two years. It was not the important part of what she said. He needed to listen and understand her needs. Then later, hope there was still an opportunity to repair things with Jane and make all this right.

"Why are you here in the grotto?"

"Mama came last night, and she said it was very important that you and Jane come back to the grotto. She said I must arrange it so that she could leave because she had been here too long."

Tatiana must have observed that he and Jane had forged a special bond and that the grotto had been a place that exemplified that bond.

"I appreciate that, little one, but you really scared me. You could have fallen in the pond without adults here to assist you."

"The pond?"

"Yes, see that green slime?"

"You mean the *vodorosli*?"

He straightened in surprise. "What did you say?"

"Mama told me that when I came to the grotto, I was to be very careful to stay away from the *vodorosli*."

A chill ran down Barclay's spine. It was not possible that Natalya had truly visited her … was it?

"Where did you learn that word?"

Tatiana shrugged. "Mama said it last night. She said she could not remember the English word for it."

Barclay rubbed his fingers over his forehead. His daughter must have heard her mother say it in the past, plucking it from an old memory. He might not be able to think of a situation in which Natalya would have been discussing *vodorosli*, but that did not mean she had not had an occasion to use the word with Tatiana. "Algae. The English word is algae."

"*Al-gee*. That is a funny word!"

Barclay smiled. Their conversation was bizarre but, in an instant, Tatiana was just a little girl again, and her simple view of the world utterly charmed him.

Brushing a frond of silver-blonde hair away from her face, he acknowledged that Tatiana had been right. She needed a mother, and he needed a wife. Not just anyone, but someone who could help him navigate the complexities of emotional intimacy. Someone sensitive to the issues his daughter and his mother faced. Someone sensitive to his own needs. Someone like—

"Jane!"

Snapping his head up, Barclay found Tatiana beaming. She was looking over her shoulder at the entrance of the cave where Jane now stood, a hand resting against the cave entrance while she panted from exertion. Across the pond, Aurora came into view as she stepped out of the woods, evidently following Jane to find them. Both women had their hair bared, apparently having hurried to the grotto without taking a moment to fetch their bonnets.

"Thank ... hea ... vens!" exclaimed Jane between pants. "I ... am so ... happy to ... see you ... Tatiana!"

His daughter wriggled off his lap, landing on the cave floor to race over to Jane and throw her arms about Jane's waist. "You came!"

"Of course I came ... I needed to ensure you were safe."

"Did you get my note?"

"Your note ...? No, I ... worked out ... where you were. You talked ... to me ... about reading *Aladdin*, but it ... took me an hour or two ... to remember that you called ... the grotto your cave of treasures. I would have ... remembered earlier ... but my head was aching ... and I could not think properly, so I searched for you ... in all the wrong places before it came to me ... Where was the note?" Jane was still recovering her breath, endearing in her haste to find his child safe and well.

"With your strawberries on your breakfast tray. I asked you to meet me here."

"Oh. I was too tired to make my strawberry water this morning."

Barclay stood. If there was anything to clarify Jane's suitability for the role of Tatiana's mother, certainly her knowledge of the inner workings of his daughter's mind was a clear sign. Not that the young woman would still consider him eminently suitable after his cloddish avoidance of her.

Nevertheless, he could not help noticing that she was ravishing—if only he could sweep her up in his arms to plant a kiss on her soft mouth, irrespective of his daughter and his mother's presence.

You cannot—the young woman may have accepted a proposal this very morning.

Barclay's gaze found the roof of the cave to inspect the composition while Aurora walked up behind Jane, also panting as she released the skirts she had been holding up to speed her progress. The women must have jogged through the woods as he had done. "Ta ... tiana! You ... scared me ... to death ... child!" Indeed, his mother had a sheen of sweat across her overheated face, but she looked overjoyed to see her granddaughter.

"I know how to look after myself," protested the girl with an indignant squaring of her shoulders.

"Of course you do, child. But you cannot stop us from

worrying after you. Thirty years from now, we shall still worry after you as if you were but a babe."

Tatiana groaned. "Adults are so fearful."

"It is true." Barclay spoke from the interior of the cave, pulling those ice-blue eyes of the woman he loved to rest on him. He could not read her thoughts, because those windows to her soul were shuttered, revealing nothing.

Was Jane aware he had dissuaded Tatiana from spending time with her—a further insult it embarrassed him to have committed? Fortunately, it did not seem to have affected the relationship between her and his daughter. He had not the right to have said what he had to the child—to interfere in their friendship, which had done nothing but bring Tatiana respite from her grieving.

Aurora looked between Barclay and Jane, her curiosity evident. "So, why are we here?"

Tatiana grabbed her hand to pull her into the cave. "It is a grotto, and it is magical. Come see the other statue."

"I have been here before," Aurora responded. "I have seen the statue. Is that why we are here?"

Jane and he both were silent. He raked his hair once more before responding. "Tatiana wanted me and Jane to speak." He flung his arm up to gesture at the interior of the cave. "She felt we might work out our differences here because ... it is magic."

Aurora tilted her head and turned her eyes up to the roof, back at Persephone, and then toward the hidden entrance to the second cave. "I can understand that. Love has grown here before, for at least one party. The other party ... he is dining at the devil's table in the halls of hell."

Barclay grimaced. He had done his best not to ponder the question of where at Saunton Park he might have been conceived, but he feared he could now guess the answer. He could imagine a young Aurora having her head turned in such a romantic spot, especially if the old earl had been as handsome in his youth as his younger sons, with their striking green eyes and sable hair.

"Shall I take Tatiana back to the manor?" His mother did not meet his eyes, aware she had offered something improper.

He cleared his throat. "I would appreciate that. Jane and I should talk perhaps ... before we return."

Tatiana clapped her hands. "First you must come see!"

Tugging on Aurora's hand, Tatiana led the way to the second cave. As they entered, Barclay was again struck by the eerie solitude of the second statue standing in its private cave, with dappled light stealing in from the opening above.

She led them to a bench in the back, where a hamper and blanket rested. Taking hold of Jane's hand, Tatiana led her forward to sit on the bench. "We did not see it before, but look."

Jane sat, then turned her head in the direction that the girl pointed, gasping in surprise. "There is a verse etched on the wall of the cave." She bent from side to side. "It is lit by the sunlight, and it can only be viewed from this bench!"

"What does it say?" Barclay's curiosity got the better of him, the question spilling from his lips before he could stop himself.

Aurora gazed at the statue in the middle, not looking at the verse but speaking its lines from the recesses of her memory.

"Doubt thou the stars are fire,
Doubt that the sun doth move,
Doubt truth to be a liar,

But never doubt I love."

Barclay smiled. "Tsar."

His mother smiled in response. "Indeed. He certainly loves his Shakespeare. I would have done well to recall that this was Tsar's creation, not your sire's. I confused the two, but"—she turned shining eyes to his—"the sentiment holds true from a mother to a son, which is why I shall never regret my time here."

He inclined his head, touched by his mother's support. She stepped forward, taking Tatiana's hand from Jane. "Come, little one. Your father and Jane should talk while we return to the manor."

"I got them here!"

"You did, child. Well done."

Aurora and his daughter headed for the cave exit, leaving Barclay to stand awkwardly in the subdued lighting. Staring at his boots, he rubbed the toe of one boot against the moss on the lit floor while he thought about what to say now that he had his chance. "I think I may owe you an apology."

He heard Jane exhale deeply. "Yes, I believe you do."

Drawing a deep breath, he walked forward to drop to one knee next to her. He was alone with Jane, and he could only pray she was not yet betrothed to that audacious little worm, Dunsford.

CHAPTER
EIGHTEEN

"You must allow me to tell you how ardently I admire and love you."

Jane Austen

J ane looked at him in surprise. "What are you doing?"

"I thought I might declare myself," Barclay answered, fascinated by her irises, which were particularly vivid in the light playing in the cave. "I might be too late, but—"

"Too late?"

"I know Dunsford intended to propose."

"Oh... I confess I did not heed your advice to wait when he spoke to me earlier in the library."

Barclay's heart fell. He had missed his chance, and Jane had accepted a proposal from another man. Feeling foolish, bent on one knee as he was so he could be at eye level with her. Now he was stuck here with nowhere to hide as she pondered him from inches away. "I... see."

He made to rise, but Jane shot out a hand to stay him. "I gave Mr. Dunsford my answer because I saw no reason to delay. I informed him that I was honored by his offer, but unfortunately, my affections were otherwise engaged, and I would not be doing him a justice if I were to agree to be his wife."

Barclay closed his eyes, his fears spent. This day had been exhausting in every way, but when he opened his eyes once more, he was invigorated with renewed energy. Jane gazed at him with curiosity as he attempted to gather his frayed wits and press forward. "I am so relieved to hear that. I would have been sorely disappointed."

She smiled tentatively. "What of you? Are there nuptials to be announced? Between you and Mrs. Gordon?"

"Lud, no!" He bit his lip. "I apologize. I just learned of the widow's philosophy on children, and I am not yet recovered."

Jane's brow furrowed in question.

"She advised me to send Tatiana away to a ladies' seminary in Surrey," he offered in explanation.

She blinked in surprise. "Why would you do that?"

"That was my question. It was in that moment that I confronted what a fool I had been. Tatiana had warned me, but I did not listen."

Jane's gaze dropped to her hands in her lap. "What happened, Barclay? One moment, we seemed to be on the road to... something special. The next, you had disappeared."

Barclay sighed before standing up to take a seat next to her on the bench. "The morning after we spoke, my mother suffered a great disappointment because of me ... Because she is ..."

"Unwed?"

"Precisely. It was harrowing to see her so upset ... The thought of something similar happening to you was too much to bear. Tatiana says I gave in to fear."

"Ah ... That explains her earlier protest about adults being fearful."

Barclay glanced up at Hades before eventually replying, "She was right. With Natalya, I loved deeply, and when she... left us ... it was devastating. I had no expectations of feeling that depth of emotion for another woman, but then I met you, and the possibility of love became a reality. Which forced me to think of all the many ways it would go wrong. The ways I could lose you. Or hurt you."

He noticed she was blushing, her hands having stilled while she gazed at them without blinking. "Love?"

Barclay swallowed hard before reaching out to clasp one of her hands in his. "Jane, I thought my heart was dead. That I would never feel anything again. And then I met you, and life came rushing back. You have captured Tatiana's heart and the approval of my mother, but more than that, you have captured ... me ... my heart."

She still stared at her hands, but a wide smile spread across her face. "I ... am ... very pleased to hear that because I must confess you have had my heart since your first night here. I ... I ..." She hesitated, but when she spoke again, it was in a rush, as if she wanted to get the words out as quickly as possible. "I confess I heard you and Aurora discussing your situation in the library, and I was utterly ensnared. I never considered what—who—my future husband would be until that moment, but when I heard you talk of your love for Natalya, I could not help falling for a man who held his loved ones in such high esteem. It was inexorable. Fated. I could not imagine anyone by my side but you."

She stopped as abruptly as she had begun, catching her breath in shallow heaves, and Barclay was perfectly captivated. Why had he ever thought she was immature? Jane was loyal, intelligent, and exuberant about life. She cared about other people and did her best to take care of them. What he had seen as immaturity was truly a woman who embraced life with her whole heart, and she could teach him a thing or two about the pursuit of happiness.

Raising her hand to his lips, he pressed a gentle kiss to her knuckles. "That was magnificently said. Much better than my paltry attempt to express myself. But then, you are the poetess, and I am a humble artisan."

Jane chuckled. "That was reasonably well said."

Barclay laughed in return, a feeling of lightness stealing over him as he released the past and accepted the future. Turning toward her, he tugged lightly on the hand he clasped to pull her into his arms. Staring down into her eyes, he gently cupped her head and brought his mouth down to hers.

IN THAT MOMENT, a tender longing awakened, and Jane sighed with elation. Barclay's lips moved gently over hers, soft and sure, his touch both familiar and thrilling. She had only recently experienced such closeness when he had kissed her in the library, and now that sweet memory blossomed anew. Jane had some understanding of the more intimate nature of affection—she had once witnessed Emma and Perry sharing a heartfelt embrace, which she had tactfully interrupted with an exaggerated snore, much to their embarrassment.

With the wrong man, she supposed such intimacy might seem unthinkable. But with Barclay ... with him, it felt perfectly right. Her heart fluttered with each brush of his lips, every gentle caress that spoke of tenderness and promise. She was captivated by everything about him—his scent of tea and leather with just a hint of spice, the strength of his arms around her, and the tickle of his beard against her cheek.

With Barclay, she could imagine staying in his arms forever.

He was everything she had imagined in a partner and so much more. His presence was strong and steady, his manner both protective and kind. Her fingers found their way to his hair, combing through the too-long strands that had captivated her from the moment they met. His skin was warm beneath her touch, and she marveled at the contrast of roughness and softness—the ruggedness of his hands and the fine weave of his waistcoat.

When he pulled back, she could not help the soft sound of protest that escaped her lips. But her disappointment was short-lived as he trailed gentle kisses along her jaw, his breath warm against her skin. When his lips brushed her ear, she shivered, feeling warmth spread from her head to her toes. The sensation was new and wonderful, sending a delightful thrill racing through her entire being. She sighed in contentment, wishing that moment could last forever.

But Barclay pulled away, his breathing uneven, and she saw the flush of color high on his cheeks. He looked almost startled by his own emotions, and Jane's heart swelled with affection at his vulnerability. She wanted nothing more than to pull him back into her arms, but she saw he was struggling to speak, so she waited patiently, hands clasped before her as she tried to contain her joy.

He took a steadying breath, his expression earnest. "I should be clear about my intentions."

Jane raised an eyebrow in playful amusement but remained silent.

"Miss Jane Davis," he began, his voice gentle but sure, "will you do me the honor of becoming my wife?"

Her face lit up with pure joy, her heart soaring. "Yes!" she exclaimed. "As soon as it can be arranged. I cannot wait to be your wife."

His smile was brilliant, his eyes sparkling with happiness. Barclay was not a nobleman, but he was a man of integrity and strength, a man who worked with his hands and built beautiful things. She admired that about him—his ability to craft and create, his dedication to his family. She looked forward to exploring his world by his side, seeing it through his eyes.

His expression grew serious, though his smile remained. "And just to be clear, you are agreeing to be Tatiana's mother as well? To love her as your own?"

Tears sprang to Jane's eyes, and she laughed with joy, nodding fervently. "I would be honored to be her mother. If she wants me, I want nothing more."

Barclay's eyes grew misty, and he shook his head in disbelief. "Tatiana wants that very much. She has championed you every moment we are together. It seems she understood the bond between the three of us far better than I did."

Jane laughed softly. "She is very bright," she agreed. "Will we be traveling with you?"

"If that is what you want, I would love to have you

accompany me. I miss taking Tatiana to see the world, and I cannot imagine a better travel companion than you."

Jane clasped her hands together, hardly able to contain her happiness. Her heart felt light and buoyant, and the future stretched out before her, filled with promise and love. "And when shall we marry?"

Barclay's smile grew tender. "As soon as we can gather our families. I want you by my side, as my wife, without delay." His expression faltered slightly. "Which does mean I must inform the earl that I have fallen hopelessly in love with the young lady in his care who has not yet reached her majority."

Jane beamed, her heart swelling with affection. "Somehow, I do not think he will mind."

Barclay reached for her hands, entwining his fingers with hers. "I hope you are right, my love. Because I cannot wait another day to call you mine."

Taking some time to enjoy the grotto with Jane while dreading the forthcoming meeting with Richard, it was all he could do to hold on to the magic of the moment as long as he could. While they were here, they were enwrapped in the magic of the caves with their silent witnesses carved from marble and stone. Once they left ... the troubles of the world would return.

So they sat together, holding hands and raiding the hamper that Tatiana had arranged. Neither of them had eaten much in their quest to find his daughter, and the cheeses and fruits were welcome refreshments. He dared not wonder how Tatiana had obtained the hamper, hoping she had not pilfered from the kitchen without permission.

An irate cook might wait for him, adding to his issues when he returned to the real world outside the woods.

Eventually, they both knew they could not delay any longer, so Jane tucked the handle of the hamper over her arm while he carried the blanket, and they headed back to the manor. Once they reached the edge of the woods, Barclay realized they could not continue together. As relations, they might relax some proprieties, but once a betrothal was announced, their being observed alone together would be cast in a different light.

Taking the hamper from Jane, he bade her return ahead of him so he might dally in the woods for a while to give her an opportunity to make her way inside alone.

When sufficient time had passed, he began his walk across the gardens. As predicted, reality set in as he approached the manor, and many thoughts clamored to be heard.

What if Richard was angry at this turn of events? The earl had no inkling of their relationship.

What if they were met with disgust or derision? Their age difference was not too extraordinary, but coupled with his status as a by-blow, there were going to be people with thoughts. Some would express them; others would display it in their attitudes.

What if their match horrified Jane's family? They had sent their daughter to have a Season in London. Surely they had hoped she would make a match with a member of the gentry, or perhaps a minor peer. Instead, they would have to settle for an architect for a son-in-law. A successful, renowned architect, but a working man all the same. The field had made great strides over the past couple of decades as a bona fide art, but it being accepted as a proper profession was slow going, and not everyone saw it that way yet.

As he strode past the ornamental hedges and the terrace came into view, Barclay firmly put these thoughts from his mind. As Aurora had advised, the best course was to be united as a family and handle adversity as it presented itself. Avoiding adversity could not be the goal of living. Love, family, and work well done were far better goals. Adversity was simply what one dealt with when it could not be avoided, but what truly mattered in life was one's accomplishments, which included the health and success of the family to whom he owed his loyalty and support.

Passing by the majestic oak tree, Barclay saw several guests playing ninepins, including Mrs. Gordon. He nodded politely but did not break his stride. It seemed a hundred years since he had played the silly game and had attempted to convince himself he could grow to like it over time. It seemed the height of obnoxious stupidity that he had tried to convince himself to make such an unsuitable match. If Natalya had been here, she would have shaken her head at his asinine behavior and accused him of cowardice.

She would have been right. He had been afraid that if he loved Jane as deeply as he had loved his late wife, he would never recover if he lost her, too. Or caused her unhappiness.

But one could not live one's life in fear. Having the courage to take a risk brought much reward. Loving Natalya had been a privilege he would choose many times over, and he would never regret the life they had shared. Natalya had known her time was more limited than most, but she had had the courage to live her life to the fullest while she had the chance and had appreciated every moment she had walked the earth.

Something he should have paid more mind to since she had slipped into the unknown beyond.

Reaching the terrace, Barclay placed the hamper and

blanket by the table of refreshments before heading inside. By now, Aurora would have informed the earl that Tatiana was safe, and he hoped he would find his brother in his study so he could press on and discuss the awkward situation they were in.

All too soon, he approached the door of the earl's study, which was ajar. Likely to catch a breeze, as the day was warm enough for the manor to be mildly stuffy.

As he reached the doorway, he heard the Duke of Halmesbury speaking. "I am afraid I will not be available to accompany you to Chatternwell in November because of prior engagements."

"Nor I. I will be too far along for such a journey." It was the countess, sitting near a window with her hand resting on her rounded belly.

Seizing the moment, Barclay rapped his knuckles on the door to announce his arrival. All three occupants in the study started, appearing distracted by something as they turned their heads to find him standing in the doorway.

Richard was the first to react, jumping to his feet to beckon Barclay to enter. "Barclay, Aurora informed us Tatiana is safe and sound. We are very relieved to hear. The duke and the other men just returned from their search not ten minutes ago."

Barclay nodded, entering the room. "I thank you for all you did. I apologize for any inconvenience we caused."

Richard shook his head adamantly. "Not at all. We are here to assist in such matters any time you need us."

Barclay took up a seat across from the duke, the earl resuming his own seat at an angle from where the duke was sitting. Silent for several moments, Barclay considered scheduling a time to talk to Richard later that day. His brother was occupied with something, based on the uncomfortable silence that had descended upon the room after his arrival.

The countess cleared her throat at the window, sitting up. "Barclay, I was wondering … My husband is to visit Chatternwell in November to … survey his local estate. Chatternwell House. We were considering having the manor renovated in preparation for Ethan."

Richard straightened in his chair, his interest piqued. "That is correct. The estate is unentailed, and I am planning to give it to Ethan when he reaches his majority. The manor is quite outdated, so it will need work. Could you accompany me in November to provide me with an estimate? I would be very pleased to have you do the design."

Barclay was mildly suspicious that there was more than had been said, but he pulled a notebook from his coat pocket. "What are the dates, so I may consult my schedule?"

"The seventh?"

He reviewed the pages. "I could manage the first week of November if I move another appointment. A few days should be sufficient to travel from London to see the place and make my next engagement the following week."

Richard's face lit up. "That would be wonderful. I am quite excited to learn what we might do with the manor. If it needs significant work, I would like to begin so that it would be ready for Ethan when the time is right."

Barclay nodded. "If the work is minor, it may only take a year or two, but significant building or renovations may take several years to complete. It is best to assess the situation early on."

"I would appreciate it. I want my boy to be well taken care of. The estate itself is prosperous, but the manor has not been occupied in many years. Once we assess the main building, I shall be able to meet with my solicitor to make arrangements for Ethan's future."

Barclay noted the date, putting the notebook away during the ensuing silence. He was aware that the others had been interrupted by his arrival and must have been discussing something sensitive. His own needs would have to wait for a little while. "I had another matter to discuss, but I can see you later this afternoon if you could give me an appropriate time?"

Richard shook his head. "No, no. We can talk now. We have settled our other matter for now."

Barclay took a deep breath. "I wish to discuss Jane with you."

"Oh, is this about Dunsford?" Richard's question caught him by surprise—Barclay blinked.

Across from him, the duke smiled benignly, leaning forward to explain in a low voice. "Ridley informed us of the young prat's intentions toward Miss Davis ... and the implied delights of London. We concluded that he will no longer be included on future guest lists."

Barclay sat back in his chair to stare at the cornices. He had never realized it was a nervous trait he had until he arrived at Saunton Park and found himself doing it constantly. "That is .... good news. But no, it is not the topic I had in mind."

He swallowed hard. This was deuced awkward, especially after he had been here while the two men had discussed the inquiry from the older lord in London. Lord Lawson, was it? Barclay felt like a green youth as he tried to find the words to declare himself. Not to mention, he had not expected an audience when he did this.

"I think Barclay wishes to discuss a different aspect." He looked over at the countess, who was smiling at him across the room. She kept her stormy blue gaze on Barclay as she addressed her husband, her red-blonde hair lit from behind to form a fiery crown. "I believe Barclay would like to announce his intentions regarding our Jane."

He frowned. How could Sophia know that?

The countess shrugged at the unspoken question. "It did not escape my attention that Jane has seemed quite taken with someone since we reached Saunton Park. I asked my lady's maid, Miss Toussaint, to find out from the servants who had captured her attentions to ensure I approved of the match." She tilted her head. "I do."

Barclay froze. From the corner of his eye, he noted that Richard's jaw had dropped. Flitting his eyes over to his cousin, he saw the Viking duke was suppressing a smile, pressing his lips together firmly.

"What?"

Sophia rolled her eyes at her husband. "I was just happy she was not besotted with that Adam Dunsford. He is charming, but he struck me as rather shallow from the outset. I needed to be sure she was becoming attached to someone worthwhile."

Richard turned to Barclay. "You and our Jane?"

Barclay grimaced while the countess turned her gaze back to the window, settling back into her seat. "I ... know ... you ... were hoping she would make a match with a younger man, but ... we are quite taken with each other, and I wish to offer for her."

Richard shook his head, causing Barclay's stomach to roil in anxiety. His brother was going to refuse his approval? Agitated, he fidgeted with the sleeves of his coat. Then he would visit the Davises to offer for her directly.

"Why do you say I hoped for a younger man? You are hardly ancient."

Barclay released his breath. He had misread the earl's reaction.

"I believe Barclay is thinking of the discussion we had about Lord Lawson a few days ago." The duke spoke in his baritone, adding solemnity to the moment.

"That? How is that relevant?" Richard appeared genuinely perplexed.

"We discussed Lawson's age and the fact that he had grown daughters." The duke gestured to Barclay. "I think your brother drew conclusions about their similarities."

"They are hardly in the same category. Tatiana is only nine years old, and Barclay is … He is Barclay. He is hardly … old. He is the same age as you, Halmesbury."

Exhaling in relief, Barclay decided he needed to be more his customary assertive self. This had been an unprecedented week at Saunton Park, but now it was time to revert to his usual state of decisiveness, which had made him the success he was. "Then you find it acceptable if I offer for her? We have discussed it, and we wish to wed."

Richard stood up to extend his hand to Barclay, which he clasped. With that, his brother hauled him to his feet to embrace him hard. "I would be delighted for Jane to make such a magnificent match. Congratulations, brother!"

While the countess rose to her feet to join them, the duke also stood, leaning over to shake him by the hand. "Congratulations, Barclay. We shall help make arrangements right away."

Sophia came over to clasp him by the upper arms. Reaching up on tiptoe, she pressed a kiss to each of his cheeks. "I am so happy for our Jane. You are a good man, Barclay."

It was at that moment that Barclay realized what he had not yet accepted. His family had grown these past few weeks. It was not the four Thompsons versus the world any longer. He had gained brothers and cousins and in-laws. Adversity would present itself in the future, but he and Jane would have many warm relations to stand by their side as they began their new life together. If Natalya had lived to this day, she would have been overjoyed on his and Tatiana's behalf.

Now all that remained was to meet Jane's parents and ask her father for permission to wed. Barclay swallowed hard, tension forming in his gut at the realization that he still had one more obstacle to overcome.

How were her parents going to feel about Jane marrying a by-blow? Who worked for a living?

Bloody hell, he hoped Mr. Davis was not too close to him in age.

CHAPTER NINETEEN

"There is no charm equal to tenderness of heart."

Jane Austen

Two afternoons later, Barclay's carriage drew to a halt in front of Saunton Park. Aurora and Jane stretched their limbs across from him to prepare for disembarking. They had left for Rose Ash Manor the morning after Jane had accepted his offer. There they had spent the day and evening with Jane's rambunctious family.

To be fair, it was her younger twin brothers who were the rambunctious ones. Her parents were convivial, and her youngest brother, Thaddeus, was a studious boy. And little Maddie was a sweet delight who had run through the gardens playing with Tatiana, excited to have a girl visiting who was close to her in age.

Beside him, Tatiana opened her sleepy eyes, having

fallen asleep against his shoulder. "Are we back at Saunton Park?"

"Yes, little one. We should find something for you to eat."

She rubbed her flat stomach, which gurgled in response. "I am hungry."

Barclay smiled down at his daughter. It had been some time since she had been so happy and relaxed as she was during their visit to Rose Ash.

Mr. Davis had graciously given his approval for the match, and Mrs. Davis had helped Jane to pack up her things in trunks, which were now tied to the carriage. There had been tears of joy, nostalgia over the passage of time, and much laughter as her family had celebrated their impending union. Jane had played lively Irish arias on the pianoforte while her family sang and danced with the Thompsons.

Soon the Davises would arrive at Saunton Park for their second wedding this month. He had sent Tsar an invitation to join them while the duke and the earl had been conspiring to arrange a marriage license during the departure to Rose Ash the day before.

"I am glad Maddie is coming to the wedding. I want to show her the grotto," announced Tatiana.

"With an adult, Tatiana. Do not go down there on your own," warned Barclay.

"Because of the *vodorosli*?"

"Yes, little one. The algae is slippery, and the pond looks deep."

"Will you teach me to swim, Papa? Maddie says she swims at Rose Ash with her brothers, and it embarrassed me to admit I did not know how."

Barclay grinned down at her, chucking her chin as the

footman opened the carriage door and lowered the steps. "You have been cooped up in Town for too long if I have not yet taught you to swim. Perhaps we should ask the earl about a suitable swimming hole while we wait for the house party to end and for all our wedding guests to arrive."

Tatiana's eyes shone brightly in the shadows of their vehicle at this news. "Truly?"

"If we are to be discreet, I will join you," Jane interjected.

Barclay smiled across at his betrothed, still in awe of her beauty. He was having trouble with his sleep—not because he was in mourning any longer, but because his dreams were plagued with the anticipation of marrying Jane.

He shook his head and stood to descend. Turning around at the foot of the steps, he assisted Tatiana down, then Jane. His mother disembarked last, an expression of contentment relaxing her face.

"Mother?" He held out his hand.

She smiled as she took hold to climb down. "You have done well, Barclay. I am pleased to welcome the Davises into our lives. Mrs. Davis is a generous woman, to have taken Ethan and his mother in when they were all alone. They weathered scandal for a boy who was not their own. I can think of no better match, and Tatiana will have aunts and uncles and cousins to support her long after we are gone."

"We have certainly extended the size of our family considerably. I am delighted that Tatiana now has relations of her own age."

They turned to watch Jane and Tatiana walking up the steps hand in hand to enter the manor, while the stone sentinels on the roof peered down to guard their progress.

"Perhaps I should have attempted to marry. So you might have had brothers and sisters," Aurora said in a wistful tone.

"Mother, you have done more for me than most in your position. I regret nothing about our lives. As wonderful as it is to unite with the Balfours and the Davises, the Thompsons are a strong family in our own right."

Aurora took his arm and squeezed it gently to express her approval. Then they followed his betrothed and his daughter into the manor.

After parting ways to freshen up after their travels, Jane and Barclay reconvened in the library, where Richard was playing his afternoon game of chess with Ethan, while Tatiana observed their play. The duke was sipping a cup of coffee while contemplating the park bathed in late afternoon light and shadows.

Barclay looked back to the door when Aurora entered, her face lit with joy. He shot her a quizzical look as the duchess and the countess arrived behind her. As theirs was a family gathering to discuss the details of the approaching nuptials, the countess shut the door to the hall so that other houseguests would not wander in to interrupt them.

"Oh, Barclay! I have the most tremendous news." His mother paused, tears springing into her eyes and her voice thick with emotion. Holding a hand over her mouth, she gestured to the duchess to speak on her behalf.

"I was telling your mother that the duke and I are involved in charitable endeavors in Halmesbury. A close friend of ours manages a foundling home, The Halmesbury Home for Beloved Children, for which His Grace is the primary patron. We provide a home and schooling. For older children, we facilitate vocational training with honest local businesses to help them explore their options. His

Grace and I had discussed creating a similar home in London, and your mother has volunteered to direct it. As an architect, I am sure you possess valuable insight about where we might establish a safe haven."

Aurora was ready to speak. "The Thompson Home for Beloved Children, in honor of your grandmother."

Barclay's hand rose to rest over his heart, which chimed with sheer happiness. He had never thought to assist his mother in creating her own society, rather than suffer the continual rejection of judgmental biddies. It was perfect. His mother would realize her own dream on behalf of the parent who had stood by her side when she had erred. "I will help in any way I can. I know Tsar will be delighted to assist."

Sophia spoke up from the seat she had taken near Richard, addressing the duchess. "Annabel, you and the duke are being so formal. I think it is time to relax the formalities."

The duchess chuckled. "It is a force of habit, I am afraid. Please, call me by my Christian name," she said to Barclay.

Halmesbury addressed Aurora from where he stood at the window. "Your agreement to direct the new home is very good news. It was imperative to find a woman with the right character to lead the project. Lady Lewis has a heart of gold and the skills to manage a household, which is why the home is a success. These days, she has a matron to assist her, but she still oversees the home. Miss Tho—" Sophia shot him a look, and the duke corrected himself. "—Aurora, you have the sensitivity to understand the children's needs, which is precisely what we were searching for."

Barclay was very pleased. His mother would fulfill her dreams to make a meaningful contribution. Aurora assisted charitable causes in London but had never acquired sufficient status to be entrusted with the type of role she had yearned for.

With the patronage of the duchess, along with the Thompsons' collective knowledge, the home was sure to flourish. Aurora had been taking care of Tatiana these past two years, but now his daughter would rejoin him on his travels, which would leave his mother with little to do other than manage the Thompson household. A project of this magnitude was an excellent opportunity for her to pursue her passion.

He felt a light touch on his arm, looking down to find that Jane had joined him. "I will help, too, Aurora. Whenever we are in London."

Barclay smiled down at her, lifting his other hand to rest it on hers.

Good heavens! He needed to spend some time alone with his betrothed. The mere hint of strawberries lingering in the air stirred something deep within him, a longing that tugged at his heart and left him yearning for some privacy.

JANE HAD SEEN Barclay's lingering glances in the library. And later, when they sat together at dinner, she had observed it again—the warmth in his eyes, the way his gaze lingered just a moment too long. It sent a flutter through her veins, her heart quickening in response.

Which was why she was not entirely surprised to hear a gentle knock on her bedroom door around midnight. Barefoot, she hurried across the room to let him in.

Barclay stood framed by the doorway, the glow from the hallway casting his tall form in soft light. Since arriving at Rose Ash, he had allowed her to trim his hair, and the unruly waves were now tamed, accentuating his handsome features. He had removed his coat and vest, his linen shirt hanging loose over his breeches, the column of his throat exposed. His feet were bare like hers.

She met his eyes and saw them crinkle at the corners as he smiled down at her. There was a tenderness there that made her heart ache in the most delightful way.

Without a word, Jane reached out her hand, which he took with gentle firmness. His palms were roughened by work, warm and familiar. She pulled him inside and shut the door softly behind them, settling against his chest with a small laugh as his arms encircled her in a firm embrace. "I thought you would never come."

His chuckle vibrated against her cheek. "I could not stay away any longer. Not if I tried."

Jane tilted her head back, her gaze meeting his. His hands came up to cradle her face, his thumbs brushing softly over her cheekbones as if she were something precious. The look in his eyes was so reverent, so unguarded, that her breath caught.

Slowly, he leaned down, his mouth brushing hers with the lightness of a whisper, a question waiting to be answered. Jane answered with a soft sigh, pressing closer, and his lips settled more fully against hers. His touch was tender and unhurried, the kiss a gentle exploration that sent warmth blooming in her chest.

Barclay deepened the kiss slightly, his hand slipping to the nape of her neck, holding her there as if afraid she might drift away. His lips moved over hers with exquisite care, tasting and learning her, and she responded with shy enthusiasm, matching his gentle movements.

When he finally pulled away, his forehead rested

against hers, and he took a ragged breath, his eyes still closed. "You taste like strawberries again," he murmured with a smile.

Jane giggled, her cheeks flushing. "I am back to making my strawberry water now that I am finally sleeping well."

"Then you must never stop," he replied, his voice hushed, almost reverent. His hand smoothed down her back, pulling her closer until not even a whisper could pass between them.

Jane rested her hands on his chest, marveling at the steady beat of his heart beneath her palms. She traced the lines of his shoulders, feeling the strength there, and marveled at how solid he was, how safe she felt. Her fingers moved back up, brushing against the crisp linen of his shirt, and she smiled up at him. "I have dreamed of this."

He cupped her cheek, his thumb grazing her flushed skin. "So have I," he whispered, brushing a kiss to her brow. "Every night since we left Saunton Park."

Her heart thudded at the confession, and she rose on tiptoe to press another tender kiss to his lips. This time, there was no hesitation, no lingering question—only the soft joining of two souls finding solace in each other's arms.

They stayed that way for long moments, simply holding each other, exchanging sweet kisses that grew in warmth but never rushed. Barclay's hands cradled her back, his touch reverent and gentle, while Jane's fingers smoothed over his shoulders, memorizing the feel of him.

Finally, when they broke apart, his eyes searched hers. "I love you, Jane," he said quietly, the words simple but weighted with meaning.

Her smile was pure sunshine. "And I love you."

It was strange to be kissing a woman in her bedroom once more. He had always been assiduous about whom he spent time with. Apprehensive of consequences might explain it, but more than that, he preferred to be with someone special. Someone of deep affection. As such, this was the first time he had embraced anyone since Natalya's passing.

Then, too, he had always been exceedingly cautious because of Natalya's weak heart. It had been a necessity, both of them aware of the need to prolong her life as long as possible. He was not sure if it was traitorous to be relieved that this was no longer a fear he would need to live with, Jane being a strong young woman with no health issues other than her recent bout of insomnia.

His time with Natalya would always be treasured—a part of who he was. But this new life with Jane would be different. He could plan on a future with her. They could grow old together, and it was such an intense joy to open this new chapter of his life.

Knowing he would not sleep, he closed his eyes to savor her presence before he left her for the night.

When Barclay opened his eyes, it was first light. His pulse quickened. He had slept for several hours, and now he could be caught in Jane's room!

He withdrew the arm wrapped around her, causing Jane to protest in her sleep. Gently rising from the bed, he quickly straightened his crumpled breeches and shirt. The servants could arrive at any moment or even be in the hall. Quickly, he raced across the room. Leaning his head against the door, he listened for any sign of activity before slowly opening it. He looked from right to left, but the hall was empty, so he exited the room and quietly closed the door behind him.

"Papa?"

Barclay was certain he jumped ten feet in the air. Looking down, he found Tatiana sitting near his feet, leaning against the wall. There was no other word for it—he blushed. He blushed like a little girl to be found sneaking from Jane's room, mortified that his daughter had caught him.

Leaning down, he lifted her up and quickly made for the door of his own room, lest others come upon them and notice what he had been up to. Once he reached his room, he carried Tatiana over to the sofa to put her down. Taking up a seat next to her, he sought something to explain what she had seen.

"What were you doing, little one?"

"I was waiting for you. Mama said if you were alone in a room with Jane, I must wait so I do not find you doing *zrelyy* things together."

Barclay shook his head, still waking up from the unexpected slumber. Again, Tatiana was using a word he did not think she knew. "*Zrelyy*?"

"That is what she said. What does *zrelyy* mean, Papa?"

Barclay lifted a hand to rake it through his hair. Could it be that Natalya had somehow spoken to their daughter? "Mature. It means adult. About your mother—"

"She came to say goodbye. Mama said that Jane is my mother now, so I must be a good girl and listen to her. I was happy for Mama but sad that she is gone. That is why I was looking for you. I ... I wanted a hug."

"Oh, little one." Barclay pulled Tatiana onto his lap to embrace her. "If I am alone with Jane and you need me, you can knock on the door. I will always be here for you."

"Mama told me that if I leave you alone, I might get a brother or sister soon. She said she would like that very much if I had brothers and sisters like she had in St. Petersburg."

These concepts were too ... *zrelyy* for a child. Barclay did not know what to say, so he held his daughter tight and wondered if all those nocturnal discussions with Natalya the past two years had been mere conjurings of his imagination. Or something else?

No, it was far more likely that Tatiana had dredged up memories during her vivid dreams due to all the excitement of the past week.

He supposed it did not signify because he, Jane, and Tatiana were a family now. His sleep had returned, and they would live long and happy. If Natalya had been visiting in truth, she was now free to start the next chapter in her journey, no longer trapped here by her concern for them.

Barclay pressed a kiss to Tatiana's silver-blonde hair. "Are you happy, little one? About Jane and me?"

"Very," she mumbled against his chest.

Soon she dozed off in his arms, and Barclay lifted her carefully and carried her to his bed to lay her down, pulling the coverlet over her before using a screen to block off the washstand from her view so he could start preparing for his day.

EPILOGUE

"If adventures will not befall a young lady in her own village, she must seek them abroad."

Jane Austen

NOVEMBER 1820

The Thompson carriage passed through the gates of Chatternwell House, starting up the long, tree-lined avenue bedecked with the colors of autumn.

Barclay folded up his designs for one of his current commissions, putting them away. Across from him, Jane scribbled with a pencil in her notebook. The duke had introduced her to a writer friend of his, Lord John Pettigrew. She was now compiling her first volume of poetry and regularly corresponded with Pettigrew, who was mentoring her.

But to his unapologetic satisfaction, Barclay was the first to hear any new poetry she composed. She was, after all, his bride.

Tatiana raised her head from the book she was buried in, noting that they were arriving at their destination. His daughter was learning some basic Russian, along with Jane, in preparation for a trip they planned the following year to St. Petersburg. It was high time Tatiana was reacquainted with her Russian relations, whom they had not visited since she was a babe.

The three of them conversed in Russian each evening over their supper, and he was pleased with her progress. Tatiana had an excellent ear for pronunciation, and her maternal grandfather would be pleased because he spoke only a smattering of broken English.

Now that Barclay's daughter had rejoined him on his journeys around England, he schooled her once more. Jane gave her lessons in the mornings, but he was able to frequently take Tatiana to his building sites to educate her on architecture and art.

Jane closed her notebook. "Remind me where we are?"

"Chatternwell in Wiltshire. We are quite close to the town of Bath, which is northwest of here."

"How exciting! I have passed through Wiltshire but never visited."

Barclay smiled. He was pleased with how much Jane and Tatiana loved to travel with him to see new places and meet new people. It was far more pleasurable to travel with his family than the solitary existence he had lived after Natalya had departed. He had commissioned a second carriage for when their family grew, and Tsar was in discussion with Sir John Soane to hire gifted new architects from the Royal Academy to reduce Barclay's travel in future periods when Jane could not travel.

"I suspect Richard has a hidden agenda for this visit. However, the building commission itself is genuine."

Jane peered out the carriage window at the passing trees. "I wonder if it has something to do with his quest to make amends."

Barclay frowned. He had forgotten all about the strange conversation in the billiard room months earlier when Lord Trafford had mentioned something to that effect. There had been so much occurring at the time that it had slipped his mind to question his brother about the oblique comment.

"Amends?"

The carriage drew to a halt in front of a small Tudor manor, and once again the subject was forgotten when the footman came to the door to lower the steps. As they descended, Barclay's new clerk of work joined them.

Marcus was an erudite young man who had a tendency to become queasy in carriages, so he preferred to ride with the coachman. This suited Barclay fine because he could spend the time alone with his family.

The front doors opened, and Richard came bounding out to join them. "Barclay, Jane! And little Tatiana! Welcome to Chatternwell House." The earl swung his arms out to gesture at the building behind him.

Barclay looked up at the façade, assessing the age and condition before heading over to the front doors to crane his head back and forth to assess the walls, examining them with his hands. Marcus joined him, a flaxen curl falling into his eyes, which he flicked back with a slender hand. They debated what they thought while Richard conversed with Jane and Tatiana, lifting the little girl off her feet in an effusive embrace.

Barclay and Marcus entered the manor without invitation to inspect the building and foundations, all else forgotten as they explored while Marcus took notes.

A couple of hours later, Barclay found Richard drinking tea with Jane in a clean but worn drawing room. The room was drab, with old furnishings and faded drapes. Barclay imagined what it would look like with a lighter color palette and rich fabrics hanging in the windows, his professional eye engaged.

Jane smiled at his arrival. "Barclay, there you are. Tatiana went to take a nap after we arrived, so she is in her room upstairs. Have you had a chance to freshen up?"

He shook his head. Walking over, he lifted her hand to press a kiss to her knuckles. "I wanted to find you first. I ran off so abruptly."

She laughed, looking beautiful in the afternoon light bathing the room. "I am not offended. Richard was telling me about a local modiste who is holding an event tomorrow to celebrate the opening of her new shop."

Barclay took a seat, noticing that the earl was tugging at his cravat. His eyes narrowed in suspicion. He had long since noted that Richard fiddled with his knot when he was nervous. *There is more to this visit than the condition of Chatternwell House.*

An hour later, he cornered Richard in the manor library. "There is more to this visit than you have disclosed."

Richard's hand rose to loosen his cravat, confirming Barclay's accusation. "It is deuced awkward to speak to ... you ... about this particular matter."

Barclay cocked his head in question.

"Because of your history. Of what our father did to ... your mother."

Remaining silent, Barclay waited.

"Very well. I used to be a glib scoundrel. A rogue. Earlier this year, I realized the error of my ways. As a result, I sought the women from my past whom I had wronged ... the ones I felt I had seduced into doing things beyond their experience. I needed to rectify any damage I may have done. It was how I learned of Ethan, which led me to search out any brothers or sisters whom our father had abandoned to their fate."

"I see. I suppose I had an inkling, considering I am aware of Ethan."

Richard broke eye contact to stare at his boots, his legs stretched out in front of him despite the agitated movement of his hands while he explained. "I have made amends to all the women I felt culpable for. One of the young women has a situation that is more complex, so I am here to fulfill part of my obligations."

"The countess is aware, I assume, considering it was her idea that I come to Chatternwell?"

"Sophia is aware of everything. She wanted to accompany me, but given her condition, it seemed unnecessarily trying for her to make the journey. Then, too, she is chaperoning Isabelle."

Barclay nodded. Their family had grown even larger when the earl had recently uncovered a young sister living in Saunton, whom he was now hosting. "Why is this situation complex?"

Richard jumped to his feet, walking over to the window to stare sightlessly into the gardens. "Are you aware I was once betrothed to Annabel?"

"The duchess?" Barclay exclaimed.

"Caroline Brown was a maid in her father's home whom I ... spent time with."

"During the betrothal?"

The earl flushed, his ears reddened, and he did not deny Barclay's assumption. "Mrs. Brown was to receive a loan from Annabel, from her pin money once we were wed, to buy a shop ... which obviously went by the boards when the duchess caught us together."

Barclay choked, coughing as he sat up suddenly to soothe his throat. Fortunately, he had not been standing at this news, for he might have fallen over with the shock of it.

"And the duchess tolerates you after catching you together?"

Richard blew a sharp breath. "Not at first. She eventually forgave my behavior once she heard of the amends I had made—to Mrs. Brown included. Which is why you are here. Tomorrow Mrs. Brown is holding an event to celebrate the shop I loaned her the funds for, and I am to show my support to help launch her new business. During our house party, the duke advised I needed to attend in the role of a family man lest I raise suspicion regarding our former liaisons. I must be seen as a patron rather than a former paramour to protect Mrs. Brown from scandal."

"And is she ... a paramour?" Barclay hated to ask, but he needed to know the character of the woman before he exposed his wife and daughter to what might be an unsavory element.

Richard exhaled. "The young woman was rather innocent when I knew her, so I would say she is a good woman who made a mistake by dallying with the wrong man. She deserves the assistance, and the duke accompanied me to Chatternwell to make the arrangements during the house party but was not available to return at this time. Instead of accepting charity, Mrs. Brown merely requested that I lend her the funds that Annabel would have done."

"Hmm ..." Barclay considered his options. "I would plant you a facer, but you have already borne the consequences of your misdeeds to correct the situation, so ..." Barclay raked a hand through his hair before reaching a decision. "Jane and Tatiana will each be delighted to order a new gown. They have both recently complained that they needed a wardrobe more suitable for traveling, and we shall be here for a few days, so there should be sufficient time."

"I shall pay for the gowns."

"That is unnecessary."

"It is a gift. And I can escort them to the fittings while you assess the manor."

Barclay realized this was important to his brother, who had brought him together with his charming new bride. Richard had also brought Aurora and the duchess together, to his mother's eternal happiness. So he relented.

"Agreed."

JANE ENTERED Mrs. Brown's Elegant Millinery and Dress Rooms on Market Street. She and Tatiana were excited to see a display of gloves and scarves by the window, set out on walnut countertops.

Bolts of fabric were fitted into neat cubbies painted in ivory, alongside drawers that soared up the walls to the ceiling. An explosion of colorful silks, velvets, cottons, and tulle could be seen in the morning light. Jane's eyes settled on the corner cabinet, marveling over an exquisite gown displayed within the walnut framework.

This was a very fine shop, and Jane was eager to leaf through fashion plates to find the newest carriage dresses.

The proprietress was elegantly attired in a day gown of rich mulberry, which offset her wheat-colored hair and hazel eyes. Mrs. Brown left two older women to examine the silks, walked over to greet the earl, and sank into a deep curtsy.

"My lord, I am honored to receive you."

Richard gave a small bow of acknowledgment. "Mrs. Brown, I would like to present Mr. Barclay Thompson." The earl had informed them during the drive to the shop that Mrs. Brown was yet unmarried but had earned the honorific when she was promoted to the role of housekeeper in a doctor's household the year before and had retained it to open her shop.

Barclay bowed, tall and dapper in his new burgundy coat and buckskins, greeting the young woman. "A pleasure, Mrs. Brown," he said in that low, husky voice that still sent shivers of delight skimming along the surface of Jane's skin.

The earl then turned to Jane, who held Tatiana by the hand. "Mrs. Thompson, Miss Tatiana, may I present Mrs. Brown? She is the owner of this fine establishment."

The young woman turned and curtsied once more to her and Tatiana.

Jane thrilled—she was still to grow accustomed to being introduced as Mrs. Thompson, but she loved the sound of it each time. She was married to Barclay Thompson, renowned architect, and she was pursuing her writing as Emma had recommended. They traveled together, seeing England, and she spent time with Tatiana, who was a child with intelligent thoughts and aspirations.

Beaming at the woman, Jane complimented her on the fine establishment and informed her that she and Tatiana were there to order carriage dresses. *Our first time ordering clothes together!*

Mrs. Brown cheerfully bid them join her at a counter to view fashion plates. Jane was soon impressed with the shop owner's overall demeanor and knowledge of fashion this far from Town. The modiste had just returned from London and clearly made a study of the latest periodicals on the subject. Jane admired the courage Mrs. Brown must possess to be running a business as a unwed woman in a new town.

Barclay and the earl wandered the shop, stopping to chat with the other patrons who were agog to be amidst such a noble visitation. Jane paid no mind, pointing to a velvet creation depicted on one of the plates. Mrs. Brown agreed it would be quite becoming and suggested a deep blue swath with a short, thick pile she had on a nearby shelf. Jane concurred and was delighted she would visit the shop for a fitting. Browsing fashion plates were a pastime for Jane, who had sewn many gowns for herself; she enjoyed conversing with someone who had pursued a trade in it. The shop was a cave of treasures for the modiste residing in her heart.

Once Tatiana went to be measured, Jane turned to find Barclay gazing out the window at the quaint buildings clustered on the street, including a post office across the road. He cut a dashing figure in his buckskins and burgundy coat, his Hessians shining with fresh polish.

"It is a beautiful town," she said as she wove her arm through his.

Barclay turned his head, his warm eyes tracing over her face with affection. "Not as beautiful as you, my love."

Glancing about to ensure no one was paying them mind, Jane reached up to buss Barclay on the cheek, causing him to grin and pull her closer against his body with the arm she clung to. Leaning in, he whispered into her ear, "I am going to kiss every drop of strawberry water the moment I get you alone."

Jane grinned in response. "There is a small hothouse at Chatternwell House, so I took the liberty of picking the strawberries."

His only reply was a slight curving of his lips, his eyes vivid with interest.

Jane sighed in sheer happiness, leaning her head on his shoulder and scarcely able to believe that she was living the perfect life that Emma had suggested just months ago. She loved visiting towns such as this one with Barclay and seeing all their realm had to offer. But more than that, she loved traveling with him and Tatiana and wanted every young lady to find their perfect partner, including the pretty Mrs. Brown.

The modiste was obviously excited about her new shop, but she had an air of reserve about her that spoke to a possible mistrust of people. It made Jane's poetic heart ache on the woman's behalf, wishing she could share the happiness that Jane, Barclay, and Tatiana had found together.

"Are you looking forward to the holidays?" The low timbre of Barclay's voice caressed down her neck, interrupting her musings. Jane beamed, nodding.

She could not wait for all their families to unite at Saunton Park for a festive house party in a matter of weeks. Aurora and Tsar would journey with them to Somerset. Emma and Perry had confirmed their attendance, and the Davises would be coming too, which meant Tatiana would have an opportunity to spend time with little Maddie.

It promised to be a joyous holiday season shared with many loved ones and her first as a married woman with a family of her own. "It is going to be a wonderful Christmas."

Learn if spending Christmas in Chatternwell can lead Caroline Brown to her own true love when she nurses William Jackson, the injured blacksmith from down the street, in *Mrs. Brown and the Christmas Gift*.

DOWNLOAD A FREE BOOK

Enjoyed the story? The adventure isn't over yet ...

Subscribe to Jarrett's newsletter to receive a book—absolutely free!

The Meddling Duke: A determined duke. Three unforgettable women. And a meddling hand in each of their lives that may just lead to true love.

Join thousands of Regency romance readers who love exclusive content, behind-the-scenes peeks, giveaways, and early access to new releases. Your next favorite story is just one click away.

AFTERWORD

While wrapping up *Miss Ridley and the Duke* last year, I hit a patch of insomnia. When I say a patch, I mean three to four months of relentless nights of barely any sleep. Still working as the manager of a sales coaching team at the time, I pasted a smile on my exhausted face, and a cheerful inflection in my voice, to start a sales meeting every morning with a team of forty to fifty people looking at me with expectant eyes.

Part of that particular job was to be upbeat and inspire the team, but I will confess by the time I made it to my desk the smile would fall as I slumped into the only thing to provide relief—my morning coffee.

Right around the time I considered becoming an extra on the set of *The Walking Dead*, I learned I had developed a caffeine intolerance. Thus, my love affair with coffee spanning three decades came to an abrupt end.

I switched to decaf espresso and sleep slowly trickled back.

Later that year, when Mr. Jarrett and I discussed the idea for *Miss Davis and the Architect*, you can figure out how I came up with the inspiration for why Jane was not sleeping.

But that is all coffee under the bridge, ha ha, and I now enjoy my Lavazza decaf espresso every morning without fail.

Aladdin was first published in 1710 and adapted into a play which was performed at Drury Lane in 1788.

The letter from the *London Virtuous Committee of Charitable Endeavors* rejecting Aurora's application paraphrases a passage from Fordyce's *Sermons to Young Women*.

Strawberry water is based on a Regency recipe from 1820, using well-ripened strawberries. It was used to soften and whiten the skin, and it had to be made fresh so it did not turn sour overnight (no refrigerators).

The dental elixir was created by a Parisian dentist, M. Leroy-de-la-Faudiǵnières. He used the ingredients mentioned by Jane when Tatiana questions her about it. Sophia's lady's maid, being French, would have known of this excellent mixture to support oral hygiene.

Did women play cricket in the Regency?

The first recorded all-women's match was reported in the *Reading Mercury* in 1746, *"between eleven maids of Bramley and eleven maids of Hambledon, all dressed in white."*

The Hambledon team won.

In 1799, the Countess of Derby personally played in a match she organized at The Oaks, her home in Surrey.

Later, in 1811, *Sporting Magazine* reported on a match between Hampshire and Surrey women, which is mentioned by the earl in the library when he collects his son for their afternoon of bat and ball.

"The ground, which is spacious, was enlivened with marquees and booths, well supplied with gin, beer, and gingerbread. The performers in this contest were of all ages and sizes,

AFTERWORD

from fourteen to sixty; the young had shawls, and the old, long cloaks. The Hampshire were distinguished by the colour of true blue, which was pinned in their bonnets in the shape of the Prince's plume. The Surrey was equally as smart: their colours were blue, surmounted with orange. They consisted of eleven on each side."

Ethan's obsession with chess is an homage to my late (and favorite) uncle who started beating adults in matches at the age of four, being something of a genius. My father would tell me about it often, when he played chess with me as a young child.

Loyalty is very important to me personally, a trait I admire immensely. It takes strength and courage to demonstrate it, and I enjoyed writing about how Aurora and her parents forwent reputation and appearances in favor of family commitment.

In Barclay's attempts to do right by his family, he had to rediscover that genuine connections with genuine people are far more valuable than worrying about other people's opinions.

Jane had to find her direction and confidence in her own abilities so she might believe in herself to pursue her dreams.

Fortunately, Tatiana is a meddling little imp who helps bring them together when their inhibitions get in the way of what they really want.

Together, in times of trouble, a family standing together is stronger than an individual standing on his own. Family, old or new, is what brings the color and joy to life.

If you enjoyed this story, I would be incredibly grateful if you'd consider leaving an honest review. Your words help others discover the book and support future stories.

The *Dazzling Debutantes* series continues when Caroline

Brown, the maid who was indiscreet with the Earl of Saunton, reluctantly nurses the brooding blacksmith on Christmas Eve at the local doctor's request.

She may want to avoid men altogether now that she has the shop she always dreamed of, but fate has other ideas when she is forced to spend the holidays with the gruff tradesman from down the street.

Discover if the spirit of the festive season will help Caroline forgive herself for betraying a dear friend, while a haunted William Jackson struggles to overcome the demons of his past.

Can these two wounded souls help each other heal? Find out in *Mrs. Brown and the Christmas Gift* if she will become the newest Dazzling Debutante.

About the Author

C. N. Jarrett started writing her own stories in elementary school but got distracted when she finished school and moved on to non-profit work with recovering drug addicts. There she worked with people from every walk of life from privileged neighborhoods to the shanty towns of urban and rural South Africa.

One day she met a real-life romantic hero. She instantly married her fellow bibliophile and moved to the USA where she enjoyed a career as a sales coaching executive at an Inc 500 company. She lives with her husband on the Florida Gulf Coast.

Jarrett believes in kindness and the indomitable power of the human spirit. She is fascinated by the amazing, funny people she has met across the world who dared to change their lives. She likes to tell mischievous tales of life-changing decisions and character transformations while drinking excellent coffee and avoiding cookies.

Stay in touch and receive a free copy *The Meddling Duke* by signing up for the C. N. Jarrett newsletter!

Printed in Dunstable, United Kingdom